The New Forest Dweller

Chapters

Chapter 01 – Introduction

Chapter 02 – The Encounter

Chapter 03 – Animal Aid

Chapter 04 – The Long Week

Chapter 05 – The Meeting

Chapter 06 – Dweller Duties Begin

Chapter 07 – Forest Tasks

Chapter 08 – The England Forest Dweller Council

Chapter 09 – Two Meetings at Fritham

Chapter 10 – The Fairy Feast

Chapter 11 – High Winds and A Highwayman

Chapter 12 – A Dwellers Final Duty

Chapter 13 – The Forest Voices

Chapter 14 – The Socks and The Hounds

Chapter 15 – Fairy Friendship

Chapter 16 – Heatwave

Chapter 17 – The Forest Folk Return

Chapter 18 – Drought

Chapter 19 – Fire

Chapter 20 – Charcoal and Rain

Chapter 21 – Local News

Chapter 22 – Walk Through the Woods

Chapter 23 – A Forest Reborn

Chapter 24 – New Years Day

The New Forest Dweller

The New Forest Dweller

Chapter One – Introduction

A bright sunny day with a virtually cloudless sky. A sky so bright blue across its vastness, that no end of day is in sight. The beams of the sun shine down on a road running along the edge of the New Forest, with trees one side, and spacious well-maintained houses the other. The greenery of bushes and grass that separated the beautiful properties, was as vivid to the eye as the blue above. The air is peaceful, and all that can be heard is the light wind making its way through the trees, with the birds' songs that twitter on high.

The far end of the road is hazy in the heat, as it bends around the corner and out of sight. Through the haze emerges a runner. It is a tall well-toned guy in his mid-twenties, with short dark brown hair, and wearing a red runners top with white shorts. He continues along the edge of the road on the forest side, keeping a decent pace, his breath labouring only slightly from the effort. Further down the straight of the tarmac he comes, until he stops at an entrance to the forest, a stoney section to park three or four cars which leads to a long wooden padlocked gate, with a separate smaller kissing gate for public use. He bends down, with his hands on his knees, trying to regain control of his breathing, and listens to the calm sound of the Forest. His green eyes look up to the gates and the stoney path beyond, that works its way through the trees. He stands up and walks over to the gate, avoiding the one small black car parked on the verge. Probably a dog walker he thought as he lifted the latch and entered the forest.

With his eyes squinting in the light, he sets off again at a good speed, his arms moving in time with the motion of his legs. He follows the winding path, and gets around five hundred metres into the forest, before seeing a dog with its owner in the distance, a lady with a white cap, walking towards him from the opposite direction. He carries on at his steady pace before smiling and nodding as he passes her, and the small black hairy dog that is running around her feet. The path continues further into the forest until, sweating now, he comes to a stoney cross road. He goes right, keeping the same pace, and after a short stretch, finds himself at a bridge over a river. The shallow depths show the rocky base of the riverbed, and the nutrient rich water creates soft splashing sounds as it folds in on itself when the banks narrow after a wider ford section at the bridge.

The guy leans on the wooden rail, letting his thoughts wash away with the water below, so that he can just take in the beauty and sound of the forest around. Only a small amount of light can make its way to the forest floor, as the vast lushness of the green leaves on the trees, does its best to soak up what they can higher up. Standing there, with his eyes closed, he feels a true peacefulness, which can only be achieved in the forest, where your body can reset, and your mind can just drink in the nature.

Just as he is getting ready to continue his run, his phone starts vibrating in his pocket. He pauses a second to let his mind return to the world, before pressing the green accept button on the screen to answer.

"Hey babe, are you still out running?" asks a woman's voice from the speaker.

"Yes, just in the middle of the forest at the minute, I'm surprised I've got reception to speak to you," the guy replies.

"Hello, hello, Ryan can you hear me?" the woman asks.

"Yes, can you hear me?" Ryan says, holding the phone up higher, trying to get a better connection.

The call beeps off. Obviously, she could not hear him. He sighs and turns back the way he came, jogging along the stoney path. No doubt she was calling to see if he could pick up some milk or something on the way home he thought, as he followed the path round to the left at the junction. He knew they had been running low on the blue milk that they gave to their one-year-old son Archie, and he needed it for his night time bottle if they were to have any success at a good night's sleep. Ryans feet continued to pound the ground for the next mile or so, until he reaches the wooden gate back at the road. The black car is still there, which must have meant the dog walker he had seen was a local, and lived in one of the nice houses along the road. The car owner must be doing the longer loop of the forest, he thought turning to head the way he had come from before.

Back on the road and running fast to use up his energy, he makes his way back to his car, parked about a mile down the road, just before a bend. He could hear the heavier traffic of the main road close by. He gets in and sets off, driving about a minute before getting to the end of the road and ready to pull out onto a busier one. His journey takes him via the local shop close to his house, phoning his girlfriend on the way, to see what she needed.

"Blue milk for Archie please" she asked in a slightly muffled voice, as she was at that moment wrestling a baby with his nappy. "Some raspberries or blueberries for his breakfast porridge too" she added, before hastily saying goodbye and ending the call.

Ryan got what she wanted and continued his journey home. He pulled into the drive, and got out to head to the front door. He had just inserted the key into the lock, when he noticed a bank card face down on the floor. He picked it up and turned it over. Becky Lewis was the name he read. Blimey, she is always losing something he thought, cleaning it off on his top, before shaking his head, and taking the shopping bag into the house. He put the fruit and milk in the fridge, before heading upstairs. As he got towards the top, he spotted a cheeky little bottom dashing about, followed by a "Dada" as a smiling little blond-haired, blue-eyed boy ran over to the stairgate.

"Hello squidge" said Ryan, opening it with one hand before lovingly picking his son up, and giving him a kiss at arm's length to not get his sweaty top on him.

"Hello babe" said Becky, stepping back from the bath she was running and coming to take Archie to start cleaning him.

"You dropped this outside the door" said Ryan, flashing her card at her as she lifted a wriggling Archie out of Ryans arms.

"Ah thanks. This baby brain has made me so ditzy" she said, giving him a quick kiss, before turning to take Archie into the bathroom. "Just leave it on the banister could you?"

"Will do" said Ryan, placing the card down on the post. "I'm going to get out of these clothes and take a shower."

He started undressing whilst walking in to the bedroom. He tossed his socks, shorts and top into his wash basket, and walked towards the ensuite. A hairy feeling at his feet made him stop, and he bent down to stroke their cat Fearne, who was making a fuss of him being home.

"You don't want to rub up against me" said Ryan, with a final scratch behind her ears. "I'm stinky from my run." He stepped over her and into the small room before closing the door behind him, keeping her out.

He takes off his boxers and starts the shower. From the other side of the wall, he can hear a lot of laughter and splashing. Smiling, he steps into the shower, and lets the slowly warming water pass over his face and neck, running down his body, freeing his mind to wander back to the idyllic scene in the forest he had been in such a short time ago. He was lost in his calming thoughts for five minutes, while he scrubbed his body clean, before stepping out onto the shower mat, pulling his towel from the rail, ruffling his hair with it, and then wrapping it around his waist. He opens to door to see Becky standing at the changing table applying sudo cream, while Archie is laid back with his thumb in, twiddling his damp hair.

"He was a little pickle, he soaked me in there" said Becky, sticking the flaps of his nappy down.

Archie tilted his head back and smiled at Ryan. "Dada" he said pulling his thumb out his mouth and raising his arms back to indicate he wants picking up.

"Wait a minute squish" said Ryan lovingly, as he moves towards his chest of drawers looking for some boxers, shorts, and a top to put on.

Archie starts crying, so Becky, who had finished the nappy change and had put his pyjamas on, picks him up, and he settles on her shoulder with his thumb back in.

"If I go and sort his bottle, are you going to put him down?" Asked Becky.

"Yep, that's cool" said Ryan, smiling at Archie's sweet little face.

He removes the towel from his waist and gives himself a final dry down before pulling on his clothes, hanging his towel back on the rail, and lifting Archie from Becky arms.

"Come on squidgy, let's go and get comfy."

Ryan carries him out of their room, and opens the door to Archie's, using his foot to stop Fearne darting past and hiding under his bed like she always tried to do.

"Say night night Fearne Fearne" Ryan said to Archie, closing the door.

"Nuh nih" was all he could manage.

"Good boy" said Ryan, giving him a kiss and sitting down in the chair with Archie on his lap laying against his chest, listening to his heartbeat.

The lamp in the room was on low, the curtains pulled shut with the blackout blind down too. It was nice and warm, and smelt of clean clothes and a freshly bathed baby.

Archie sat, with his thumb in, his other hand holding his daddy's ear.

"Do you want a story?" Asked Ryan, knowing the little boy loved to hear them.

"Muhm" came the response past a thumb.

So Ryan cuddled him closer and began. He calmly talked about the forest, the trees, the wildlife, and the cheeky squirrels that like to run along the branches and telephone lines. Archie sat contently listening, more for the familiarity of his daddy's voice then what he was saying.

Becky enters with a bottle of warmed milk, and Archie immediately reaches out for it, pulling it quickly into his mouth before sucking away. Becky gives him a kiss, and tells him to have a nice sleep before she closes the door carefully to keep a waiting Fearne out.

Ryan continues his story, talking about the mythical Fairies and the Pixies of the forest, and the rumours of a figure that walks the less trodden paths, and who is said to take care of the forest. This last one had actually been rumoured for years. A brown cloaked figure that had been seen carrying water with cupped hands, providing for plants when the rains have been scarce, and clearing the debris and fallen trees after the storms.

Every once in a while, a very pixelated brown blur on a background of green is captured and printed in the local papers, mainly thought to spread the mystery and stories to attract tourism to the area. Now and again these pictures pop up on social apps, with people swearing blind they saw 'the old man of the forest' going about his work. Ryan kept talking as Archie's eyes slowly started to close, and the sucking became intermittent, only happening when he felt the bottle dropping slightly.

"You're my good boy" said Ryan, bending over slightly to kiss Archie's forehead. Once finished, Ryan lifted the empty bottle out of his hands, and the thumb went automatically straight back to the mouth. He placed the bottle down on the floor, and slowly got up, cradling a sprawled out one year old in his arms.

"Night, night bub" said Ryan, bending over the cot and lying him down, resting his head on the pillow, before pulling the small duvet over his body. It would not stay on for long, as Archie liked to wriggle and roll over in his sleep, but for the minute, he looked so comfortable all wrapped up. Carefully, Ryan picked up the bottle, turned off the lamp, and left the room, while making sure a fluffy black shadow did not pass him as he opened the door. He crept down the stairs, aware of every time the boards beneath the carpet squeaked, hoping it was not loud enough to disturb Archie. He got to the bottom and walked over to the kitchen to put the bottle on the side. Becky was in there, in her pyjamas, stirring their dinner which was on the stove. A creamy chicken pasta from the look of it.

"Ah, good job babe" said Ryan, putting his arms around her waist and resting his chin against the back of her head. He held her for a few seconds as she stirred, before he reached his hands up to get a couple of plates down from the cupboard.

They dished up and took their plates into the lounge, each with a cold can of coke zero, and slumped down onto the sofa and began eating. Ryan flicked the Tv on, and they settled into the next episode of the latest crime drama they had been watching. Becky finished first, and rested her plate down next to her.

The New Forest Dweller

"I've put my card back in my purse" she said, as Ryan continued to eat. "I must have dropped it when I brought Archie in earlier and didn't realise my bag was open."

"At least it was just outside the door" said Ryan, through a mouthful of pasta.

"Yeah" said Becky, looking back to the screen.

They sat in silence for a while as their show played out, before the credits started with the option to watch the next episode.

"I'm so tired, I might just have an early night" said Becky with a sleepy exhausted smile.

"That's fine" said Ryan, "I have a bit of work to do before bed. And yes, I will take the plates out and lock up," he added with a smile.

"Thanks babe" she said with a kiss, "and fill up my water bottle?" she added cheekily with a smile.

"Blimey, talk about taking the Mickey" Ryan said laughing.

He got up balancing the plates and cutlery, and with his other hand grabbed her water bottle from the side and headed to the kitchen. He placed the plates down on the counter above the dishwasher, and emptied her bottle, filling it up with fresh clear water. Not quite the same as the stream in the forest he thought, as he tightened the lid, before walking back out to see her waiting at the foot of the stairs.

"Thank you babe," she said taking the bottle and giving him a kiss, "don't stay up too late" she added, turning to head up the stairs.

"No, I won't" he replied. "Night, night."

He stood there, waiting for her to get to the top of the stairs, before he headed to his office to get his laptop. He had to finish off a quotation for a customer, and it meant he would not have to rush tomorrow to get it done when Archie was up and wanting his undivided attention.

Laptop retrieved he sat back on the sofa and filled in the details for the work. He owned a building company with his business partner, and also a couple of labourer friends that helped out occasionally.

Writing on the quotation what the cost and breakdown would be, he slowly filled all the information needed. He worked for about twenty minutes, before saving the document, attaching it to an email, and scheduling it to send at eight o'clock the following morning.

He then flicked up his internet browser, and checked to see how Southampton had gotten on that night. Draw, not bad away from home against a good Leicester side he thought. Continuing to scroll through the results, he then clicked to check the latest news on the main BBC page. Always doom and gloom in some part of the world, bad news sells better than good. All the major stories were talking about the conflict in the middle east, the immigration coming illegally to the UK, and the interest rates which never seemed to stop rising, which intern was making people have to cut back to possibly avoid homelessness. Nothing new then he thought, scrolling down to the local news for Hampshire and the Isle of Wight. The article he noticed and clicked on, was about the fourth one down on this list.

'Big foot spotted around the New Forest?' Read the headline.

Snorting, Ryan looked at the title, and began reading the story which went all the way down the page, finally revealing the blurriest picture in the world. Of course it was tactically located at the bottom of the page to make sure people read the article. But again, a brown blur, half behind a tree, and seemingly caught on the first camera phone ever created from four miles away in a blizzard. Hardly worth the effort to write he thought, as he clicked off and closed his laptop down. Just more advertising for tourism and adventure hunters.

He stretched his arms out, and looked around the dimly lit lounge. Fearne was lying on the floor, eyes carefully closed, with her paws tucked up under her belly so she looked like a furry sledge.

"Oh Fearne" he said as she opened her big eyes. "Do you want some biscuit?"

She got up and bent down to stretch her legs out. Ryan got up too, putting his laptop back in his office. He plugged it on to charge and closed the door with Fearne hot on his heels. He climbed halfway up the stairs, and poured a cup of her biscuit into her bowl and she immediately descended upon it. With a little scratch behind her ears, and a stroke along her whole body, Ryan stood up, and climbed the remaining few steps to the landing, and crept quietly into their bedroom.

Beckys gentle snores were breaking up the monotonous whirling noise of the fan, which sat on the chest of drawers. Ryan took off his top and shorts and got into bed. He plugged his phone in, and quickly checked his socials before bed. Someone has shared the BBC article about the sighting in the forest, and the comments below were all laughing or sarcastic about the picture that accompanied the story.

Ryan clicked his phone off and placed it down on the floor. He laid back in the darkness, his eyes purposefully closed, thinking about how much peace being in the New Forest brings him. It had been a beautiful hot spring day, and all the nature had shown itself to be thriving. Comforted by the pictures in his head, the sun shining in his mind, he rolled onto his side, and drifted into a deep sleep.

Chapter Two – The Encounter

Ryan awoke to the sound of silence. At least for a second, he was unsure what had awoken him. For the sun had risen, but the room was dark thanks to the blackout curtains that were closed. Then a sound came from the baby monitor on Becky's bedside table. A crying out from Archie to signal he was awake and so should everyone else. Smiling while rubbing his eyes before ruffling his hair, Ryan sat up and got out of bed. He walked over and pulled on some sports shorts and lifted a top over his head, before turning towards the door. Looking over to Becky, he saw her eyes flicker shut, almost as though she hoped he would be the one to get up first to sort their son. He smiled as he opened the door. Fair enough. After the countless nights she'd had to deal with his hunger, teething, the nighttime nappies, and whatever else that needed to be done, he did not mind doing the mornings. He went into Archie's room, leaving the door ajar as he opened the curtains and pulled up the blind. Fearne jumped up to the window ledge staring out, no doubt trying to see the birds that sometimes nested in the eaves of the roof. He turned and saw his smiling little boy sat with his arms in the air.

"Hello bub, did you have a good sleepies?" Ryan asked reaching down to pick up the happy little boy.

"Dada, cheeky" said Archie, pointing to the cat on the windowsill.

"Yes, she is cheeky" replied Ryan, smiling as Fearne started to paw at the window. "Come on, lets change that nappy and then go downstairs for breakfast." Archie let out and excited chuckle at this.

He changed the nappy quickly and set off downstairs, placing Archie down when the stairgate was secured. The little boy ran off to find a toy from his play pen, and Ryan watched him from the kitchen as he made his breakfast. Today was porridge with some raspberries mashed up and his vitamins mixed in. Once made, he set up the high chair in the lounge and fed Archie his breakfast.

Fearne came down after a few minutes, and made the most of Archie being strapped into his seat, by sprawling herself out on the floor where he could not get her. When he was free, he liked to chase after her, stroke her, and twiddle her tail between his fingers. Fearne was not the most loving of cats, and certainly did not like his often sticky fingers running all over her. She endured it for only a few moments before trying to escape his clutches. Whenever he got too much for her, she would paw him back by standing on her hind legs which was usually enough to get him to stop. If he persisted, then she would hide out of reach, either in the conservatory, Ryans office, or upstairs, which she got to by climbing through the banister poles. But she never attacked him.

After breakfast Ryan put Archie's cup, bowl and bib in the kitchen, and returned to him still sat in his highchair in the lounge. He could hear Becky upstairs carrying out her morning routine, as he walked over and unstrapped his babbling son, lifting him out and down to the floor. Immediately Archie let out an excited laugh and ran over to see what Fearne was up to. She already knew how accidentally strong his stroking could be, and leapt up, walking over to the conservatory door that Ryan had opened to put Archie's highchair out of the way. She ran out and Ryan put the latch on so that she could come and go as she pleased, but Archie could only watch her from the glass window and try to entice her in with his toys.

The footsteps on the stairs started as Becky descended, and Archie, upon hearing this, ran over smiling, calling out for his 'Mama.'

"Good morning my beautiful little squidge" she said, opening the stairgate and picking him up, before delivering a big kiss to his cheek. Archie tried to return the kiss with his mouth open wide, and started sucking on Beckys cheek making her laugh out loud.

"Ah, I love you so much my little boy" she said, prising him off her cheek and looking into his forever happy face. "Have you had a nice breakfast with daddy?"

Archie just laughed and pointed to his Dada.

"Morning babe" said Ryan walking over. "Did you sleep alright?"

"Yes" she replied, trying to hold onto Archie who was now contorting to get down to go and get one of his toys he had seen from up high. "He slept through which was good."

"One night out of about four hundred and eighty's not too bad" said Ryan, and they both chuckled while watching Archie lifting a heavy book of noisy animals towards them.

The rest of the morning passed as usual for them. It was Archie's day off from nursery, and a non-working day for Becky, as they both only went in three times a week. Ryan worked from home whenever he had paperwork or emails to do and tried to only be on site as little as possible, usually only when a job was too big for his guys to do alone and it needed overseeing and directing. It was not the steadiest of work, but it provided enough income to help support their house and lifestyle.

Ryan checked to make sure his quotation from the previous evening had successfully been sent, and saw a reply already, asking when they could start and how long after could they begin using the area again as they had some large orders being delivered at the end of the month. He replied to them, and a couple of others who had contacted him as well.

Around midday he sat back in his chair and relaxed. He could hear Archie's little feet running around, often accompanied by his excited squeals and basic speech to Becky, trying to convey what he wants. She was trying to tell him it was lunch time and his sandwich and sliced tomatoes were ready, and a few seconds later he started making yummy noises as he saw his food was coming. Ryan got up and went out to see his son stuffing a finger of sandwich into his mouth while his mum was telling him to "only take small bites." He pulled most of the soggy bread back out of his mouth, and bit down on the very end bit as she had shown him.

"What a good boy" said Ryan, walking over and placing a hand on Becky's shoulder, giving it a squeeze to assure her she was doing a good job. Archie smiled when his daddy spoke, as he had not seen him emerge from his office.

"I'm thinking of going for another run in a bit if that's ok?" Ryan asked tentatively, knowing that Becky had spent most of her morning chasing Archie about. "I have only got two weeks before my five-k" he added, subtly reminding her it was for a good cause as he had raised about four hundred pounds towards a diabetic charity. His brother had type one diabetes and his dad had type two which is why he had chosen that specific charity.

"Yes, that's no problem babe" said Becky, smiling as Archie took another dainty bite of his sandwich. "I might take him over to see my parents after lunch and possibly stay the night if you don't mind?" she said looking up into his face.

"No problem" he said, "It is poker night after all" he added with a smile. Every Thursday he played a friendly game of poker with his friends at the local pub in Lyndhurst, a beautiful village that he and Becky used to live, before buying a house a few miles away in a slightly more affordable location.

"Hmmm" was the reply that came back. That was usually the reply he got for an expected night of drinking and gambling with his friends.

"Don't worry, I won't have too much to drink. I don't want to ruin my progress with my running." He said as he started climbing the stairs to get changed.

Another "Hmmm" came from Becky, but this time with a slight smile that Ryan would never see.

Ryan got changed into another running outfit. A mid length pair of light grey shorts with pockets for his phone and keys, a dark blue lightweight top, and some sports socks. He brushed his teeth and quickly shaved off a few loose hairs from his beard that were messing up the shape. He then headed back downstairs just as Archie was finishing his tomatoes and being given some sliced banana as a pudding.

"Mmmmm" he said as Becky tipped the fruit onto his highchair tray.

"You won't be here when daddy gets back" Ryan said to the little boy, who was happily jamming squidgy banana into his mouth, half of it sticking to his fingers from gripping too tightly. "Quick kiss before I go" Ryan added, bending down to kiss the distracted boy's forehead.

Standing up, he walked over and bent down again kissing Becky on her lips.

"Look after my little boy won't you?" he said, looking her in the eyes. She smiled and replied, "Of course, and you make sure you take a drink and look after yourself. Where are you going? Back to Ashurst again?"

"No, it was beautiful there yesterday, but I think I'll go out towards Burley this time."

"Ok, well take care and we'll see you when we're back tomorrow."

"Yes, see you babe. Be good for mummy!" he added, looking at Archie whose tray was empty, but his mouth was full to the brim.

Ryan grabbed his running shoes, phone, keys, and wallet leaving just as Becky started telling Archie off for stuffing it all in. Chuckling, Ryan pulled the door open, slipped his shoes on, and went out to his van. He would have to take the van as Becky needed the car to go to her parents. He pressed the keys, opened the door, and chucked his stuff onto the passenger seats. He climbed in and reached down for one of the small bottles of water he kept under the seat, placing it next to his phone and wallet before turning the key and setting off.

They had bought a house on the very outskirts of the forest boundary, but still under the New Forest district council governance. The place they lived was Ashurst bridge, a small peaceful area that was connected to the village of Ashurst via a few long roads of houses. It was a beautiful place to live. So close to the forest, the beach, and the city of Southampton.

Ryan drove to the main road that ran through the forest, with the radio playing a funky tune on the local station. Ryan turned it up just as the song finished and the hosts filled the gap between songs with interesting chat before playing a request, Baba Orielly by the Who.

"Great song," said Ryan to himself, dropping the windows slightly and turning up the volume again so that those he passed by could appreciate a few notes. He kept driving on the A thirty-five, through Ashurst and Lyndhurst, before heading out towards Christchurch. Burley was about halfway through the forest and accessed via a road off the main route. It is a quaint and beautiful village, full of history and stories of witches that supposedly used to gather there.

The journey took about twenty-five minutes in total, until Ryan got to a forest car park just on the outskirts of the village. He reverse parked up to the edge of the stones and got out. The weather was very much the same as the previous day, bright and blue with only a few whisps of cloud. Unusual to have two good days in a row in England Ryan thought, smiling to himself. The trees and vegetation here was just as green and luscious looking as it had been in Ashurst the day before.

There were some horses grazing on a small green plain the other side of the road from the car park, occasionally stepping forward to chomp at a fresh patch of grass.

Ryan crossed the road, going past the horses, and scouted out a pathway through the wilderness. He stretched whilst walking slowly along the first section, which wound through some large trees that blocked out most of the direct sun, creating a nice cool calm environment. Ryan stood still for a few minutes, appreciating the coolness whilst completing his leg stretches, before setting off. He could feel his keys and phone bouncing against his legs in the pockets of his shorts, his wallet he had left hidden in his van, and the small full bottle of water was clenched in his right hand as he ran.

He ran for about thirty minutes through the undergrowth, losing the barely trodden path quite quickly, and instead forging his own route through the trees, following animal tracks whenever he encountered bushes or long grassland. His breathing had become very rapid, and when he came to a stop, he doubled over, staring at the soil. He stood like this for around a minute, the only sound was the squarks of some birds nearby, and the gentle wind in the leaves above. After staring at an ant walking between his legs for a few seconds, he stood up straight again and checked his phone. With the one bar of signal he had left, he saw on his running app that he had ran five point three one kilometres in that time. He had done a sort of a wide loop and was only a couple of kilometres, as the crow flies, from where he had started. Not bad considering he still had two weeks to train. Ryan had set himself the target of twenty-five minutes to do the five-k run, but thinking about it, his build was probably a bit too muscular to achieve as quick a time as that without some serious changes to his diet and lifestyle. As long as he can do it under twenty-eight, he would be happy.

He began to walk around the wooded area to keep his muscles active while he regained his breath. He unscrewed the bottle, and took some big gulps in between equally large recovery breaths of air. He had only taken a couple of sips of water during his run, as he thought he would probably finish the bottle when he stopped. He decided to save a small amount for on the way back, and feeling slightly recovered, began to walk back the way he had come.

Snap!!

He stopped. One foot in front of the other in a frozen pose for walking, his head had turned quickly, looking over his left shoulder trying to find the source of the noise. Thinking he was about to see a deer, he waited, holding his controlled breathing to not make a sound and scare off what was there. He moved his legs slowly together, and turned gently towards the direction he thought the noise had come, eyes scouring the trees.

Slowly but steadily, a figure appeared. A thick brown cloaked figure, hooded over with cupped hands and exposed arms stretched out in front of it. It moved slowly, with shuffling feet beneath the cloak that slightly draped on the forest floor. Ryan remained as still as he could, not daring to breath or believe his eyes, for he thought he knew who this figure was. The temptation of reaching for his phone to capture a picture, disappeared as quickly as it was created, and he just stood there, motionless, as the figure bent down to a young sapling, and poured the water from the hands gently into the soil around it. Then the figure stood up, turning around before it froze still as well, a pair of eyes from within the hood focused on the person stood about twenty metres away, silently watching. Slowly, the figure stretched out its arms and gripped the edge of its hood, gently lowering it down behind.

Ryan released a long slow breath. It was like being caught in a predator's sight when the figure had first noticed him, and he was unsure whether to remain rooted to the spot or start running as fast as he could. But now, stood here before him, was a kind faced old man, with short white hair sparsely spread across his head.

The old man lowered his arms to his side, surveying the young man watching, with a satisfied smile spreading across his face.

"So, it is time." He said, in a warm friendly tone.

He began to slowly walk towards Ryan, who's senses had still not returned to him from shock, his mouth hanging slightly open still.

The old man came right up to him, about a head shorter, but with his arm outstretched to shake his hand. Ryan instinctively reached out and gripped the old man's hand, noting the dampness from where he had carried the water. His grip was strong though, and they shook for a couple of seconds before Ryan found his voice finally.

"Err, umm, hello, I'm Ryan" was all he was able to say, still quite bamboozled by the appearance.

"Hello Ryan, I am, well, I used to be called John. I must say, it is very nice to meet you" he said, smiling and clasping their joined hands with his remaining free hand.

"I can't believe it" said Ryan suddenly, and the old man smiled wider almost breaking into a laugh. They released hands and Ryan took a small step backwards. His mind was racing now, and the words just seemed to tumble from his mouth with very little direction from his brain.

"I've heard rumours about you in the papers and on the news, but I always thought you were a hoax, or a myth or legend" he said looking at the old man. This did cause the old man to chuckle.

"Legend eh" he said through his laughs. "I am not too sure about that. I consider myself to be a helper or guardian, a dweller of the forest if you will" he said scratching his chin. "Yes, I am The New Forest Dweller" he said, bowing his head slightly.

"But how? why? what do you do? where do you live? How long have you been here, looking after the forest?" Sputtered Ryan, releasing all the questions that had built up in him from the rumours about old man of the forest. Could it be that they were about to be answered?

"Well let's start with why" the old man said kindly. "Shall we walk as well?"

"Yes" replied Ryan, noting how his legs ached now from the very little movement they had done over the last few minutes.

They walked through the trees together, and the old man began.

"Why, why, why?" the old man said, more to himself than to Ryan. "Well, I love the forest. I love the trees and the wildlife, the communities that you know about, and the ones that are hidden from the world. It is a great task to be a guardian of the forest, and one that I take great pleasure from doing every single day," he said smiling as he thought about the life that he had.

Ryan, noting the small break in speech whilst the old man thought, continued with his questioning.

"Well, where do you live? How long have you lived here?" Asked Ryan, trying to get the answers quickly in case it was all a dream and he woke up without the information he craved.

The old man paused before answering.

"Well, I suppose I live in the forest, I walk its paths and carry out my duties, and when I am tired, I either sleep against a tree, or on the plain, or even under a log house that children make when they come to the forest. Occasionally I visit the Forest Folk and camp there, or else with the Pixies or even sometimes with the 'Sisters of the Wreath'." He said to Ryans stunned silence before continuing.

"And as for how long, I am not too sure to be honest. I have been here carrying out my duties since I was around your age I suppose" he said, looking round at Ryans face.

"Blimey" said Ryan glad he could still speak from shock, "Don't you get lonely sometimes?"

"Not really" he said, "I feel at one with the forest, and I communicate with the wildlife and hidden communities around it. It feels like I have a very full life," he said with a satisfied finish.

"But how do you look after the whole forest?" said Ryan, perplexed but yearning to know how one person could tend to such a colossal place.

"The 'How' will have to wait I'm afraid" said the old man coming to a standstill near the edge of the tree line before saying, "You are the first person I have talked to since I started this work, and now you have found me, I am afraid it signals my time is coming to an end. You are the one chosen to be my successor. Someone who has an affinity for the forest. For its life and eco systems that thrive at different times of the year. I guarantee that the work is not easy, and that leaving your life will be difficult at first. But the forest needs a Dweller. All forests need a Dweller" he finished, looking hopefully up into Ryans face, almost eager for an immediate response to this request.

Ryan stood still. Mind boggled and racing. Why him? Had he just been in the right place at the right time? It never even crossed his mind that this might be a hoax or a trickster, his mind so willing to believe in the Forest legend that he had already accepted the old man to be him.

How could he accept? What about his life, Becky, and Archie, even Fearne, his friends and family, and the life he was building for them. It was too much to think about.

"I can't," he stammered stepping backwards slightly, trying not to look at the reaction his words had with the old man "I mean, I just can't. I have a baby, and my fiancé. I love them both so much. I am sorry, I just can't" he said, looking over to the old man and feeling regret grip his stomach.

The old man's features did not change. He stood there silently for a few moments.

"Tis not I who has chosen you my son, but it is the forests choice. It sees you as someone with the best heart and lifeforce to help keep it safe. You would be looking after millions of animals, insects, trees, and plants, and they would see you as part of them. This is no small task, it would require one hundred percent of your time rendering any relationships you have, for what of a better word, irrelevant. But please think on it. Take your time to decide. For my time on this earth is now ticking towards an inevitable end, and someone does need to takeover" said the old man, channelling the feeling of the forest through him and his words to try and persuade the young man that this is his destiny.

Ryan was scared. Not of the responsibility, nor the prospect of hard work, but scared of the thought of leaving his family. But deep down in his gut, he was most scared of saying no.

"I'll have to think about it" he said after some time. "Do not take this as a yes. I need time to assess my life and make the right decision. Would I be able to bring my family here?" he asked, desperation puncturing his voice.

"Take the time to think it over, but no Dweller has ever had a partner in the Forest. Duty must come before relationships, and one cannot be fully committed if their time is taken up elsewhere. Therefore, I am afraid you would have to leave your family, as many of us have had to do before" said the old man, pausing to contemplate what he would say next. "You will have just a week to decide. My time is limited and I will need to train you in the ways of a Dweller, the 'How' question that you asked. The deepest secrets and magic of the forest. Once you have made your decision, meet me on the green in Nomansland at midday, seven days from now." He said, willing Ryan to remember this all and make the correct decision.

"I will" said Ryan, "I'll see you in seven days," and he turned and walked past the last few trees and out of the woodland onto the grassy strip next to the road opposite his van.

He turned back to try and see the old man, but his eyes could not detect him in the wilderness. He walked over to his van, clicked the key, and threw his phone and almost empty bottle back on the passenger seats. But instead of leaving, he just sat there, hands on the steering wheel, staring out onto the forest, not quite seeing it, instead picturing in his mind the hurt he could cause to those he loved the most. It was too much think about now. He turned the key and set off back home.

Chapter Three – Animal Aid

Ryan got home without even remembering the journey. He picked up his phone and wallet and went inside. He kicked his shoes off as Fearne ran up to him, rubbing her body along his legs. The car was gone so he knew Becky and Archie were not there. He bent down and absentmindedly scratched Fearne behind the ears, making her close her eyes and roll on her back, tempting him to try it on her belly, before she would respond with her claws. Ryan did not even notice, but stood up and headed upstairs to start his shower.

Once undressed and standing under the cascading warm water, he shut his eyes, trying to relive the whole afternoon in full. It seemed like such a blur. The encounter, the talk, and the request had kept him shocked and confused throughout. He was sure he was going to think it all a dream in the morning.

So, after he had scrubbed his body, washed his hair, and stood on the mat reaching for his towel, he decided to write down all the information he could remember. Wrapping the towel around his shoulders, with his lower half dripping, he picked up his phone and went onto notes. He then proceeded to type everything he saw and talked about with the old man. After a while, and having reread what he had written, he clicked his phone back off. His lower half had given up waiting on the towel and instead airdried in the time, so Ryan hung his towel back on the rail and went into the bedroom. It was only mid-afternoon now, but he felt tired. The mental exhaustion along with the physical one weighed down on him. So, he put on a pair of boxers, set an alarm for a couple of hours, placed his phone on charge, and then laid down on the bed, closing his eyes and almost immediately drifting off to sleep.

He dreamed of floating through a green leafiness, in a comfortable silence, as the branches of trees pointed the route to him. He made his way down several different paths that he knew, but ended up in a different part of the forest than he expected. He wound his way down the path, surprised at seeing a badger sat on a log, waving at him. Around the bend and in the distance, he saw two people of very different heights, just standing there. He floated nearer until he made out who it was. Becky and Archie stood, the height difference making sense, and they were holding hands. They smiled at him and reached out their free hands, but as Ryan reached back, they seemed to move away slightly, just out of reach. "No" said Ryan desperately reaching out, flipping over whilst floating, twisting onto his belly to try and get closer. But now they were moving away quicker, their smiles turned to sadness, he looked round and saw that it was the trees that were holding him back, stopping him from getting to them.

He awoke with a start, cold with sweat and in almost darkness. He sat up and saw the sweaty outline of himself remain on the bedsheet. That had been a bad dream! He turned and rested his legs on the floor, before grabbing his phone and standing up. Seven fourteen was the time. He must have turned the alarm off without even realising. There were a few missed calls as well, one from his dad and a couple from Becky along with several messages. He looked through what had been sent to him. Becky had text saying they had got there ok and how did his run go, and then sent a new text saying are you ok, as he had not replied to the first one a couple of hours before, and then that is when she had tried ringing. His dad had also text asking if he was picking him up for poker. Ryan got up and turned the light on. Stood in the dim light of an energy saving bulb, he text his dad back first saying 'Yeah, he will get him in twenty minutes'. Then he phoned Becky back, putting her on speaker and starting to get dressed.

"Finally," came her exasperated voice through the speaker "I'm guessing you've been asleep."

"Maybe yeah" he replied, careful not to sound too suspicious. Now was not the time to tell her what he thought had happened. "How are you? How is my little boy doing? Is he being good?"

"He's a little pickle as you well know" she said, and he could hear excited giggling in the background of the call, as it sounded like Becky's dad was chasing Archie around the lounge which was one of his favourite games. "So, you've had a nice afternoon then. I never seem to get time for a nap anymore," she added in a slightly disgruntled tone.

"I know" he said, rubbing deodorant under his arms and spraying on aftershave. "It must be bedtime soon though?"

"Yes, as long as he sleeps all night. At the minute, Dad is getting him all worked up chasing him about. Bumped his head once already since we have been here," she added slightly guiltily.

"There's always some bumps and bruises" Ryan replied pulling on a top, "I'm sure he'll be worn out from all that running" he said, again hearing a squeal, louder this time.

"Ouch, Archie! Dad, leave him alone now he needs to settle. Just climbed all over me trying to get away from Grandad," she said, her tone turning angry.

"Ok, well I'm just about to head out, so I'll say bye and have a good night."

"Say night, night to daddy" Becky said to Archie.

"Dada!" Archie exclaimed.

"Ah, he's looking round for you" said Becky, her tone soft again which happened much quicker with Archie than it ever did with him.

"Ah my good little boy, be good for mummy tonight won't you" he said sitting on the edge of the bed and pulling his socks on.

"mhmmmhmm" came the response.

"He's sucking his thumb" said Becky, before the sound of a kiss travelled out of the speaker.

"Ok babe, well I'll see you tomorrow, I love you both," Ryan said, standing up and heading for the stairs.

"We love you too daddy, have a good night" said Becky, before making a kiss kiss noise down the phone and then clicking off.

Ryan headed downstairs, stopping halfway to put a pouch of food in Fearnes landing bowl, and checking her water which was full before continuing to head down. He turned a couple of lights on, grabbed his keys, wallet, and hoodie, before slipping his shoes on by the door and heading out.

As he got into his van and headed off, he noticed an owl fly overhead, its form caught briefly by the light of the street lamps before it vanished into the darkness. Ryan continued his journey, and after five minutes got to Ashurst and turned down Woodlands Road, the same road he had parked on the previous day for his run. His parents lived down there, but their drive had been full yesterday which is why he had parked further down the road. There was darkness to the left in the grassland that led up to the trees, which was very contrasting to the well-lit houses on he right. Lights which showed off each angle of the large properties and gardens.

His mind was still elsewhere, when about halfway down the road, a squirrel jumped out of the grass in front of Ryans van. He broke hard to not run it over, and could hear some tools in the back sliding forward.

"Blimey you stupid little thing," he said at a complete stop. He waited a second, but did not see it come past his side, and he had not seen it go back into the grass. So, with his lights on and checking his mirrors, he opened the door, jumping out quickly. Walking around the bonnet, he saw the squirrel. It was dancing about in the most unusual way, almost beckoning Ryan into the grass before leaping off into it. After what had happened earlier in the day, and with his dream still fresh in his mind, he paused. The squirrel then darted back, looking at him before lurching back in. Checking quickly to make sure no cars were coming and that his door was shut, but with the engine still going and lights on, he slowly walked through the grass, careful not to stand on top of the bushy tail that only just poked up past the top of the blades. Flicking the torch on his phone, he came to a stop about seven metres in. The squirrel was hopping around, trampling the grass down, and there in the middle of its weird movement, was another squirrel, motionless. The squirrel stopped hopping and started motioning towards the lifeless body. Ryan understanding immediately, knelt down and rested his phone against his thigh, torch shining light over the small scene. He reached out and nudged the squirrel, but nothing. He then shook it gently, but still nothing. Not knowing what to do he started rubbing its chest, gently squeezing where he assumed the heart must be. Nothing happened at first. The other squirrel had stopped completely and was watching, its paws resting on Ryans leg, quivering gently. Then, all of a sudden, the life came back. The arms reached out as it tried to flip onto its legs. Ryan let it go quickly, and the other squirrel darted in and began sniffing it, rubbing its paws all over the other ones face. The squirrel sat motionless for a second, allowing the frantic one to check it out, before sniffing it back and then rolling about together in an unmistakeable show of excitement. Then they stopped and ran at Ryan, jumping and bouncing off his legs with the same excitement.

"Haha, no problem little buddies" said Ryan, astounded at what he had just been a part of, but pleased it had worked.

The squirrels stood on their back paws looking up to his face, and then both turned and started leaping through the grass, back to the dark woodland, leaving Ryan still kneeling, staring after them.

A minute later, and after a lot of confusing thoughts, Ryan got back to his van, and immediately reached for the antibacterial sanitiser that he kept in his door. Rubbing copious amounts into his hands, he then brushed down the knees of his jeans which were slightly wet and green. Getting back into his seat and thankful that this was not a busy road, he continued down it for another hundred metres, before pulling into the driveway.

His dad was by the door kissing his wife goodbye. As he walked over, she waved to Ryan who returned one back to her before she closed the door.

"Alright Son" He said getting in and pulling the seatbelt round, "How is my grandson? Granny Marie says give him a kiss from her."

"Yeah, he's alright" said Ryan, carefully backing out onto the road, still very aware he was breathing quicker than normal due to the recent events. "He's gone with Becky to her parents tonight."

"Ah what a sweetie" his dad said smiling. Then sniffing, he said, "What's that chemically alcohol smell in here?"

"That's my hand sanitiser" said Ryan, hoping there was no follow up from this.

"Ah I see. You know you shouldn't use it too much though, it is good to have some germs about, helps the immune system. You only really need hand sanitiser if you have touched something really filthy," he said in a very parental tone.

"Mmmhuh" agreed Ryan, happy to leave it there.

He then turned the conversation to work, and his dad bored him with his stories for ten minutes while they drove, and he was still going when they parked up in the main carpark in Lyndhurst.

"And then if you will believe, they go and place the order that afternoon. I could not believe it. I told Debbie in the office, I had only thought that morning we haven't heard from them for a while."

"Crazy" said Ryan, in a gently sarcastic tone that was missed. He locked the van and they walked over to the rear of the pub.

"Ah Ryan, Steve, what you having?" Came a voice from the smoking shelter, as the two of them approached.

"Alright Paul?" Asked Steve going through the gate and shaking his hand.

"Alright mate?" Said Ryan following him in and shaking his hand too.

Paul was slightly younger than Steve, but he was their best friend and Ryans business partner in the building company they owned together. A bald, happy go lucky guy who lived in Lyndhurst with his kids.

Paul smiled at having his mates here, stubbing out his fag as they all went in, and they were greeted by Mark, Dave, Luke, Steffan, Greg, and Jim. All the guys were about Pauls age apart from Jim who was Ryans younger brother, another of Steves sons. Greetings were carried out and drinks ordered, they all sat down and setup the poker table, carefully passing money to the banker in exchange for chips, keeping the cash out of sight of the bar staff.

It was a fun night. It was always a fun night to be fair. They laughed, drank, and made stupid bets to try and bluff each other off the pots. Jim ended up winning the 'Best hand of the night pot" with his Full House of aces on eights, scooping forty-nine pounds as they put in a pound each hand for the winner of this.

Paul overall came out biggest winner, and thankfully no one lost too much in the process. Ryan, who had decided to only have one pint before starting on the diet cokes, finished packing up the chips about eleven-thirty. The rest of them, who had had six or seven pints each, Mark had ten, were all merry, saying goodbye with lots of hugs as they left to walk back to their homes.

Ryan and Steve left out the back and walked to the van, discussing the night they had just enjoyed. A few minutes later they were leaving Lyndhurst on the dark road through the forest back to Ashurst. It was a sixty zone which was what Ryan accelerated to, waiting for the inevitable warning he got every time he hit this bit of road with his drunk father.

"Watch out for deer along here," came the line about a second later. In fairness, Ryan secretly thought he would probably be disappointed if it wasn't delivered one time.

"Yes" he replied, flicking his headlights up to full beam after a car went past them.

Actually, thought Ryan, if any night it does happen, it is probably likely to be this one. This made him chuckle to himself.

And then, just like that, about twenty metres ahead of them, a deer stepped out into the road. The vans brakes got their second good test that night, and from the sound of it, whatever had not slid forward earlier, definitely had now!

"I told you," said Steve. "I told you, I told you, didn't I tell you. I definitely think I am a bit Psychic."

Steve kept talking, although Ryan had stopped listening. He was staring at the deer who was illuminated in his headlights only a few metres away now. It was a stag, with great thick antlers that seemed almost too heavy for its head. It looked almost angrily at Ryan, its brow slightly creased and eyes narrowed, but seemingly not taking notice of the blaring headlights. Luckily no other cars were coming from either direction as they sat there watching. The stag looked behind him, and another two deer bounded out onto the road, a doe with a small white spotted baby. Once they had joined the stag, they all continued to cross, and with a small backward glance at the van, they hopped into the darkness.

The New Forest Dweller

"You've got to be careful at this time of night, especially with the deer" continued Steve, as Ryan put the van back into first gear and set off again. This time he stayed at forty until he dropped his dad back, and then drove carefully home. Pulling into the drive, and with no further emergencies, he turned off the engine.

Getting out and going into the house, he was greeted by Fearne who wandered over for a fuss like normal. Giving her the usual attention, he then got a drink of water, before going up to the bedroom to sit in bed and watch a bit of tv. He did not really focus on what was happening on the screen, once again delving into his memories, trying to structure his thoughts so they made sense.

Is this how it is going to be? Is this the forest showing me it needs my help? He would be hurting everyone he loved if he was to accept. So why was he even considering it. It would ruin his life not to be with Becky, Archie growing up without him, Paul having to run the business by himself, his family, his friends, Fearne, their finances, their future plans, the house.

Overwhelmed and starting to get upset, Ryan rolled onto his side. A tear dripped down his cheek and made a soft splashing sound as it hit the bedsheet. How could he even tell anyone. Surely, he was not meant to reveal what he was planning on doing. The New Forest Dweller was just a rumour, a tourism attraction, much like the Loch Ness Monster and Bigfoot. Who would believe him anyway? He would sound like a madman. I am going to live in the amongst the trees and take over from the legend of the old man in the forest. I am going to feed the plants and look after the wildlife in a secret community unknown to the outside world. He would be sectioned.

Unsure how to even approach sorting all his problems, he drifted off, the television still playing, Fearne curled up on her bed in the corner, her eyes resting on one of her favourite people, as she purred softly into sleep too.

Chapter Four – The Long Week

Ryan woke earlier than usual from an unsettling dream, but not remembering why it had made him feel so bad. Rubbing his eyes, he wondered how could he had such a feeling of dread in his stomach. And with a bump, his thoughts reminded him of the previous day. Another bump. This time on the side of his head made him look around. Fearne was up on the bed, her paw outstretched, from tapping him on the head so he could get her breakfast.

"Morning Fearne Fearne" he said, used to saying the name twice as that's how he referred to her in front of Archie.

She meowed at him, turning and leaping down, as if to say follow me. Ryan remembering the strange behaviour from the encounter with the squirrels the night before, shot up out of bed, and followed her slightly sceptically. She led him out of the room and halfway down the stairs, waiting by her bowl, impatiently looking up at him before meowing again. He honestly did not know what he expected to happen, she was just a hungry cat. He poured out some kibble for her, and she ate hungrily. He went back upstairs, closing the bedroom door before slumping down on the bed.

He reached over for his phone and looked through his notes. It was still there. It had not been a dream then. Could it be brain tumour then or something? What else could rationally explain what he remembered?. He could not think of anything.

So instead, he changed his thoughts to why did he feel so bad? Should he rewrite his whole life's future, knowing it would cause those he loved so much pain? After a few minutes of thinking and staring into space, he concluded that it was because he did actually want to accept the offer. To join the forest and help maintain it, care for its creatures and plant life would be a dream fulfilled. He felt horrible for thinking it, but he knew that it was not an opportunity he could just pass on. The next question came to him, his mind trying to rationalise the decision. How? How could he? Surely if he just disappeared it would be noticed by everyone around him. People would be searching and Becky could be suspected of having some involvement in it.

He needed to come up with a plan. If he was certain he wanted to do this, he wanted to find a way to keep Becky and Archie in his life. He was sure that he could not live without either of them.

So, he set to work. Opening his laptop, he arranged all his work files, writing out simple sequences for what to consider when pricing and scheduling jobs, and for processes that needed to be done to continue running the business successfully. Then he noted down all the works banking details, passwords, memorable answers, email addresses, health and safety updates, and all relevant information that when found, would allow Paul to continue without him. It would seem to an outsider, if they ever questioned it, that he was just extremely well organised.

Next, he made sure to setup a direct debit from his account, to the joint account with Becky. His account would be empty in around seven months, but hopefully by that time his life insurance would have paid out to allow Becky to continue to be supported financially.

He had made up his mind on how it would need to look. It would cause a lot of people a real shock to hear that he was missing, but done on a day where Becky would be at work in the hospital, therefore alleviating suspicion that she had anything to do with it, whilst also providing her with enough money to pay off the house. She would not struggle to raise Archie financially if it came to it. It would be the best for them both he thought, if the chat he was planning to have with Becky did not go as well as he expected.

Leaving nothing to chance, Ryan then made sure that all the house details were organised together for Becky. Mortgage documents, life insurance, all his personal email addresses, his bank account, and all the other house information, listed together in a folder, labelled neatly. Double checking his list and making sure all his passwords online were correct, he placed the folder on his office desk, next to the work one for Paul. He could not give them the documents directly, it had to be that they found them to make it believable, but everything was there for them that they would need.

It was around five thirty in the afternoon that he felt he had got everything sorted if the time came. He had planned to empty his van into the garage, but time had escaped him during the mounds of paperwork sorting. It would have to wait until tomorrow now, as Becky and Archie were due home soon. Ryan walked into the kitchen, and started to unload the dishwasher before filling it with all the dirty plates and cutlery, before sticking it on. Next, he started prepping something for dinner. He had decided he wouldn't tell Becky, at least not tonight. He would need her to focus and realise what he would be doing, and what that would mean for them. He did not want to rush it and come across as crazy.

Around twenty minutes later, a crunch of tyres on stone sounded from outside, and soon after the front door opened.

"Dada" was the first thing he heard, and it pulled on his heart strings to know that the times he could be hearing him say that were numbered.

"Hey my little man" he said, walking over to the running boy who raised up his arms to be held. Once Ryan had picked him up, Becky returned to the car to get their bags and bits, managing to get it all unloaded in just a couple of trips back and forth.

"Ah, it's nice to be home" she said, sounding exhausted as she dropped the last bag down, pushing the door shut behind her.

"Hello babe" said Ryan, walking over to her and giving her a kiss on the lips, succeeding at acting normal despite his insides lurching about.

"Ah something smells good" she said, taking off her shoes and walking through, sprawling out on the sofa. "Oh I just need to relax for a minute" she said, pulling out her phone, and flicking through her socials.

Yes, definitely not tonight, thought Ryan. He looked at the little boy in his arms who was smiling so cheekily back at him, and gave him a big kiss on the neck. Archie giggled. Why would he leave this all behind? At this specific moment, it seemed crazy.

***

The following day Ryan could not work an opening without it seeming unnatural. He also needed to think about the best way to deliver it, having not settled on the correct wording in his head. So, over the next couple of days, he played out scenarios in his mind, trying to cover what questions she would ask so he had the right answers. With regards to her emotions, he could predict these quite easily, she said on numerous occasions that she was born with waterfalls behind her eyes, so he wasn't expecting much else other than confusion, anger and tears.

During the days where he was off, he phoned his siblings and parents. It did not seem suspicious to any of them, as he had been calling much more frequently since Archie had come along, but this time he used the Archie excuse to call again and catch up, possibly for the final time. He loved his family, and knew he was going to miss them, but the prospect of losing Becky and Archie was all he could think about, which naturally put his feelings for everyone else on the back burner.

Three days before he was due to meet the old man, and with every scenario he could think of run through his head multiple times, he planned his talk. He would wait for Archie to go down for his nap at around eleven in the morning, and then they would have a couple of hours if they needed to discuss the offer Ryan had received. He knew it was never going to go how he had planned but it needed to be done.

So, at eleven, he made up a bottle for Archie, and Becky took him up to put him down in his bed. Ryan tidied away the toys he had been playing with that morning, straightened up the cushions on the sofa, before sitting down and turning Archie's tv programme off. After a few minutes, he heard the door open and close from above, and then her slow creaking footsteps coming down the stairs. She appeared, holding the baby monitor. Walking over, and sitting down, finishing her nearly cold coffee that she had gotten from the mantel piece which handily kept things out of Archie's reach.

"Ah he is so cute. He held my ear and gave me a cuddle before pointing to his bed. I put him down and he just rolled over with his thumb in." she said, her voice so full of love.

"Yes, he is" Ryan agreed, a nervous energy building up inside of him.

They sat in silence for a moment. If he left it too long, he knew Becky would start looking at her phone or switching the tv on for one of her programmes. So, he swallowed his nerves and began.

"Hey, do you remember we talked a couple of years ago about the 'Old man of the Forest'? When we went for a walk that time, we said wouldn't it be weird if we ever saw him?" Ryan said, trying not to sound too unnatural.

"Yeah, you said he was just a myth though to get people to visit the forest? Has another blurry picture been posted somewhere?" she replied casually, unaware of the fight raging inside of him.

"Yes, there was another picture in the BBC, but they were saying it was Bigfoot" he said quickly, not wanting to waver from his point. She snorted at this before falling silent again.

"Well," he said, pausing as she looked at him slightly quizzically. "I met him."

"What?" She said slightly startled. "Oh, wait a minute" she said laughing, "you're having me on."

Her laughter quickly died when she saw how serious he looked, almost tearful. Her bottom lip quivered in response. Ryan continued talking slowly, but purposefully.

"I met him out on my run when you left to go to your parents. I had run for about half an hour, and was just heading back, when this figure in a brown cloak appeared, watering the plants with his hands."

"What? His hands made water?"

"No" he said realising how that had just sounded. "He had his hands cupped and carrying water for a small sapling. It wasn't just that though, he spoke with me, and told me that he was the one who looked after the forest, and that me being there signalled his time was over, and ..." he built himself up for this "and that I was the one to continue the work." He said finishing the story. This is where he was most worried about not being taken seriously.

"I don't understand, you met a man in the woods and he told you he wants you to work there? Is that it?" She said, sounding very unimpressed. How could he blame her? He spoke with more haste.

"No, that is not it. He is not just a man, he is the New Forest Dweller, the guardian of the forest, the legend of the woods, the old man of the forest. It is him, I know it."

"But wait. What?" She said starting to get frustrated that the person she loved was coming out with this. "I don't know what you mean. I mean, I know what you are saying. But how?"

"I don't know. All I do know is that I have been asked to do this incredible thing by someone everyone thought was just a rumour, a myth, a legend, but it turns out he is real, and the forest needs him, and now it needs me" he said, his voice tailing off.

"Well, let us say for a minute it is real and you want to do it. What does it pay? What hours would you do? Do you have weekends off?" She asked, a bit more frantically seeing how this was affecting him.

He paused, staring at her, his chest breathing like he had been running again. How could she understand? How could he say that the job would take all his time effectively meaning he had to leave them.

"It's not that sort of job" he said quietly, not wanting to continue but feeling like he had too now. It would have been easier to just disappear. But he loved them, and Becky deserved an explanation.

"It would take all my time, with no pay or time off. I don't know exactly what it entails, but I think if you wanted to see me, you would have to come to the forest." he said, not really sure he could look at her.

She didn't say anything right away. She just looked at him, her face unreadable.

"Have you been taking drugs?" she asked calmly.

He let out a surprised groan of pain. If she was questioning him like this, it meant he couldn't do much more to make her understand.

Suddenly, in his quiet desperation, an idea hit him.

"No of course not" he said, thinking this new plan might help show her what he meant. "Forget it ok, but let's go for a walk this afternoon after Archie's lunch. I haven't been out for a few days and we could all use the fresh air." He said, hoping that what he thought might happen, would play out.

"What?" she said getting really annoyed now. "What was all that before then? Are you going mad? Have you bumped your head?" she said, still wanting to get answers to this sudden change of behaviour.

"Let's just go for a walk this afternoon," he repeated wishing to have had this idea first instead of opting to just talk and coming across like a madman.

"Ok" she said slowly, eyes narrowed and sounding highly sceptical.

Ryan got up and headed to the kitchen to get a glass of water. He knew now this would be the way to do it.

***

Once Archie woke, was fed, and had his boots on, they got in the car and headed off. Ryan had tried to act normal the last couple of hours, but he was now getting excited and thinking this new plan would be all the proof he needed, providing it worked. Becky who had been highly suspicious of his behaviour since their talk, kept giving him funny looks as though assessing whether or not something was seriously wrong in his head.

They drove for about seven minutes, parking in the small car park at the entrance to the forest in Woodlands Road, Ashurst. Ryan knew his parents would be at work, confirming this when he drove past and the driveway was empty with the gate closed. There wasn't even anyone else parked by the forest entrance, so he reversed onto the side verge so that others could get in too if needed.

Ryan started to get Archie unstrapped, and was just about to lift him out when Archie pointed and laughed at something over Ryans shoulder. He stopped and looked round. There, sat on the car door, was a fat red breasted robin. He felt a tingle on his insides, it was starting to work.

"Oh, wow look Archie" said Becky only just seeing the bird "how friendly. Don't scare it Ryan" she added warningly, as if he might shoo it away.

It was simply just there, looking at them, but after a few moments of staring at one another, it turned to Ryan flapping its wings. Ryan leant forward, looking closely, and saw a small stick trapped in the fluffy feathers under its wing. He reached out carefully.

"Don't touch it," cried Becky, "it has probably got a disease, that's why it's come up to us."

Ryan ignored this, gently digging his fingers in, and very slowly, pulled the twig out. Flicking it onto the ground, he looked back at the bird, which gave a happy tweet, fluttered its wings, and sped off into the trees. Becky was silent now.

"Can you come and hold him while I get some hand sanitiser?" Asked Ryan, moving out the way so that Becky could pick up the unstrapped little boy. Ryan reached into the side of the passenger door, giving his hands a good few squirts of the liquid. Rubbing them together well, he pocketed the bottle in his jacket, then shut the door before turning to Becky and Archie. Becky looked slightly shocked at the interaction, not having said a word since, as Ryan walked over to the gate and opened it for them all.

"Thanks" she said as she passed through, putting Archie down on the path and holding his hand so he could walk along beside them.

Within ten metres of setting off though, a hedgehog popped out of a bush beside the path, beginning to slowly walk out into the middle of the stones.

"Ooohh" said Archie pointing whilst trying to walk towards it.

"Oh Archie, it's a hedgehog" said Becky pleased, before freezing still. She was holding Archie back, but looking sideways at Ryan who was calmly watching the little creature. Slowly, and very tentatively, it walked over to them, stopping right at Ryan's feet before flipping onto its back. Becky gasped. Ryan, pleased his plan was indeed in motion, bent down, seeing one of its paws had a thorn embedded quite deep in it. Holding its soft little leg, he used his nails to grab the end, pulling quickly. The thorn slid straight out, and Ryan pressed his thumb over the hole it had left for a few seconds. The hedgehog had tensed slightly when the thorn had been pulled, but just lay there comfortably afterwards until Ryan let go. He then carefully flipped the hedgehog back up the right way, trying not to get a spike to the hand, thinking it would just go on its way. It did, but not before nudging his shoe a couple of times with its head, before scurrying away into another bush and out of sight.

"Ooohh" said Archie again wanting to carry on walking.

Ryan reached into his pocket and sanitised his hands a second time. Becky seemed unable to speak again. After a few moments spluttering and trying to gesture, she finally managed to spit out.

"I just don't understand what is happening!"

"I know" said Ryan calmly, fully believing it himself now, "but you will soon." He reached down to take the struggling boy's hand before continuing to walk. They made it almost twenty metres this time, before a badger crossed their path, its head stuck through a plastic bag which was now twisted round its neck.

On and on they went, all the way down to the bridge by the river, by which time Ryan had helped sixteen different animals, including a pair or ladybirds that had clumsily flew into him as they had accidentally joined their legs together in tree sap. Each time something appeared, Becky and Archie would stop and watch as Ryan figured out the issue and helped sort it. After a couple of minutes at the bridge, when they had not been interrupted again, Becky turned to him.

"I get it now." She said in quite a defeated tone. What Ryan had tried to explain to her earlier had sounded like the crazy delusions of a mentally unstable person. But each animal that appeared seemed to hammer what he had said further into her rationale. There was no other explanation for it.

"I'm sorry, I tried to tell you, but how could I mention this and you believe me without seeing it" he said, glad she was able to see the predicament he was in. He was holding Archie in one arm so he could look into the water, but grabbed her hand with his other, pulling her close.

"I'm sorry, but as you can see, I think this is something I have to do." He said looking longingly into her eyes.

"I know" she said, her eyes filling up with tears.

"Oh babe, it will be ok. Why not come with me? We can live here together? Raise our son together? And look after the forest?"

She looked at him, tears rolling down her cheeks.

"I…, I don't think I can" she said lowering her gaze.

It felt like the wind had left him, but he continued anyway, breathlessly.

I am meeting the old man of the Forest on Thursday at midday. I don't know all the details yet but I will see what I can do. I don't want to lose you both" he said feeling a tear leave his eyes too.

"Please do" she said hugging him tightly. "Archie loves his daddy. So do I" she whispered.

They stood there holding each other for what seemed an age, with Archie caught between them, sucking his thumb. Before they silently held hands, walking back to the car, only getting stopped eight more times along the way.

Chapter Five – The meeting

They didn't talk much after they got back from their walk, quietly letting their thoughts and feelings settle in. Becky had work that week which usually meant an early bedtime, but because of what he had told her, and what she had seen, they ended up spending the following evenings having some long, deep discussions. In the mornings, she felt exhausted, knowing she had a full day ahead, whilst also having to get Archie up and ready for nursery.

It was good to discuss it together though, and they had needed to talk about their options. It also helped Ryan immensely to see her talk about it seriously, making it much clearer in his mind what he should do.

During the days, he finalised anything that he had left to be completed. He wrote out a will, back dating it so as not to look too suspicious. He placed it in the safe in his office, locking it, and placing the key in the top draw of his desk. Next, without being able to delay the task any longer, he emptied his van out. He put all the expensive tools in his garage so that if he had to stage a disappearance or murder, Paul and the business would not suffer too much. After that he filled out invoices for all the works they had completed that month, attaching them to emails and sent them off. Next, he emailed the following couple of weeks work schedules through to Paul so that everything would look like it was completed as normal. Finally, he completed a list of house chores Becky had left for him. Putting up some shelves, picture frames, and the new curtain rail in the dining room. These were things he had promised to do previously but had just never found the right time. Well, they are done now he thought, grimacing slightly as he saw the shelf was ever so slightly off level. He put his tools away and went to the kitchen to get a drink. He was only nineteen hours away from his meeting time, Becky and Archie would be back shortly, and he wanted to enjoy tonight with them, not knowing what tomorrow would bring.

***

He was up at seven thirty, and gave a normal goodbye kiss to Becky and Archie whilst also making her swear not to mention anything to anyone about where he was going and what he was doing.

"Yeah, like anyone would believe me." Becky said as she left to drop Archie off to nursery before work.

The plan they had made together was different to the one he would be carrying out. He had not told her that it was unlikely they would be part of his life if he accepted, which burned his insides to think about, as he had to lie slightly during their discussions. She would never want to live a life without having contact with her own family, as they spoke almost every day, seeing each other as often as possible. No, he was going to have to talk to the old man, to see if something could be worked out where he got to see them, but knowing what the outcome could be.

He had considered all options now though, planning how he would carry out the meeting. If it came to the worst, and that the forest needed him so much that Becky and Archie would have to be removed from his life, then he regretfully felt he could not take the position. If he did accept, he knew it would mean causing Becky a huge amount of pain, and he just could not do that to her. He loved them both so much. In this instance, he did not care about his own feelings, only for those he loved the most. The sacrifice of his life to the forest to save so many more that needed help every day would be a selfless act, he thought, knowing Becky would not see it that way.

So he set off, taking the key for his van, a ten-pound note in his trouser pocket, an old wallet with his driver's licence and a bit of loose change in it, and his phone, which had been backed up to the cloud so that all his pictures and memories would be safe for Becky. He had turned it off so it could not be tracked. He drove into Southampton, and parked on the Industrial estate around the corner from the Southampton football stadium. He left his old wallet in the glove box, locking the van and making sure to walk past a few cameras to capture his image so if anyone had to check, they would see he had been there. Then, knowing the route he would take, he swapped his top and trousers for spares hidden underneath, binning the old ones. He then walked about three miles and caught a bus back towards the forest, having to change just once for another that went out towards Salisbury, with a stop near Nomansland on the way. He had done this so that his disappearance would look suspicious, meaning his life insurance would have to pay out to Becky. If the old man agreed that they could move with him and be part of his life, he would return to pick up his van without anyone being any the wiser. He felt he had prepared for every option.

He arrived in Nomansland at around eleven thirty, having had to walk for forty minutes through the woods where the bus had dropped him off. He kept back from the village green, staying under the shade of the trees, keeping watch. At five to twelve, he walked out of the trees and waited. A couple of cars went past, but other than that, the place was very quiet.

Twelve came, with Ryan constantly looking round expectantly. He was still alone on the green. Starting to feel dreadfully foolish with every passing moment. He walked about a bit, trying to see if he was in the right area.

Five past twelve according to his watch, a sinking feeling was swallowing his nerve. Had he dreamt it, surely it had been real. It must have been, he thought hopefully, remembering the animals, that could not have just been coincidence. Relaxing slightly, he then noticed something out of the corner of his eye. On the grass, near his feet, were about a dozen flies all facing the same way. More landed, and then another lot. Around three dozen, all facing the same way, and all forming the shape of an

"Arrow" Ryan whispered to himself, warmth spreading through him. This was real, he had not gone insane.

It pointed directly south, into the woods the other side of the road. Ryan strode quickly, trying to keep true to the way they had pointed. After a few minutes, he found himself surrounded by thick trees. Moving slowly now, so as to not miss any signs, he carried on what he thought was straight, and a minute later, found himself in a clearing, but not alone any more. A figure, in a brown hooded cloak stood with his back to him, peacefully still.

"You found me alright then?" Asked the old man turning around to view him. His cloak helped him blend in well with the trees, his hands stood out slightly though, as they were clasped out in front of him.

"Yes" said Ryan walking toward him with relief.

"I take it this means you accept the position?" Followed up the old man, smiling.

Ryan paused before beginning slowly.

"I simply can't leave my fiancé Becky and son Archie" he said, and this comment caused the old man's smile to turn into a look of unhappiness. Ryan carried on, knowing he had to ask,

"Is there a way for them to be here with me in the forest, so we can be together when my work is done and we can raise Archie together whilst looking after the forest?" he said, his voice layered with hopefulness.

The old man knew what it was like to leave people behind, he'd had to do it, and it did not feel good to do. He chose his words carefully.

"I'm afraid of repeating what I have said before. In this position, the forest above all else comes first, its needs are great, and you will find you have little to no free time. Therefore, I think having them move to the forest with you, would not be possible," he said, taking a firm stance. It was true, if one had to devote their full attention to something, there could be no distractions.

Seeing Ryan was faltering with his decision, the old man said

"Come with me and let me show you what I really do. You will see it from a very different perspective. However, we cannot possibly know all the secrets that are hidden here, I do not feel I have uncovered even half of them." He said, knowing the temptation he himself had to know more as a young man. There was a pause. Ryan felt like he wanted to be convinced this was the right thing to do, and to be shown something that would make his decision easier.

"Show me then," said Ryan suddenly. "Show me what needs to be done, and I'll decide if I can."

The old man smiled widely.

"Wonderful, ok firstly" he said walking over to the nearest tree, Ryan followed. "You will need to be able to get around the forest. Out there you have cars. Here we have what I call, root transport. And it goes like this." With his arm flat on the tree trunk and with a very faint pop, he disappeared. Ryan jumped back in shock. What the hell, where had he gone?

"I'm over here if you're wondering," said the old man from behind Ryan.

Spinning on the spot, Ryan gasped. There he was, leaning against the next tree along.

"Root transport" continued the old man. "It's complex to explain, but simple to do. Now you must place the palm of your hand on the tree, bush, plant, or grass, close your other fist and think about where you want to end up. The forest is all connected you see, deep down beneath the ground it forges a connection. The better you know the forest, the more places you can transport to. Now mine works because of my title, The New Forest Dweller. In order for you to be able to do it, you will need to agree to train as my apprentice. Do not worry, it is not binding, well yet. It is so not just any human can use the network. Go on, you try. Aim for, um, that tree over there" he said pointing at an oak about ten metres away.

"I accept your training" said Ryan loudly, hoping the trees could hear this. The old man smiled again. Turning back to the tree, Ryan placed his palm against the cool bark. With his mind, he thought about the tree he wanted to connect to. With a pause and feeling of complete disbelief in this working, despite already having seen it done, he squeezed his spare fist shut.

Pop.

"ARGH" cried out Ryan, tumbling to the ground.

Righting himself, he saw that he had in fact moved to the tree he wanted, albeit arriving upside down.

The old man burst out laughing.

"I forgot about that," he wheezed, doubling up slightly. It took a few seconds for him to stop cackling, returning to a sensible voice, but with tears in his eyes. "You must picture where you want to go, and turn slightly as you clench your fist.

That is so the momentum follows you, and you arrive the right way up. Try it again, back to the first tree."

A bit shocked, but glad it worked, Ryan concentrated again. This time he twisted slightly just before he clenched and with another pop, landed right side up, back where he had started.

"Very good" said the old man with a clap or two. "Took me nine times to do it as well as that when I started."

"Thanks" said Ryan, a bit shocked still. The transporting did not feel like anything really. The only thing he noticed was a slightly sweet smell, like honey.

"Ah pollen power" said the old man breathing in deeply. "Ok, now you've got the hang of that, you need to be clothed."

Looking him up and down he continued with

"Yep, I think I gave the sisters the correct measurements."

"Which sisters?" asked Ryan, a little confused.

"Ah" said the old man smiling, "witch sisters indeed. The 'Sisters of the Wreath'."

***

They travelled together with linked arms along the root transport, as Ryan had no idea where he would be going. Within a millisecond of leaving the ground, they had both returned to it. The old man took his hand off a very bulbous, blackened, oddly shaped looking tree. The tree was so strange, that for a moment Ryan didn't even notice the large cottage wall a couple of metres behind it. That being said, the old stacked stone walls and tiled roof were almost completely covered in moss and ivy, and hidden by the bushes surrounding it.

"Where are we?" Asked Ryan, not able to recognise the location. They were stood in a little pocket of land, with the trees either side and the cottage and its small grassy garden in between.

"On the outskirts of Burley. They have been here for years now. Come on, follow me around here" said the old man, walking carefully round the side of the cottage.

They passed a small brick water well, which had a wooden bucket on a rope attached to a pulley, making their way to a very slanted wooden door inset with bolts and a large black knocker.

The old man reached up to the knocker, and rapped it six times on the door.

There was a pause. Ryan was certain he saw a netted curtain twitch in the window above them. Then the door slid open a crack, revealing complete darkness within.

"Yesssss?" came a sinister female voice, sending a shiver down Ryans spine.

"Oh, stop trying to scare him," said the old man chuckling. "We're here to meet you and to get robed."

The door swung open fully showing a large purple curtain which was pulled back to reveal a bright cosy interior. The cottage was full of old wooden beams, thick armchairs, and a fire crackling away in a fireplace which separated the two downstair rooms of the cottage. A large black cauldron was hanging above the fire, and Ryan noticed a few very twiggy brooms resting in the far corner by a metal umbrella stand. A plump happy looking lady with orange hair stood across the doorway,

"Oh you," she said smiling at the old man, "ruining our fun. Come on down sisters" she said, calling over her shoulder.

Appearing at her side almost immediately was a thin taller lady with purple hair, and an older shorter woman with crazy white hair stuck up all over.

"Come on in Dweller" said the older lady with the crazy white hair, and the others stood back to let them pass beneath the wooden beam above the door.

Ryan followed the old man in, and was hit by a wall of warmth sprinkled with the scent of many herbs and spices. Coughing slightly as the hot fumes penetrated his lungs, he moved further forward into the room.

The door shut with a snap behind them, and the curtain was pulled back across.

"Ah the new one," said the purple haired lady, eyeing him up and down.

"Oh, he is a handsome," said the orange haired one, giggling.

"Just like you were when you started," said the white-haired lady, winking at Dweller.

"Sisters, this is Ryan, my protegee to take over from me as the New Forest Dweller" said Dweller holding his arms out in presentation.

"Maybe" Ryan corrected him.

"Hmmm" said the white-haired lady. "Unsure are we?"

"Yes" said Ryan, feeling sad for the first time since he had met with Dweller in the forest, as he thought about Becky and Archie.

"Oh, my dear" said the orange haired woman pulling him into a hug. "We can help with that. I'm Flo by the way, this here's Gwen," she said releasing him and pointing to the purple haired lady who smiled. "And her over there, that's Dotty" she finished, pointing to the white crazy haired lady before adding "and we are."

"The sisters of the Wreath." They called in union, holding up their right arms, with index fingers touching together.

"Nice to meet you," said Ryan smiling back at them, but still feeling down inside.

"Now a little spell I think is needed," said Flo, looking past Ryans smile and into his eyes. She walked over to the bookcase and slid her finger along five or six books before stopping at the right one and removing it.

"Yes, here we are" she said holding it out in front of her and ruffling through to about the middle page of the book.

"Two spells for a new dweller in training. One for himself, and one that will help his loved ones." She said looking up from the book to Ryans face.

"Spells?" questioned Ryan apprehensively. "For what?"

It was Gwen who replied.

"Well, they will not change you in any way, or your loved ones. But they will stop missing you as much, and it will make them forget about where you have gone. They will be a bit upset, but not like they would be if you just do not return. Also, it helps keep The New Forest Dweller a mystery, not like in the fourteenth century when everyone knew the Dwellers. No, best be just a rumour, especially now in the age of phones and photos." She said with an understanding smile.

A moments silence before Flo took over.

"The spell for yourself, that is so that you do not miss your family as much. The forest would be your home now, and you will become part of the cycle, putting its needs first."

Ryan paused, letting this all sink in. It probably would be best for Becky, if he decided to stay, to receive the spell. He knew how worried and distraught she would be if he didn't come back, and this would alleviate a lot of his own concern, knowing she would not be suffering. Archie is too young to remember anyway, Ryan wouldn't want the spell put on him. As for himself, he wanted to remember them, he loved the memories, and could not lose that even if he would be losing them.

"Could the spell be broken in the future?" He asked trying to sound innocent.

They all looked at one another.

"Yes," said Dotty slowly. "If it comes a point where your loved ones see you, and knows where you are, then the full force of their feelings will return for you. But this shouldn't be something that should be considered." She added in warning.

"Dangerous having all those feelings flooding back" said Flo, her voice full of worry. "Not something that should be thought about really."

Silence followed as the ladies and Dweller all looked at Ryan, who was staring at the ground. The ground being a large thin, threadbare rug that covered almost the entire flagstone floor.

"Did you have to use the spells?" Ryan said, looking to the old man.

Dweller returned the gaze, slowly nodding.

"Just the one for them, not for me." He said quietly.

Ryan thought for a moment, he wanted to do good in the world and the spell quelled a lot of his worry. He pictured their faces again in his mind, his eyes shut. I love you, he said to them in his head, wanting to be able to tell them and kiss them. He settled on a decision and looked up.

"Ok then, the spell for Becky only, to help her. But not for me or anybody else" he said, knowing he was making the right decision, glad he had planned his disappearance so thoroughly.

Relief broke out in their faces, and the old man Dweller patted him on the back.

"Welcome to the Forest family," he said smiling.

"Thank you," said Ryan trying to smile. "Shall we proceed with the spell?"

"Absolutely," said Dotty taking the book from Flo and placing some bejewelled glasses on her nose. "Ah yes here we are. Uh Hmm, ladies if you please." She said holding a pointed finger aloft.

Flo and Gwen both moved about collecting items from jars and draws before returning to Ryan. Gwen lifted a withered daisy chain up and over his head so it sat loosely around his neck. Flo ground some pepper on top of his head before sticking a sprig of lavender up each of his nostrils.

"Hold your breath dear," she said with a wink. "Think clearly about who it is you want the spell to work on."

Then they all stood back. Dweller moved over to the fireplace, casually looking down into the cauldron that was occasionally releasing a bubble from within. Dotty walked forward, resting her finger on the centre of his forehead. Ryan, holding his breath and trying hard to picture Becky, went slightly cross eyed looking at it.

"Ready?" she asked, smiling at him. He nodded gently and her smile widened. In a loud voice she read.

"Forest Dweller you shall be, when Dwellers time has come to pass, the forest you will protect, from biggest oak to withered grass, and all the animals that do belong, will look to you for love and support, as the ones who currently cherish you, their pain be gone, Dweller forgot."

A tiny static shock from her finger to his head was felt by them both. Removing her finger and stepping backwards she said,

"It is done."

Flo and Gwen moved forwards and together they removed the lavender from his nose, took off the daisy chain, and ruffled his hair so little crushed peppercorns dropped to the floor. Ryan released his breath through nostrils that still retained some of the lavender scent, sucking in some fresh air through his mouth.

***

The New Forest Dweller

A long way away, in a department in Southampton hospital, Becky's mood suddenly became much more cheerful. Her shift was almost finished and she would be leaving soon to pick Archie up on the way back to see Ryan at home. Little did she know now, that he would not be home.

***

Back in the cottage, Ryan was still stood where he had been for the spell. He didn't feel any different himself, but he now knew that Becky would be ok. As Dotty sank deep into an armchair by the fire, Flo and Gwen bustled back over holding brown fabric much like Dwellers cloak.

"Here we are dear," said Flo, laying the longest piece over the back of the armchair. "This is your new cloak, and Gwen here has your, well, undergarment should we say," she said giggling.

"Thank you," said Ryan a little surprised but taking the fabric from Gwen.

"We promise we won't look," said Gwen with a wink as her and Dotty turned away.

"I'm not promising that," said Flo with a small laugh before proceeding to cover her eyes.

Ryan started to strip off, folding his clothes neatly on the floor by his shoes. The undergarment was just a triangular strip of cloth to be worn around his waist and then through his legs and tucked into the back.

"All self-cleaning material," said Gwen, all eyes still averted. "You can do all your business in it without taking it off and cleaning. The nutrients etc will be transported into the soil around the forest."

Ryan who was slightly surprised and disgusted by this, looked over to the Dweller whose face turned slightly sheepish.

"It takes a little getting used to," he admitted, knowing it felt weird at first to fight every instinct you had always relied on not to go when clothed, "I'm peeing right now if truth be told," he said smiling.

A little unsure, but definitely going to check it worked before soiling himself, Ryan started on the cloak. At least the prospect of possibly embarrassing himself in front of them all had removed Becky and Archie temporarily from his mind.

"Like the undergarment it is self-cleaning, inside and out. If you sweat or get covered in rain or mud, it will keep you clean, comfortable, dry, and warm. It will keep you healthy and free from colds, bugs, and disease, giving your full body a cleanse to keep you as fit and active as possible. No need for shoes either, the cloak should reach to the floor and not fray or get caught in thorns or branches, bushes, or wire fencing." Said Flo, peeking between her fingers as she heard the cloak dropping over him, very slightly resting on the floor. Removing her hand completely she said,

"Ah, the perfect fit."

Ryan felt a tingle all over his body, as though being tickled by a thousand feathers. He could feel it on his insides too, he knew was being cleaned from head to toe.

"Excellent," said Dweller looking round to him. "Also, Flo forgot to mention that the material also can remove hair, for instance if it starts getting long on your head, beard or anywhere else, simply put your hood up and think about what you want."

"So why do you have that haircut" asked Dotty swiftly, making the other two laugh and drawing a smile out of Ryan for the first time in a while.

"My dear Dotty, I am no spring chicken. I saw my reflection in a pond a little while ago and decided I needed something that better befit my age."

Trying to hold back a grin, he turned back to Ryan and continued.

"You'll find large deep pockets either side of the cloak" said Dweller, showing Ryan the pockets on his one. "These are magical also. For the one of your right, you have any tools and equipment you might need for the forest, simply think of what you want with your hand in your pocket, and pull it out. But please remember to put it back in so we are not leaving things all over the place." He added, and Ryan nodded. He continued.

"Your left pocket is similar, but with food and drink. Anything you can think of is at your request, but before you try, please remember you need to think about a plate or cup too. My first time wanting a Bolognese, started with me and a handful of spaghetti with pasta sauce." He said laughing.

Ryan tried the right pocket first, pulling out a needle and thread, a lighter, a shovel, a first aid kit, and a six-foot wooden fence post. Chuckling while tucking them back in his cloak he noticed the post seemed very light. It would appear that the cloak enhanced his strength too.

"Light eh?" Said dweller with a sparkle in his eye. "Makes you quicker too. These cloaks are essential though to get everything done around here."

Ryan reached back in and pulled out a wooden box with a small silver clasp. Opening it, he placed his clothes, shoes, phone, watch and keys inside, before closing the lid and dropping it back in his pocket.

Satisfied with this, he thought what next, before remembering the left pocket and instantly wanting to try it. Out of it, he pulled a slice of pepperoni pizza. He took a bite. It tasted as good as any he had eaten before. He placed the rest back in his pocket, not feeling it hit the bottom. Oh, he liked this! Next, he reached in and grabbed a glass on freshly squeezed orange juice. After drinking heavily, he once again dropped the glass back in, and turned to them all.

"Well, happy? Asked Flo, smiling widely.

"Oh yes," replied Ryan, trying to decide what obscure food he could try when he was alone, caviar sprung to mind.

"Well, thank you ladies" said Dweller bowing to them all. "We'd best get moving. A lot to see and teach, and not much time to do it," he said grimacing slightly.

"Please feel free to pop in anytime" said Gwen looking at Ryan. "And please look after the forest well. We all rely on it for our magic and existence," she said giving him a hug goodbye. Flo rushed in to give him one too.

"And you, Dweller, make sure we see you again, multiple times, before you are gone" demanded Dotty, getting up and following them over to the door.

"I will do of course" he said, pulling back the curtain and unlatching the door.

"Bye, see you soon" said Ryan, stepping out into the bright natural light which contrasted the fire and candle light from within the cottage. Squinting slightly at Dweller, he heard the door snap shut again.

"Ah, nice to be back to the fresh air," said Dweller rubbing his hands together.

"Now let me show you my forest" he said grinning.

Chapter Six – Dweller Duties Begin

Over the next few hours, Dweller took him to some of the main spots around the forest. From Burley they travelled to a large tree by Beaulieu, from there to Cadnam, and then to Bramshaw, Sway, Bransgore, Frogham, Brockenhurst, Ashurst and finally, Lyndhurst. They did not appear in any of these village centres, but on the outskirts, where eyes could not seek them out.

As they went, Dweller kept up a stream of information about each area, and about the groups of people or things that lived there.

Night had started to draw in, darkening the sky slightly as they silently walked along through an area of boggy marshland. They didn't sink into the mud thanks to their cloaks, but instead seemed to walk across it as though it was solid ground.

Ryan thought about the day, it seemed as if he had been there an eternity already because of what he had seen and learnt. Other than the 'Sisters of the Wreath', they had also met with the Forest Folk. They were a kind simple people who smoked long pipes, lived off the land, and travelled around the forest, usually on the plains with their horses and carts. They were a tribe of around sixty or so, with mixed ages from the elders, down to baby Holly who giggled and waved at them from within the cloth which was wrapped around her mother's shoulders. They had also met the Pixies in the woodland around Brockenhurst, and the tiny King himself had expressed delight that the forest would be in good hands still with this new Dweller looking after it. There were thousands of them, all around four inches in height, and each with a shiny clear pair of wings which allowed them to make their homes near the tops of the trees.

They trudged on further into the wooded area before Dweller stopped in the Darkness.

"I think we should rest here for the night" he said, sitting down with his back to a tree. "I have shown you a great deal of the forest today. You have done well in keeping up, but I, well we now, have been shirking our duty. Tomorrow, I will show you what we do and how we can help in the forest." He said closing his eyes almost immediately.

Ryan paused for a moment, and walked over to another tree a few metres away. Laying down beside it felt weird at first, but the cloak seemed to comfort him no matter how he lay, as if a memory foam mattress was built into its cloth. He reached into his left pocket and drew out a glass of water and a slice of cherry pie, which tasted delicious. He had been testing the pocket all day, but each time it had produced the goods. The tin of surströmming, the rotten herring, was a particular favourite of the day ,and the old man Dweller had gagged at the smell. Ryan dropped it back into the pocket after he'd opened it, hoping it would not ruin the cloak, but no, the magic that imbibed the cloth had sent it into an abyss within the pocket. Now with his hand in his right one, he drew out his box with his personal belongings. He longed to turn on his phone and speak to Becky, but knew that would not be possible now. For things at his old home were not nearly as peaceful as they were in the forest.

***

Becky's better mood had well and truly vanished. She had picked up Archie and was on her way home, assuming under her spelled state that Ryan would be there. As she pulled into the drive, and saw his van was gone, she called him. Twice the phone rang through with no answer. She then phoned Paul to find out if Ryan had been at work with him. He hadn't, so she tried him again. Still nothing, so she text him. After she had fed and bathed Archie, finally putting him to bed, she decided to phone his dad. But again, he hadn't heard or seen Ryan that day. Starting to panic now, Becky thought she would try him one last time before phoning the police. The same as before, straight to voicemail. Heart sinking, she pressed nine, nine, nine on her key pad, asking for the Police when the options were given.

"Hello, emergency services, you're through to the Hampshire Police Department" came the professional voice down the phone.

"Oh hello" said Becky, wondering if she was doing the right thing "I'm just calling as my partner hasn't come home today and I can't contact him and no one seems to know where he is" she said, the words bringing tears to her eyes.

"Ok, I'll just ask you a few questions if you don't mind?" said the voice. A woman's voice, Becky thought, although it was quite deep. She could hear the sound of a keyboard tapping away in the background of the call.

They went through all the basic details, with Becky providing her name, address, and contact information for herself and for Ryan. She had answered about thirty different questions before they got to 'What vehicle does he use?'

"His work van" said Becky, managing to keep her cool throughout the talk, hoping Ryan would just text or call now so she could answer him and make sure he was alright. She followed on with,

"It's a sign written building company van that he uses for work" she said, thinking that maybe she should have mentioned this sooner.

There was a pause down the line.

"Give me a moment" the lady said. Becky had confirmed during the questioning that she was indeed female.

"Is it registration YG63 XPB?" She asked. "A white ford transit?"

Heart racing Becky replied,

"I know it's a white ford yes, but I wouldn't have a clue what the registration was"

"A sign written building company vehicle was reported damaged after someone smashed some windows and broke into the rear compartment in Southampton earlier this afternoon. I would say from these pictures in front of me, it would unfortunately appear to be your Fiancés vehicle."

Becky's heart seemed to stop.

"I just don't understand" Is all she could remember saying, over and over again. The thoughts of why he had not answered her calls now seemed to play out in her head like a terrible dream. Had he been kidnapped or killed? Had he committed suicide?

"Hello? Becky?" The voice said, a bit more panicked that there was no response at first. "I'll send a car around to talk to you, if you could get someone in the meantime to come over and support you, that would be best," she said.

"Ok" said Becky half dazed at what this all could mean, "Thank you," she added before ending the call.

Ryans parents got there about a minute before the police.

They all sat down in the lounge and went over details, saying that they were checking all the CCTV in the area and asked what did she know about his activities that day. But due to the spell, she knew nothing of what he had done since she had left for work that morning.

They continued for about an hour, until the police got a call confirming Ryan had been spotted on a camera walking towards Southampton.

"That almost certainly rules out suicide," said the officer, trying the help ease Becky's worry.

They stayed for another half an hour, talking about procedures and what a search would involve before saying their sombre goodbyes and leaving. Another Police car would be stationed outside in case Ryans family were targeted from whatever had happened to him.

Steve and Marie stayed that night in the spare room, and a very tearful Becky had the worst night's sleep, her dreams of losing Archie as well and not being able to find him, made her shiver and weep alone in bed.

***

Ryan awoke from a the most peaceful sleep he could remember. The daylight was just breaking, and the birds seemed to be serenading them. He lay there for a few moments, admiring the gently swaying of the leaves above him.

"Morning" said Dweller walking over, "How did you sleep?"

"Wonderfully" said Ryan, stealthily getting to his feet and pulling a tea with two sugars from his pocket.

"Ah, good, drink up quickly then" said Dweller, chomping on a Croissant, "We've got a lot to do today."

Within a few minutes Ryan had drank his tea and placed the cup in the pocket. Dweller had finished too, and was wiping some crumbs away from his mouth.

"Right then" he said rubbing his hands together and pushing up his sleeves.

"There is a whole lot of the forest, and not a lot of you. How would you know if there was a sick squirrel ten miles away for instance? My way for dealing with this and other emergencies is this. When you have a free moment, where you are not clearing up debris from storms, or cultivating an area, rest your hand against the tree with your other one squeezed shut, but do not think of a destination. Instead, think 'emergency' and you will be transported where you are needed." He said, the palm of his hand still placed against the tree. "Almost all the time there will be something to help, and it is one of our duties to the forest to do this. We will do the first one together. I know you have had some practice already before you came here, but you are a Dweller now so it is your duty. Go on, ready yourself and place your hand on the tree. WAIT, let me grab your other hand."

Ryan did so, palm to tree, feeling the ridges of the bark beneath it, his other fist clenched with Dweller holding on. The moment he thought 'emergency' they vanished.

They reappeared in the grass along a road Ryan recognised, the B three zero seven eight to Fordingbridge. They were right alongside a small pony, who had unfortunately been hit by a car, and was lying, shaking convulsively on the tarmac. There wasn't any sign of the car, or indeed anyone else around. Good thing too thought Ryan.

"Ah poor thing" said Dweller kneeling at its side. "We're too late to help I think."

A large patch of blood was leaking out from beneath the animal, and Ryan noticed that its front left leg had been bent severely away from where it was meant to be. It didn't even seem to have the strength to make a noise to the other horses, who were just a few metres away grazing. Dweller put his hand on the horses' head, and the animal became still, then the head slowly drooped until it lay motionless.

The nearest horse let out a whinny and trotted over. It stood by the side of the foal and nudged it with its nose. With no response, it turned its head and walked back to the others, to continue eating the grass.

"We've got to go" said Dweller quickly, as Ryan stood there looking down, wondering why he felt tingling in his feet, "People coming." Dweller said warningly.

He grabbed Ryans hand, making him hold his clenched fist before putting his palm on the grass and they vanished in an instant.

Back in another wooded section, they released hands, stepping back to look at one another.

"Sometimes, the body is too far gone and the soul is in too great a pain" Dweller began looking at Ryan who was quite upset the first animal they tried to help had died. "To help ease its pain, you need to touch its head and use your thoughts to comfort and guide its soul, so that it releases and becomes part of the forest cycle." He said, making sure Ryan was following. "Also, you might have noticed the tingling in your feet?" He said and Ryan nodded at this. "We get this whenever a human is approaching, so that we can disappear, for it would be more harm than good to reveal ourselves to the world again."

"What happens if we accidentally transport to an area where humans can see us?" asked Ryan, thinking about all the dog walkers and people out and about across the forest.

"Ah, that is when the forest takes over. It knows where the people are, and would not let you appear in a place where you will be caught. What is more, there have been numerous cameras and drones around the forest recently, capturing the spring time, and stopping would be thieves pinching the wood from the log piles. Thankfully our cloaks distort the images so we are not really seen. You were only able to see me" said Dweller, smiling before continuing, "because you must have been the chosen one."

Ryan thought about all this for a minute or so, as Dweller helped himself to a drink of what looked to be ginger beer.

"Ah, another thing." He said, as if it had only just occurred to him. "The transport will also take you to the most urgently needed emergency first. So, as you could see, that foal was the most in need throughout the forest. Sometimes I end up helping hundreds of plants, trees, and animals a day, usually in the aftermath of a storm or during a drought" he said, taking another swig from his bottle.

They stood there for a minute more, Ryan deep in thought, the birds tweeting overhead, and a slow breeze whistling gently through the trees. Dweller finished his drink, returning his bottle to his pocket.

"Now, I think we will go off separately, sorting emergencies, over the forest. I imagine there has been a few as we didn't do any yesterday afternoon" he said striding over to the nearest tree. "We'll meet back at sunset, in the woods by Nomansland where we started out yesterday."

And without waiting for a reply, he placed his palm on the tree, and with the faintest of pops, vanished. A light waft of honey hit Ryans nostrils again.

Slightly surprised that he would be on his own all day sorting emergencies, Ryan readied himself, before disappearing to his first location. On arrival, he was greeted by a deer with a broken leg, standing gingerly in the middle of a light woodland area that Ryan did not know.

"Oh, you poor thing." Said Ryan approaching.

He spent the next twenty minutes or so strapping up the leg and attaching a splint to support it comfortably. The pocket seemed to provide a see-through bandage as standard, which made sense to Ryan as it would look extremely odd if someone were to see a deer all strapped up like a human. It was amazing what he could demand from his right pocket. He had spent about five minutes trying to make a splint from scratch before realising he could just ask for one, the correct size and fit for the animal. He stood back looking pleased, and the deer rubbed its head against his arm in thanks, leaving a slight stain from its nose before the cloak magically cleaned it. Then the deer turned and trotted gently through the trees to the rest of the herd that was waiting uncertainly, a little way away. He assumed that when the bandage and splint he had used eventually dropped off, it would be absorbed back into the forest. He would ask Dweller just to be sure. Satisfied with his first one, and happy it wasn't to put down an animal, he left for the next.

Straight away he appeared on a slight hillside out in the open, beside a small shrub that looked beige and parched. Ryan bent down and took a glass of water out of his pocket, pouring it onto the plant. Well, that was easy he thought smiling at the simplicity of this one compared to the last, before noticing that the water had disappeared before it had hit the ground. He tried again, but with the same outcome. Standing back up, and scratching his head, he noticed the twinkling of a pond at the bottom of the hill. Remembering where the plant was, he went down, taking a bucket out of his right pocket as he went. But the water from the pond would not stay in it, jumping out as if alive, back into the rest of it. Very odd thought Ryan, bewildered again.

Thinking hard now, he then remembered when he had first met Dweller, he had been carrying his cupped hands full of water.

That was it. Rolling up his sleeves, he plunged his hands into the cold liquid. He turned and then jogged gently back up to where the shrub sat. Pouring the water into the soil around it, the plant gave what appeared to be a very faint shiver, and Ryan was hit with the smell of pollen. Not sure if this was good or bad, he turned and headed back down. After the fourth trip, and when a greenish tinge had returned to the plants colour, Ryan assumed that the pollen smell had been it saying thanks. So, he pressed his hand onto another slightly better-looking shrub nearby, and vanished once again.

This continued to happen for the remainder of the day. Thankfully around midday though, the most serious ones had all been dealt with, and he was left with simpler tasks like helping a group of baby birds that had fallen out of their nest. He had thought it would be tough to get them back up so high, before he remembered his pocket. From its depths, he extracted a tree winch, and thanks to a lucky throw, got it over the nests branch, returning the squeaking chicks to their thankful mother. She allowed Ryan to stroke her gently on the head, before turning to her offspring, and seemed to berate them for giving her such a scare.

It was not until later in the day when the sun was lower in the sky, and after he had helped a rabbit which had some barbed wire stuck around its tail, that he appeared at another serious one.

A hedgehog laying half squashed in the road, a car in the distance. Ryan quickly bent down to it and saw that it had little hope of recovering. Its feet and rear end had been caught, meaning its bowels had squeezed out, still attached somehow, but flat on the tarmac. Ryan noted the feeble attempts at movement from the front end, so gently placed his warm hand on its head. It was such a strange feeling to connect to an animal like this, to try and guide it to peace so its pain ended sooner. He felt he led the hedgehog on a long journey, not having done it before, and had taken a while to find the right feelings to send it on its way. Its limp lifeless body just lay there now, finally at peace, but still in prime tyre squelching position. He carefully scooped up its body in cupped hands, guts dangling down under it, and placed it by a thorny bush away from the road. Standing up and staring at its little body, Ryan started getting a tingling in his feet that could only mean one thing. He reached out, and palm to thorny bush, disappeared once again.

When Sunset came, he had to admit he was knackered, both physically and mentally. Finishing up with a frog which was lost, before he reunited it with its pond family, he headed back to Nomansland. Well, he tried to. His hand on a tree like usual, his other clenched, imagining himself the right way up on the tree he travelled from in Nomansland. But still, it didn't work. So, he picked another tree, one by the village green, so he could walk along to the spot and see what the issue was.

That worked. He arrived by the village green just as he imagined. Keeping in the tree line and walking quickly, he made it close to the spot he had originally intended. Through the air though, he could hear children's laughter, and a tingling in his feet meant he was close to someone. Carefully creeping through the undergrowth to take a look, he saw four kids around the age of eleven or twelve, playing on a rope swing they had managed to hook over the branch of a tree. Knowing Dweller would not be able to appear here either, he waited a while, just watching as the kids took turns swinging and pushing with such innocent happiness. Then out of the corner of his eye, he spotted Dweller signalling to him across the other side of where the children were playing. He was pointing to a tree near him. Understanding immediately Ryan touched the closest one to him, and appeared beside the old man.

"Shhh" he said, a finger pressed to his lips. "This way."

Half crouching, half walking, they made their way through the thicker trees to an area less likely to be disturbed.

"The kids will probably be back home now" said Dweller stopping by some big oak trees. The darkness had descended almost completely, with the normal sounds of the forest seeming slightly eerier at night to Ryans ears. Sitting down and pulling a lantern from his pocket, Dweller turned to Ryan and said,

"So, how was your first full day? Learn a lot?"

"Yes indeed" said Ryan pulling a plate of sausage, mash, peas, and onion gravy from his pocket along with a cold bottle of beer. It seemed pointless offering Dweller one too considering he could produce his quicker than Ryan could ask. He followed on with,

"There was one this afternoon, with a hedgehog, where I had to help guide his soul to peace" he said, looking the old man in the face who had, in the meantime, magicked up a paella and glass of white wine.

"How did you find it? Weird at first, isn't it? Just remember that if the animal is putting up too much of a fight, in their head that is, they probably will make it with some help." He said, sipping his wine.

"This one was past saving unfortunately" Ryan replied confidently, knowing he had done the right thing, even if it was slow. He had a few mouthfuls of his food whilst laid back against a tree.

"Seen anything weird today then?" said the old man.

To Ryan, the whole day had been weird.

"Nothing too strange" he lied, not knowing what was normal and what was strange yet "did you?" he added.

"Nothing much out of the ordinary. It would take something really peculiar to beat my most memorable emergency." He said tucking into his food.

"What was that then?" Asked Ryan, eager to hear Dwellers past stories of the forest.

"Well," said the old man, and then paused momentarily to swallow his mouthful. "I suppose the deer had sat down in the evening to get some rest, oh umm, out near New Milton way" he started, his eyes glinting, a smile forming at the corners of his mouth. "But little did he know that a certain mole had been digging up the area all day. Well by the time I got there, the deer was knackered from running, and the mole, who had tunnelled up and become lodged headfirst in its bottom, was still in a right panic."

Ryan began laughing loud, Dweller too for a minute before he continued.

"Thankfully the deer froze when it saw me, and I was able to prise the wriggling little soil muncher from its behind." He said trying to hold back a laugh again. "I had to apply cream to the deer's bum for a week, and clear out the moles nose with a suction cup." He finished, breaking out into a happy cackle.

Ryan was still laughing hard, trying not to choke on his food, and hoping his cloak would come to the rescue if he did.

"Brilliant" he said when he had managed to swallow.

"Yeah" said the old man wiping a tear from his eye, "It is nice to get a funny one sometimes. Unexpected, as more often than not they are serious" he said sombrely.

They sat in silence for a while with just a few flies buzzing around the lantern, the clinking of cutlery as they ate their meals, and the low drone of the wind through the trees.

When he had finished his dinner, and placed his utensils and plate back in his pocket, he thought about the withered shrub he had helped early in the day.

"Hey Dweller, why can't we produce water for the plants? I helped a plant this morning, but had to carry the water in my hands, like you did when we met. What's with that?"

"Well," said Dweller, lying back against a tree and pulling his hood over his head so his face was cast in shadow. "We are here to help the forest. The cloaks powers of food and drink are limited to us, to sustain us, and allow us to focus on helping and protecting those in need. The water and rain in the forest has its own magical properties, that the ancient Dwellers would say helps spread the feelings and news of the world around to the forest. By providing water that is fresh and unused, we could break the chain of life, and alienate plants and creatures from the rest of them."

"Wow, I never knew the forest was so complex and connected" said Ryan, his mind never fully comprehending that the forest could be so in tune with its surroundings. Then something else occurred to him which he thought he knew the answer to but asked Dweller for confirmation.

"What happens to the bandages and other medical things we use on the animals? Do they drop off? What happens to them?"

Dweller responded immediately, the question one he assumed would be asked. "Sometimes we are called back during another emergency session to remove them. Other times they fall off when healed. But yes, they disappear, their duty is done."

Pleased at the answer, Ryan moved on to the next query that they were both aware of.

"When I tried to appear in Nomansland, the transport wouldn't take me directly" he said, looking over at the hooded figure. "This because the children were playing there, wasn't it?"

"Absolutely" Dweller said sounded tired. "The forest wouldn't allow you to transport somewhere you'll be discovered right away."

"Ah yes, I remember" said Ryan, recalling their conversation from the morning. A few minutes passed as he thought about what a long day it had been, and wondering what tomorrow would hold. Seemingly reading his mind, Dweller began speaking again.

"It is late now, and we have got another big day tomorrow. Firstly, we will take care of the emergencies, and then I will show you what else I do to keep the forest, for what of a better word, tidy." He said, his voice becoming slower with tiredness, before announcing with renewed vigour. "And I cannot forget, in two days' time, we have the great annual meeting of the four main Forest Dwellers of England. It is our turn to host in the forest. It will be my last one" he said, tone dropping slightly. "Anyway, let's get some sleep" he added lifting the lantern into his pocket which threw the whole area into blackness, "goodnight."

"Dweller, just one more thing" said Ryan hesitant to ask what might be an obvious question to someone who was desperate to sleep. "If I drank the forest water, would that make me more connected with it?"

Silence, for a second, before he replied with,

"Some secrets of the forest, you are meant to discover for yourself, but only once I have gone" he added, and within seconds descended into light snores, with Ryans starting not long after.

***

Becky had experienced one of the worst days of her life. Search crews were looking in the areas he was last seen on camera, posts on social media had started and were being shared with a picture of Ryans face and a heartfelt plea to return to Becky and Archie. They also had divers out, looking for a body in case he had turned towards the water somewhere to end it all. The spell that had been cast upon her had worked in regards that she had forgotten where Ryan had gone, and that her initial pain associated with him becoming a Dweller had eased. But these feelings she was having now were as real as ever.

She had been interviewed twice with the officers, who were reassuring her she was not under suspicion as she had a stone clad alibi from the hospital CCTV. It did not help her case though that he had been the only one of them to have life insurance, as even though he had reminded her several times, she had never gotten around to doing it for herself. She had argued though with the interviewer, that he had gotten it because of his job, working on building sites. He was after all the main bread winner, implying it would be worse financially for her and Archie if he were to perish without it than it would be the other way around.

Archie was at home being looked after by Steve and Marie, as Becky did not want him in nursery with his father missing and all the questions or accusations that came with it.

After assisting the police the best she could, they dropped her back home. But she was in such a state now with scenarios running through her head, it brought on a migraine, so she had to go and lie down for a while.

Archie, who wasn't sure what was going on with 'Mumma', was happily playing with his toys, oblivious to his grandparents' distress and concerns about his 'Dada'. He was just a happy little eighteen-month-old without a care for adult problems. His only ones were about yoghurts or strawberries, and why could they not be eaten with every meal in copious amounts.

Fearne seemed to notice more that something was amiss. Ryan had been her favourite before Archie had come along. She sat on the window sill, looking out over the driveway as she often did, awaiting a large white van to reverse back and reveal one of the few people she loved. But such a time did not arrive.

***

Rain fell. It pitter pattered through the leafy surroundings, managing to equally soak the forest floor even without being able to directly hit it due to the trees. The thick dark clouds overhead managed to keep signs of dawn at bay from the forest, meaning Ryan and Dweller both slept for longer than their previous night's sleep. Without time to govern them in the forest, they relied on the sun and the seasons to determine how long they had during the day to carry out their tasks.

It was Ryan who awoke first. The noise from the rain was very loud in the forest. Getting up and admiring how his cloak had magically stopped any water hitting his face or getting him soaked from the ground, he looked over to Dweller. He was still laid back and snoring gently, a branch from beside him on the ground had been used as a makeshift pillow, to which the cloak provided the comfort and the branch the elevation.

This was handy thought Ryan. It seemed an urge had awoken him from his sleep. An urge he had not felt in the two days he had been in the forest. But an urge it most definitely was now. Walking away and trying to convince himself that it would be the same as when he pees, he squatted down slightly. This seemed more natural to do then just standing, he thought, disregarding all natural instincts, and very gently, pushing.

SPLAT. Blind panic. Then a feeling of cleanliness washed over the region accompanied by immense satisfaction and relief. The undergarment worked as it was meant to then.

Feeling a lot better and confident that it was not just a trick to soil himself, he returned towards Dweller who was still laid out. Ryan sat down, his bottom feeling like it was comforted by the softest cushioned chair, even though he was just on the ground. He pulled out a full English breakfast with a cup of tea and immediately started tucking into it, safe in the knowledge that when it did finally come out, it would be dealt with. Failing to notice the lack of snoring, he continued to make his way through sausages, bacon, beans, toast, tomatoes, hash browns and black pudding. He did not like eggs or mushrooms. The continuing rain poured down, but Ryan and his food were safe thanks to the leaves above. Apart from the odd drip here and there which vanished soon after, he finished his breakfast and went over to wake Dweller.

"Theres nothing like eating heartily after going for the first time, is there?" Came Dwellers voice to Ryans amazement. They both chuckled, and Dweller got to his feet.

"I thought you were sleeping" said Ryan who realised his awareness must have been lower than usual when he had awoken, mainly due to the apprehension of finally needing to defecate.

"Oh, I remember my first time," said Dweller laughing harder now. "You are a lot more trusting than I was. I had to go in the forest a few times before I was able to believe the undergarment would work sufficiently." Ryan started laughing hard at this.

Looking up to the dripping forest canopy, Dweller pulled a glass of apple juice out and started drinking.

"Ah a good bit of rain" he said "just what the forest needed. Pretty much means all the plants are taken care of for the minute. Might have a few cold baby animals, and if it continues this heavily, some flooded burrows, but overall, rain is good for all the wildlife."

They both stood there, listening to the drips and pattering, warm and cosy in their cloaks.

"Ah" said Dweller stowing the empty glass away, "That is better. Now then, let's do a few emergencies each to get the worst ones helped, and the we will meet back here and I'll show you the rest of our duties."

"Sounds like a plan" said Ryan striding to the nearest tree, "see you in a bit," he said to Dweller before disappearing.

Dweller chuckled.

"Keen to get at it, I like to see that" he said to himself, before he too touched the same tree, and was whisked away to a different part of the forest.

***

After around an hour, they both arrived back at the spot.

"How'd it go?" Asked Dweller, knowing that as Ryan had gone first, he'd have likely seen the most serious case. He himself had been able to help every animal he had attended. It had only been animals that were in need this morning, as the rain took care of most of the trees and plant's needs.

"Yeah fine" said Ryan looking slightly saddened. "First one was another road collision, a fox this time with a very bruised and battered body. I managed to apply some ice and sew a few cuts up. This one was definitely not on the way out though." He said smiling slightly.

"Ah yes, the roads around the forest often claim a lot of animals at night. It was fortunate you were able to help it. We do not get emergency transport to the ones that have already passed," said Dweller. "My first one was a quadriplegic spider."

"A quadriplegic Spider?" Repeated Ryan a bit confused.

"Yes. It had lost four of its eight legs. Must have been in a fight or something. It seemed ok enough, still had two either side. I rubbed some soothing gel over its missing sections and then placed it higher up so it does not have to climb far to make its web." He said before continuing with, "and the last one was just a stag beetle with a leaf stuck around its body. I knew we had covered the worse ones when that happens" he said smiling.

"So mainly we only have to sort the worse ones?" Asked Ryan.

"Yes. The beetle would have figured his way out of the leaf eventually, so it was not in any real danger. We just must check emergencies periodically as you never know when a serious one may happen." replied Dweller, having a glass of water before continuing,

"Right then, we've covered some of the main locations, and a few of the locals."

"A few of the locals? Are there more then?" Asked Ryan, surprised.

"Oh yes" said Dweller happily. "We still have the Fritham Fairies, and the spirit in Wilverly. There might even be others I have not met or discovered yet. I know there used to be the Bisterne dragon, but I've never met any of its ancestors if it had any. The Fairies are very busy this time of year pollinating alongside the bees, and the spirit is rather a dour sarcastic old highwayman, but he can be useful at times as he knows a lot about the forest. He only appears at the full moon though."

Ryan had struggled with this new information, especially the mention of the dragon.

"Er, a dragon?" Said Ryan, sure he had misheard.

"Ah yes, The Bisterne Dragon. Killed by Sir Maurice Berkeley, laid to rest where Boltons bench is on the outskirts of Lyndhurst." He said scratching his chin thinking, "must have been about six or seven dwellers ago now since a dragon was last seen in these parts" he said, finishing with a nod to himself.

"Right then back to it. So main locations," he held up his thumb, "the locals," he extended his index finger, "emergencies" his middle finger went up. "So, we have human activity, weather extremes, and finally Other forests and their Dwellers." He said holding up his outstretched hand and holding his palm to his chest. "This is what the Dweller who trained me did" he said seeing Ryans slightly confused look. "It signifies the five main priorities of the Dweller, the sixth being the Dwellers."

"Ok" said Ryan committing this all to memory. "So, it's main locations for forest protection, tidying and duties, the locals for socializing, news and help, emergencies to help those in desperate need, human activity, what does that involve?" he asked looking into the old man's face.

"Let me show you," he said, getting Ryan to hold his arm before he touched the tree.

The New Forest Dweller

Chapter Seven – Forest Tasks

They appeared at a treeless area, surround by spiny gorse bushes that had little yellow flowers poking through. The rain had ceased, but it had left endless dull grey clouds overhead.

"We're on the outskirts of Burley" said Dweller, releasing Ryans hand as well as the bush. His cloak quickly healing the spines that had stuck to his fingers when they had travelled there.

"From here I can show you most of the human activity that affects the forest" he said, walking through the maze of bushes until coming to a stop at a barbed wire fence.

Turning to Ryan he said "So, here is the first one. A nice new fence. But you see there, and there" as he pointed to a worn-down strip of grass that passed through the fence, fading out the other side. "This is stopping the animals moving about as they might do normally. We must give them a slight helping hand and bend this bit of the fence up just enough for them to still get through. That way the routes that they have been tracking for maybe hundreds of years, are still accessible to them. This is just one way that human activity has changed the forest over the years. If you think about the roads too," he said walking along the fence a few hundred metres before hiding behind a bush and pointing out to the tarmac strip that stretched out and into the forest. "These are killing so many animals each year, and with cars getting quieter and faster, I'm seeing many more fatalities than before." He said with a slightly annoyed look.

"Next, we have telephone lines and electricity pylons that stretch across the forest, the train track, the farm land, and the towns and villages that seem to only expand. Human influence on the forest is nonstop. Then we have the walkers, cyclists, dogs and campers. These are all fine usually, but they bring litter, dog poo, barbeques and bonfires which can greatly hurt the forest and its animals," he said, as if reading a prepared speech. "You need to be aware of each of these things and how they affect our forest. We want to make sure everyone can use and access the land, but without it being harmed."

"I understand" said Ryan, slightly ashamed of people and how they treated such a beautiful environment. Dweller continued,

"Often, I walk the popular trails at sunset, collecting rubbish along the way. I have had to put out numerous barbeques and bonfires that get left by wild campers, usually with a fire blanket as our water will not work and often it is too far to carry cupped handfuls of it from the nearest source" he said, sharing his experience with his apprentice.

"Good thinking" said Ryan, processing all the information as it was provided. And then with a sudden thought, slipped in a question before Dweller could continue.

"Have you ever had to save a person?"

The old man stopped before he spoke.

"Twice, I have succeeded, once not" he said suddenly quiet.

They both stood there in silence, Dweller half positioned to gesture what he had been talking about, but without continuing. After a few moments, which made Ryan feel very awkward, the old man spoke again.

"A little girl, who was lost in the woods when I happened to be doing my emergencies. I appeared out of sight from her, but the forest seemed to have decided she needed saving, as it was getting cold and dark. So, I lead her back to her family who were panicking by their tent. She only saw me, for I hid and watched as she ran back to her mother, who cried out loud with relief, thanking the heavens that she had returned alright." He said, pausing while collecting his thoughts.

"The second, was a man older than I am now. He had taken his dog for a stroll in the woods behind his home, tripping on a root and not able to get back up. So I helped him back to his cottage, and bound the small cut on his forehead with a bandage, made him a cup of tea with his kettle, and left him to recover. He thanked me, promising to take my secret to the grave. Which he did, a year or so later" said Dweller pensively.

"And then," started Dweller before faltering slightly. A few seconds passed before he decided to continue, but a quiver had entered his voice. "And then he came. The, the man I had loved in secret from my school years and who had reciprocated the feeling. The man I had chosen to leave to become a Dweller." He said almost breathlessly. "He came into the forest about a year after I started. "His secret had come out when he tried to meet someone new, and they had exposed him for what he was, a homosexual. It was all too much for him. He took a revolver and and and..." Dweller said, trying to go on. "Shot himself in the side of the head" said the old man, tears streaming down his face. He paused, and Ryan unsure how to comfort him, patiently waited for him to continue.

"I got to him too late. I held his head in my hands as his blank eyes looked up into my face." Finished the old man, his voice filled with sorrow and regret.

Ryan, who had remained motionless listening to him speak, stepped closer, giving the old man a hug. It took a good few minutes for the old man to regain control of his speech. Ryan guessed he had never said this story to anyone, and keeping the regret with him for around sixty years would have eaten him up inside.

"It wasn't your fault" said Ryan, knowing the very real pain that was also burning away inside of him. "Love is a funny thing, but you cannot blame yourself for anything that happened. You became a Dweller for love. For the love of the forest, the animals, the nature."

He paused as the old man wiped his eyes with his hands, because, just noticing it for the first time, for some reason the cloak didn't clear up tears. "I have given up everything in my life that I had been working for, to do this. I knew it would not be easy, but it is my choice. I want to do good. And you did too. You have selflessly spent your life looking after this place. How many animals have survived because of you? How many plants lived to see another spring? You saved two people from almost certain death. You are a real-life legend for this forest." He said, finishing with awe in his voice at the old man's dedication and service, waiting for Dweller to ready himself for what was next.

The old man seemed to pull himself together, sniffling slightly.

"Thank you Ryan, that was a nice thing to say and good to hear. I have spent almost all my life caring for this place. But I am glad I was able to say what I needed too, and hopefully it helps me find peace before I move on."

He straightened up slightly and turned towards Ryan once again. Starting back with his speech as he knew how important relaying the information was.

"Right, where were we? Ah yes. So, there is little we can do regarding large scale human interference in the forest, but with regards to litter, dog poo, fires, and forest boundaries for the animals, we must try our best to keep on top of these, especially fire when there has been a lack of rain and everything is dry" he added.

Ryan nodded, showing he understood the severity of what could happen if he failed at his duty.

"Right then, a quick tour of the popular tourist routes and trails" said Dweller, back to his usual tone. "Take my arm."

Ryan did, and for the next couple of hours, he was transported all over the Forest. Usually, they would start at the beginning of the trails, so that they could be walked in their entirety to clean up any rubbish and dog poo, but it all depended on what people were about. Dweller also explained about the hundred or so car parks dotted over the forest that attract the walkers to more abstract spots. He also said to watch out for the orienteering groups, as a lot had been about over the last few years and he was not sure why it was so popular again.

"The have to do it for school" said Ryan, glad he could help Dweller understand this query. "They have to demonstrate the ability to get from point A to point B within a certain amount of time."

"Ah I see" said Dweller, bowing his head in thanks. "It just makes things a little bit more difficult as they do not seem to mind penetrating the deeper sections of the forest, quite like the people that collect the mushrooms that grow here I suppose." He said thinking for a minute.

"Ok, we will call a halt on human activity. We have covered the major points and there will always be changes to what they do and how they use the forest. I have found there will always been new problems to consider."

Ryan nodded again, pleased to have got through that duty.

"Right then, I think we'll each do five emergencies and meet back at that tree near the Pixies in Brockenhurst for lunch, to discuss the weather extremes." He said reaching for a fern that was near him.

Ryan followed once he was gone, and the second he disappeared, he found himself on the edge of a large hilly field, feet tingling, watching a couple of dogs chasing after a hare.

Ducking down in the long grass and keeping an eye on the animals streaking across the field, he did not know what to do. The hare was obviously terrified with two powerful dogs at its heels, slobber from their jowls flying in their wake. There was a roar. Someone nearby had fired up a dirt bike and was racing after the animals. Think Ryan, he commanded to himself quickly, not wanting the hare to be caught. Then it hit him. He reached into his pocket and pulled out a small silver whistle. Blowing hard, he saw the dogs stop immediately, leaving the hare to race as far as it could from them, before diving through a gap in the hedge at the opposite end of the field. The dogs, had looked around at the whistle, and began pounding the ground directly towards him, paws hitting the earth with incredible speed. The dirt bike rider, annoyed that the sport had been stopped by his dogs changing focus onto something behind them, turned the bike to follow them and accelerated. Ryan was frozen still, fear making his mind race. His hand was already on the grass, all he needed to do was think and close his other one. With great focus, and the dogs almost upon him, feet tingling like crazy, he squeezed his hand shut and thought 'emergency'. He vanished.

A few seconds later the dogs stopped in the spot he had been, the rider close behind and yelling at them for losing the hare. They paused, before running off back to the pickup and trailer they had arrived in.

Ryan reappeared in the open on almost the opposite side of the forest. Breathing heavily and thinking it was a miracle he had managed to get out of there in time, he for a moment, forgot why he had appeared there. All of a sudden, he heard a noise, causing him to look round sharply. It was a cow, head tilted towards him, stuck in a fence, waiting patiently for him to help. Smiling in relief, he went over and spent a few moments repositioning its horns until finally it came free. The cow gave him a grateful 'Moo', and then headed along the grassy plain to the rest of the herd, who seemed to be oblivious to their missing member.

After another three less important emergencies, he transported to the tree Dweller had said to meet at. He was the first one there so sat down and enjoyed a cool bottle of beer. He ended up waiting around fifteen minutes, and was even considering going to another emergency when Dweller appeared.

The old man immediately pulled a bottle of stout from his pocket and started drinking.

"Alright?" asked Ryan knowing the answer.

Dweller took another swig before answering.

"Tough" said Dweller, sipping again. "Deer got hit in the open and was trying to hobble back to the forest. I couldn't get close as there was a walker nearby watching it go. So, I had to sit and wait deeper in the trees for it to come to me. It made it, but was exhausted. I strapped it up, cleaned and sewed its cuts, and applied some cream to its nose that was sore having scraped along the tarmac. Spent all my time on that one and when I went to the next it was just a ladybird that's wings had been bent slightly so it couldn't close them properly. I thought you must have tackled any other serious ones, so I helped fix the wing, before transporting here."

He finished his bottle and tucked it away before pulling a new one out. He sat down, having another few gulps which left Ryan to speak about his first one with the dogs, the biker, and the hare. Once he got to the end of his story, when he appeared by the cow, Dweller interrupted.

"That was good quick thinking with minimal interaction" he said proudly, "from the sound of it, you made completely the correct decision."

"Thanks" said Ryan, pleased the dog whistle idea had come to him so quickly considering the danger to the hare.

They both started pulling out food, relaxing and enjoying the noises of the forest. Ryan, who was halfway through a burger and chips, felt a nudge on his leg. Looking down, he saw a black bird, its wing bent out of shape, the feathers pointing the wrong way.

"Ouch" said Dweller through a mouthful of cheese and pickle sandwich. "Dislocated wing, here let me show you what I've learnt." Putting his half-eaten sandwich back in his pocket, he got up and walked over. Ryan put his burger back on his plate and watched as the bird hopped happily into Dwellers outstretched hand.

He held the bird up to show Ryan how and where he gripped it carefully, pulling the wing and twisting it round in a single motion. The bird squawked loudly but ended up gently rubbing its beak against Dwellers thumb, before flying up and out of the trees.

"Good job" said Ryan, impressed at how quick Dweller had worked to fix it.

"If you do ever get stuck, and you will," admitted Dweller a little sheepishly, giving up his secret. "You can pull out a how-to walkthrough from your pocket to make sure you're doing the right thing for the animal."

"Ah excellent" said Ryan, mightily relieved that his cloak would support him in this as well as everything else it did.

They both sat down again, Dweller pulling out a new sandwich and Ryan finishing the chips before eating the last few bites of burger, all well again in their surroundings.

"Ah lovely" said Dweller, drinking deeply from a glass of water. "Right then, let us go for a little walk then shall we."

"Sure" said Ryan, following him along a pathway between some large trees, and crossing a small bridge that went over a stream.

"So, extreme weather." Said Dweller, marching with purpose. "Basically, we have the seasons, Spring, Summer, Autumn, and Winter. They all overlap, but there are significant dangers each pose. Let us start with Spring and Autumn as they're generally the easier times. Flooding and wind can be an issue though, and it is especially bad if strong winds follow lots of prolonged rain" he said seriously, looking sideways at Ryan to make sure he was keeping up, both with walking, and what he was saying.

"Yes, strong winds after a lot of rain means that it is more likely for treefall, right?" Asked Ryan,

"Correct" said Dweller, pleased Ryan had a keen mind. "This leads to blockages around the forest, birds needing new homes, animals at risk of being squashed and flooded, and trees and wildlife being destroyed."

"Ok" said Ryan, not quite sure where a Dweller fitted in with all of this.

"And it is our responsibility to help where we can. Usually, I will be on emergencies all night, lantern out, helping where I can, but it can get overwhelming. The focus should be on animal welfare over trees and plants, simply because they can move and relocate to higher ground or a different area. Emergencies are nonstop, so it's at your discretion when you need to rest or have food. Believe me, it can be relentless. After the emergencies have calmed down, and you are left with the devastation of the forest, you can rest temporarily, but there is still a lot of work to be done. Trees that have fallen need moving and chopping up, so that new plants and trees can grow in their place, consult the Pixies and Fairies to help with this work. Animal tracks need clearing, the Forest Folk can help wherever they are travelling, and birds need new nests. The Pixies usually take care of this around the forest as well." He said glad to have tackled half the seasons.

They walked along a bit further, following the stream further up. Dweller stopped for a minute looking at the river. Then, carefully he climbed down the small bank to the edge, holding out his hand just above the running water. Almost at once, a small fish leapt into it. Ryan could see a tiny elastic band caught around its waist which Dweller carefully removed, placing in his pocket. Gently, he released the fish back into the water. A little fountain of liquid popping up to the surface in thanks before it swam away, camouflaging with the pebbly basin of the riverbed. Dweller climbed back up the bank to Ryan, his hands and knees getting muddy temporarily, before he was stood again, breathing slightly heavier.

"Right, Summer" he said, carrying on from before as if with no distraction. "The heatwaves are the obvious threat as these can cause forest fires. Rarely it happens naturally though, usually there's a human cause. The barbeques and bonfires we mentioned earlier are the main threat. There is little you can do if fire spreads before you can contain it. Best to find a phone and make an anonymous call to the fire fighters who have the best equipment for this. Then you tackle emergencies again, but be careful, you can still die. Our cloaks are not impervious to attack. Also, be careful carrying out a rescue in a fire, it can be hard to find a plant or tree to use for travel if they are all burning" he said, warning his young apprentice.

"I understand" said Ryan, acknowledging the danger and taking the advice.

"Lastly, we have winter. What a cold and terrible time it can be." He said sounding glum. "On the whole it is not too bad in our cloaks, but for some of the animals, it can be too much. Many a winter we lose animals and insects due to the freeze. What I have found best is to stack logs up like the children do in the summer to make little shelters, and layer them with the fallen leaves. Usually, I make between one to two hundred, in late autumn, all around the forest for animals to shelter together, out of the wind, rain and snow. I have seen them work really well, and last year we had our fewest casualties since I started." He said proudly.

"The plants and trees normally bear up well to the cold, so rarely is there any emergency relating to them. The only added thing is often the ponds freeze over, not allowing animals to get a drink. Sometimes it is best to break the ice if you can. I find that this either frees trapped water from below, or just helps it melt quicker."

"Right" said Ryan, thinking he had taken all this on board.

"Confident?" said Dweller.

"Yes. Well, sort of" said Ryan, slightly unsure how he would do when his mentor was no longer there.

"You'll be fine on your own" said Dweller smiling. "It'll make you see the place in a whole different light, then you'll be truly in love with the forest and what each season brings."

Ryan hoped so. Then, deciding as Dweller had sort of brought it up, he thought he would find out.

"Dweller, how long do you think you've got?" Asked Ryan tentatively.

Dweller paused, his smile faltering slightly

"Well, from what I can remember. Once you have found your apprentice, you have one full moon cycle left" replied Dweller calmly, as Ryans eyes opened wider. "Also, if we hadn't been meeting with the England Forest Dwellers Council tomorrow, I would have had to take you to meet the Council Leader, so you'd know who you were meeting with each year." He said, thankful that he would be able to say his farewell to his fellow Dwellers in his own forest.

Ryan was shocked at this. Less than four weeks they would have together, well three actually thought Ryan, his heart sinking as he realised, he'd had a whole week to consider the position. Now he understood why Dweller was keen to make him choose as quickly as possible.

"I'll be finished just after the next full moon" said Dweller, carefully watching Ryans expressions of worry with a gentle smile. "So, I will be able to introduce you to the Spirit in Wilverly before I pass, and the Fairies of course" he said, giving Ryan a show of confidence that said he was not scared that the end was in sight. Which in truth, he wasn't.

"Ok" said Ryan, not sure how to change the conversation from here, opting to go with another question.

"What about the other forests and their Dwellers? Are you going to tell me about them?" He added, trying to sound eager.

"Well, as we're meeting them tomorrow, I'd hate to do them an injustice today" said Dweller, smiling toothily. "Right, so we have now covered the five duties of a Dweller, main locations, the locals, emergencies, human activity, and finally weather extremes. We will cover all the main locations before my time is up, so now I think we should spend the afternoon handling some emergencies before the sun sets, and get a good night's sleep before tomorrow."

"Yes indeed" said Ryan, pleased to start helping again instead of just learning.

"When the sun is low in the sky, we'll meet by those Gorse bushes we first transported to this morning" said Dweller, seeing Ryan was almost at a tree already.

"Perfect" said Ryan, turning to look back before he disappeared to across the forest.

"Ah, we've got a good one here" said Dweller, smiling to the listening trees.

Chapter Eight – The England Forest Dweller Council

Morning broke. Mildew adorned the grassy tips of the untouched ground so that millions of tiny spheres shined in the rays of the sun. There was a very light mist rising gently over the forest, heading towards the pale blue cloudless sky. Multiple birds punctured the silence by singing with delight.

The two Dwellers were lying comfortably, between separate thickets of gorse bush which mostly hid them from view, not that anyone came this way that often, and definitely not at this time of day.

A little time passed until they both began stirring. Ryan yawned and stretched out his arms, pulling then back quickly as he hit the edge of the bush in surprise. Sitting up slowly, he looked over to Dweller who was indeed awake as well, sat eating some jam on toast with what looked like a cup of coffee. Ryan reached into his left-hand pocket, and drew out a plate of pancakes, strawberries, blueberries, and golden syrup. Tucking into this quickly so that he wouldn't hold Dweller up when he was done, but also pulling a thick chocolate milkshake from his pockets depths to accompany his food. Eating and slurping away, he got through it in only a few minutes.

Feeling the urge again, and looking over at dweller who was just finishing off his coffee, he tried to push gently without making it look like he was doing anything at all. Thankfully the undergarment seemed to gobble up what it could the moment it was produced, leaving Ryan to feel much happier and more confident, as he stood up the same time as Dweller, and they walked towards each other.

"How'd you sleep?" Asked Dweller, some crumbs disappearing from his mouth and chin.

"Yes, not bad. You?" Responded Ryan, pondering some questions he had been thinking about before he'd fallen asleep.

"Yes, all fine" Dweller replied, shaking his cloak down slight so it sat normally, as it had hitched up slightly from when he had been laying down.

Ryan quickly took advantage of this silence to start asking some of the questions he had been thinking about.

"Dweller, what happens if there is someone out walking at night that comes across us?" he said, thinking about the people who like to explore the forest with torches at night.

"Basically, the same as what happens in the day" Dweller replied simply. "Your feet tingle, and it should wake you immediately, letting you escape. A few times I have hid behind a tree to watch, and occasionally during the day, in front of the tree." He added, realising that he had not mentioned this fact before about the cloaks.

"In front of the tree? Did the people not see you?" queried Ryan, perplexed.

"Oh, I forgot to mention. Your cloak will blend in perfectly so you will match the trunk of the tree, providing its wide enough of course. Yes, it will imitate the bark, moss, and any other affectations on it. You must make sure your hood is up though for this." He added, Ryan nodding as he continued.

"In fact, I have had this hood down more in the last few days than I can ever remember. When you are by yourself, it's good practice to keep it up." He said, absentmindedly nodding as well this time.

"Right. Just a couple more questions if that's alright?" Asked Ryan. "When I first came to the forest to become a Dweller, there were flies forming arrows for me to follow. How did you get them to do that?"

"Ah," said Dweller happily. "When the time comes of my passing, you will drink deeply from a forest pond. You will find out then." He said with a finality to this query.

"Ok" said Ryan, slightly confused but intrigued. "And just a last one, quickly." He said pausing slightly as it could be a delicate reminder of returning to the emotional conversation they'd had the day before.

"Yes, go on" said Dweller calmly.

"Well, why is it that our tears don't disappear?" Ryan asked, seeing Dweller freeze for a second knowing what had triggered this question. He took several moments to think about this before replying.

"Tears for us, are formed due to emotion. Whether it be happiness, pain, or sorrow. They will simply drip down, finally hitting the ground beneath. This is because our emotions are a more powerful magic than anything that the cloak possesses." He said, finishing with a slightly surprised look.

"You know what? I feel better already from our talk yesterday."

"Ah, that's good" said Ryan, pleased not to have brought pain to his much older friend.

"Those were very good, deep questions." Dweller said looking proudly at the young man stood before him. "But now we must get back to business. Emergencies, lets tackle these until about midday, and then we will meet at the tree we appeared at when we met the Forest Folk" he said, and turned towards the nearest gorse bush. He looked back as he grabbed the bush and said "have a good morning," before vanishing.

Ryan did the same.

***

Appearing at the tree, and looking about, Ryan saw the Forest Folk had moved on to a different spot in the forest. Realising how difficult it must be to hide themselves from the rest of the world, Ryan made a point of remembering to ask Dweller how, when he appeared. And within a few moments he had that chance.

The old man popped calmly into view, with the smell of honey spreading gently as he did. Breathing deeply for a moment and saying 'Pollen Power' under his breath, he walked over and sat next to Ryan, who was starting on a club sandwich with a can of coke zero.

"Not bad today, eh?" He said, whipping out a pie, mash, and gravy on a plate, with a glass of orange squash to accompany it.

"No not at all" said Ryan, in between mouthfuls. "My first one looked a bit painful though, a woodlouse that had bent the wrong way. I had to use a pair of tweezers to realign its scales when I put him right."

"Ah yes, I've seen a few of them in my time" said Dweller, chewing the crust and revealing what looked to be a steak and ale filling. "Mine was a deer that was tangled up in barbed wire which started to cut into its neck. He got out ok in the end with just a couple of little scratches." He said tucking into the enticing looking inners of the pie.

They both sat and ate their lunch in peace. Ryan deciding to follow up his sandwich with a nice warm bowl of apple crumble and custard, which Dweller liked the look of and decided to do the same.

Bowls empty and dropped in pockets, and finishing their drinks soon after, Dweller turned to Ryan and said,

"That was just lovely. Right, so later this afternoon we have the meeting with the council. We will need to pop in to see the Sisters of the Wreath, to borrow a charmed object to place at the meeting spot. This will keep humans at least a kilometre away so we do not have to worry about interruptions. We only need to borrow it, as we do not want to stop people going to that spot altogether." He said gesturing.

"Ah" exclaimed Ryan to Dwellers slight shock, "do the Forest Folk have a charmed object like this?" Asked Ryan, suspecting he was correct and happy to know his query would be answered so quickly.

"Yes indeed" replied Dweller pleased at the ingenuity and thought process of his young apprentice.

"Right then, we'll do that and drop it off, and then I want you to lead me to the main locations I showed you around the forest, so I know you have remembered those ones before I show you the rest of them," he said smiling. "Then we'll do some emergencies again, before heading to the meeting."

"Perfect, I'll meet you at the Sisters cottage then" said Ryan, and they both reached out for separate trees and within moments appeared together at the trunk of the blackened bulbous tree.

The charmed object turned out to be a statue, purchased from one of the stores in Burley by Flo, when she was out shopping. 'She hides her hair so that she doesn't stand out too much' Gwen had said, pointing to what looked like a selection of patterned head scarves hanging on a hook near the door. The statue had been charmed by the ladies together, and stored in a magical bag in a cupboard, so that it wouldn't keep people away from their cottage. Not that people wandered near there anyway. It was on private land, and often only the postman who dropped off letters or parcels was the only human to venture there. Also, they lived too close to Burley, and the charm would make everyone keep away from the area which is what they didn't want. Best kept undetected rather than have inquiries about why there had been a mass migration from the village.

Ryan and Dweller thanked the ladies, and holding Dwellers clenched hand, travelled to a spot in the wooded area outside of the town of Ringwood, right on the border of the forest. From there they walked to a wooded area where, amongst the trees, was a small ring of grass surrounding a large moss-covered stump. The tree which had previously stood there, was lying down on the grassy edge, still quite solid even though it must have lain there a long time. The lack of it upright and attached to its base, had allowed the area to have a mini opening to the sky above. Removing the bag, Dweller placed the statue on the stump surface. Nothing happened. Ryan assumed the spell was working its magic as Dweller placed the bag in his pocket and led Ryan back to a good tree, saying,

"Ok, that small task is done. Actually, slight change of plan I think. Yes." He said talking to himself more than anything. "I think I'll show you the remaining Main Locations, and then I'll get you to take me back to all of them." He said to Ryan this time.

"No problem" said Ryan, before reaching out to Dwellers outstretched arm, and immediately transported them around the forest.

Over the course of the next couple of hours, Ryan took them back to almost all the places Dweller had taken him to, only forgetting one spot. Dweller mentioned that he had missed one, and Ryan immediately took them there, showing at least he remembered which one he'd missed and how to get there.

"Very good work" said Dweller, pleased he had gotten the hang of it so quickly.

"Thanks" said Ryan grinning, "I did forget the one around Minstead though. Knew I was one short as well." He said, slightly annoyed he'd miscounted and had to be reminded.

"Twenty-eight in total" said Dweller "spread over the forest for easy access to the areas, and to make sure every part gets looked after as it should be. Ok well that was good. Now let's do ten emergencies each and then meet at the site near Ringwood."

"Ok" said Ryan, pleased Dweller was happy with his progress and looking forward to helping the forest again.

"You go first this time" said Dweller, gesturing for Ryan to step to the nearest tree. "That way you are on point for the worst one, just so you get the experience of them on your own. I can then assist you in how I would have done it, afterwards when we meet again."

"Sure" said Ryan confidently, and strode towards the tree, palm up, fist clenched, 'emergency'! And he was gone.

***

When they met back together, the sun had passed the peak of the day, and was slowly making its way back to the horizon. Ryan had appeared about thirty minutes after Dweller, and was quickly filling him in on the first one he had gone to. It had been for a Rabbit that had been killed instantly by a car, but this had meant that it had left its babies stuck on the wrong side of the road as you enter Lyndhurst from Ashurst. Ryan told Dweller he had appeared in a thicket, having to crouch down the moment he felt his feet tingle. Seeing the bunnies in distress, but not able to get them without being seen had caused a mighty dilemma. So, he had waited for the road to be clear, before making himself visible to them, holding a carrot he had pulled from his left pocket. At once they became calm at the sight of the him in his Dweller cloak, before all five of them leapt off the curb and ran across the road. He had stowed the carrot back in his cloak, and carried them safely back, across the more open ground, whilst trying to avoid walkers. He had headed for a large bunny he had seen, nibbling some food on a little hilly section of grass. Seeing another Rabbit, the babies had jumped out of his hands, wiggled their fluffy tails, and shot off into the burrows that Ryan could see once he had gotten closer. Knowing they would be accepted here, Ryan had proceeded to the second emergency.

"Excellent" said Dweller "Excellent indeed, you kept calm and unseen, and managed to lure the bunnies to you safely. Do you know what a group of bunnies is called?" He added.

"No idea" replied Ryan, pleasantly surprised at the question.

"A Fluffle, a Fluffle of bunnies. Now isn't that cute?" Said Dweller happily.

"That is very sweet yes," said Ryan, thinking about another emergency. "Also, my seventh one must have only just happened. Two stags fighting had their antlers locked together. I had to cut a few bits off to get them separated. One had a punctured eye that I could only drip some drops in and patch up, and the other, a great slash across its chest that seemed to be making it weaker and weaker. I cleaned and sewed it shut. I hope it was enough." He said slightly worried.

"Those deer just do not give up. I must have to pull them apart three or four times every year. You would think they would learn." Dweller said slightly exasperated. "Well, good thing you got to them, or I'd have given them a good piece of my mind. As if we don't have enough to be getting along with without pulling apart some randy deer."

Ryan laughed at this. Dweller gave a wry smile.

"I suppose I shouldn't be too hard on them," he said walking over to the fallen tree and sitting down.

"Ah, well, our company should be joining us shortly. I suggest we have a quick bite to eat before they get here" he said, as Ryan came and sat beside him on the tree.

Ryan opted for a lasagne, chips, garlic bread, and salad, with a pint of San Miguel beer to wash it down. Dweller went with a funny looking simple stew, with thick cut bread which he said was the same as his mum made him and his siblings growing up. This was accompanied with a large glass of merlot, that he most certainly would not have had when he was younger.

Once eaten, they got up and removed some of the sticks that littered the ground, stacking them by a tree a little further away. Then Dweller produced four large lamps along with poles to hang them on, as it had started to get darker. Finally, he moved the statue from its prominent position, laying it down beside the fallen tree. And then they waited.

Flies, bugs, and other insects were flying about, attracted by the bright light from the lamps, but Ryan noticed they didn't bother him like they would have a week or so ago. This must be because he was a Dweller now, A New Forest Dweller he thought proudly. He did not know why, but at that moment, he felt a wave of emotion pass over him, and a feeling of longing for Becky and Archie. He had tried not to think about them over the past few days, but it was impossible to keep them out completely. He wondered how they were getting on, and really wished he could see them and be with them again.

Trying to bring his mind back to what was about to happen, Ryan didn't notice at first the moss-covered tree stump begin to glow. Slowly his eyes got drawn to it as the light became brighter and whiter. Then atop the stump was a door sized portal, shining white and gold with shifting blurry black figures who were starting to take shape, until they began bursting out onto the forest floor.

First came an old, gingery haired Dweller in a dark green cloak, smiling and holding a nobbled stick to help walk with. Then popped out a handsome well-toned Dweller, with thick blonde hair swishing around his chiselled face. He looked in his late forties, but had managed to keep his looks even though creases were appearing in his brow and neck. He adorned a light brown cloak with an Pine tree leaf clasp that matched the cloak in colour. He was lastly followed by a tough looking blackish grey-haired Dweller who was balding on top, but sporting a mid-length beard and wore a light green cloak. Once he had stomped out of the portal, it dropped down into the stump and disappeared.

"The New Forest Dweller has an apprentice I see," said the light green cloaked Dweller to the others in his deep commanding voice. "Well, that is a bit of a shame. I thought you would live forever."

"I'm perfectly happy with how this has turned out thank you," said Dweller smiling, reaching in to hug him. The light green cloaked Dweller placed his large arms around him, allowing Ryan to see his tough working man's hands holding his master lightly in the welcome hug.

"Well, I guess I should introduce everyone" said Dweller when they released. "Ryan this is The Forest of Dean Dweller" pointing to the ginger haired Dweller with the walking stick in the dark green cloak.

"Just call me Ash" he said in a high voice that surprised Ryan who had leaned in and shook his free hand.

"And this is the Dweller from Thetford Forest" continued Dweller, pointing to the blonde-haired Handsome Dweller who smiled confidently back. Ryan returned the smile and shook his hand feeling a good grip and strength.

"Call me Pine," he said with a cool calm voice that was strong and friendly.

"And I'm Spruce, from the Kielder Forest." Said the blackish haired bearded one, in the light green cloak. "We four are the England Forest Dweller Council," he said with authority.

"And my Dweller name is Oak," said Dweller to Ryan, who hadn't heard him called this before and was slightly surprised. "You will be called Acorn until I have passed, upon which you will transition to Oak yourself. Spruce here is the leader of the council and manages the largest forest in England. He has another dweller at all times who helps him manage his forest as he has to attend Dweller meetings with the heads of Scotland and Wales, and he also overlooks the other half dozen or so Dwellers who maintain areas of woodland and nature all around the country. We are the four biggest Forests in England who make up the Council, but I believe there are around ten of us in total."

"I didn't realise there were so many of us, let alone Dwellers in other countries too" said Ryan, amazed at prospect.

"Yes" said Dweller, his eyes twinkling, "and rumour has it that there are Dwellers in the forests all over the world."

"Wow" said Ryan amazed at this.

"We only deal with Britain though," said Spruce in his deep voice. "To meet the others if there are any, we would have to travel there overseas through the human transport system, and this hasn't been done in over three hundred years. No, best stick to our land and the root network that connects us."

There was a momentary pause during which Ash pulled a bottle of amber fluid from his pocket, and gulping a few mouthfuls. They all stood around the moss-covered tree stump they had appeared from, using it as sort of a meeting table. They then all placed their outstretched hands, Pine was the only one using his left, over their chests, holding it for a few moments.

"Right" said Dweller, holding up his hands and formally saying, "Welcome to The New Forest, this of course is my young protege, Acorn. He will be taking over from me in around two weeks' time. I believe this is now your tenth visit here Ash, your fifth visit Pine and your eighth Spruce. I am pleased to be able to host what will be my final Council meeting before handing over the reins to my youthful apprentice. I will now pass over to Spruce, to lead this Council meeting."

"Thank you Oak. I am glad to see your forest doing so well. It is a pleasure to have you in attendance for your last meeting. Last time a Dweller passed, he and his apprentice, Pine here, had to travel to meet me so that Pine would know the protocol for the when, where and who he would be meeting. It is a pleasure to meet you, Acorn. We hope you can be as wise as Oak, and as long lasting as he has been" he said. Dweller smiled at this.

"Right then, to business" continued Spruce beginning the meeting.

And so it commenced, lasting well into the evening. Spruce talked about what they discussed at the annual meeting with the heads of the Wales and Scotland Forest Dweller Councils. Pollen levels over the year had remained consistent around Britain for the last few years, with Fairies working hard to support the bees during tough times. Temperatures were still rising however, causing more need to water plants and trees in the summer manually. Flooding had been an issue in some parts of Britain, with the humans building on what once were flood plains, which meant that on average more water sat elsewhere, including in the forests. Thankfully, the tree cycle managed to soak up and evaporate the excess, keeping up with the increase. He then moved to talking about his own forest and what problems and issues he'd had to resolve, and other things that he had noticed. After about an hour of talking, Spruce then invited each Dweller for updates on their forests. Ryan sat and listened intently, very interested in hearing what problems the others faced in their work.

Ash started into a longwinded analysis of The Forest of Dean, and how the behaviour of the wild boars was causing destruction on a daily basis. He spoke for around twenty-five minutes in his high voice, before Spruce cleared his throat to signal for him to wrap things up.

Pine then followed in his cool calm voice with an update on Thetford Forest, saying about how the deer population was running wild again, and that the humans were culling them in their dozens. He spoke about the dry summer they'd had the previous year, and how all the saplings, the ones that hadn't been eaten by the deer, had unfortunately perished. He spoke for about fifteen minutes, ending on a summary of the insect population.

Dweller was next, taking a sip from a glass of icy water before he spoke. His slow quieter voice seemed to be a comfort to them all, making them realise how much they would miss him. This was at least the sixtieth meeting he had attended after all. He had seen them all join the Dweller ranks, swearing allegiance to their forests, to protect and conserve the wildlife and its secrets. Dweller spoke on the tree population, the impact that the humans were having on the forest, and the changing of the weather during his tenure. He talked for over forty minutes, trying to cram as much into his last meeting as possible, mainly so that Ryan could see all the things to consider and monitor around the forest. He ended with a thanks to them all, for their support during tough times, and the meetings which helped show that they were all doing a good thing for the world.

Once he had finished, they all put their hands into the middle over the stump, Ryan just watched as they said 'Dwellers of the country united as one, may our forests continue to thrive.'

"That concludes the England Forest Dweller Council Meeting for this year" Spruce said, looking a little saddened. "And now to a toast" he said, pulling a silver goblet of red wine from his cloak. The others followed suit with the same goblets and liquid, Ryan included this time. "Here's to the New Forest Dweller, may he find peace in his passing," he said looking at Dweller. "And to his apprentice" he said, nodding to Ryan. "May you continue the fine work that Oak has carried out for over half a century, I am sure he is teaching you well. To Oak." He called, raising his goblet to the middle. They all joined drinks together, before gulping deeply.

"Right then my friends. Tis time for us to return to our homes" said Spruce, placing his palm down on the tree stump which started to glow.

"Goodbye old friend" said Ash, hobbling forward on his stick and giving Dweller a hug. "You beat me to the passing, but I don't believe I have too many years left before I catch you up." He said smiling at his old friend, who mirrored one back, eyes shimmering.

Ash then hugged Pine and Spruce, then gave Ryan a quick squeeze, before hopping onto the stump and walking through the portal, back to the Forest of Dean.

Pine next approached Dweller, pulling him into a hug as well. "Thank you old man" he said. "You have helped me so much over the years. I have wondered for a while now when would be your last, and now it is here, I'm gutted" he said, his voice losing a little of its cool calmness, instead starting to sound upset.

"Do not worry for me Pine, Acorn is a good replacement. I'll join the other Dwellers of the New Forest past, in the great ghost council. So please feel free to visit when we appear each January first." Dweller said kindly to him, to Ryans immense surprise.

"I will" said Pine, pleased it was not goodbye forever. He turned and hugged Spruce, before doing the same to Ryan.

"You've got big experienced boots to fill kid" he said letting go. "I hope you're up for the task."

"Absolutely" replied Ryan confidently. Pine squeezed his shoulder, and then climbed on the stump. With one last look back at Dweller, who raised his hand in farewell, disappeared through the portal and back to Thetford Forest.

"Right then. Take care of yourself old man" said Spruce, his tone wavering very slightly.

"It's been a pleasure to serve with you on this Council" said Dweller, trying to keep his voice normal as it quivered slightly. "Keep my apprentice in check, although I'm sure he's got the making of a future Council leader," he said with a tiny wink towards Ryan.

Spruce turned to Ryan and pulled him for a strong hug.

"I look forward to meeting you as the new Oak" he said. "I'll be in touch before the next council meeting so you know the protocol," he added turning from them both back towards the portal. Hopping up and turning back slightly to raise his hand and saying, 'Thank you for your service' before vanishing, taking the portal with him.

They stayed still for a moment. In the light of the lantern Ryan could see a tear roll down Dwellers cheek.

"That, that was a very nice end to it all" said Dweller softly. "I am glad to have had this chance to serve the council and my forest. Please do look after it well." He added, but with the knowledge he had been given the best replacement.

"I will of course" said Ryan, touched at the old man's emotions.

They paused there for a little while. A number of questions were going through Ryans head, but he decided to wait until the morning to ask them. They then collected up the lanterns and the statue, with Dweller placing it back in the bag he produced from his pocket, Ryan dropping the lanterns and poles into his own.

"Ok" said Dweller, who had found control of his emotions again. "Let's find a couple of those shelters out towards Rhinefield to sleep under tonight."

Gesturing for Ryan to hold his arm as he placed his other against the nearest tree, they vanished, appearing moments later in a very dark covered wood. Massive thick trunked trees were in abundance, with their canopies almost blocking out any view of the star lit sky. Ryan took a torch from his pocket, and within only a few minutes they had found a couple of shelters that children had made, each choosing which one they would sleep in.

Sitting down beside his, Ryan pulled out a hot chocolate. Dweller had settled on one a few metres away, and was himself having a cup of tea, seemingly content to be just sat in the darkness in silence. Ryan, turned his torch down, his eyes struggling for a few moments to adapt to the lack of light.

"Good night" said Dwellers voice from the darkness. "See you in the morning."

"Yes" said Ryan. "Goodnight, Oak" he added, before hearing a little chuckle. No long after, he heard that the soft snores had started, and Ryan feeling tired himself, settled down for a good night's sleep too.

Chapter Nine – Two meetings at Fritham

A group of six teenagers lay around their burnt-out campfire in the woods by Sway. There were some beer and vodka bottles strewn about, and a few wrappers from their food was trapped in the bushes, unable to blow away in the wind like their other ones had. Their bags were by their sides, and a pair of speakers sat on a log, its blue light showing they were still on, even though the music had stopped. Slowly the light flickered and died. The teenagers slept on, not waking until around midday, before taking their bags and speakers, and heading home, leaving the rubbish, bottles, and the ash remains of their fire behind.

***

Ryan awoke first. Staying still, he looked up to the stacked sticks and logs above that formed the small shelter. He yawned, before lying motionless again. His normal morning urge had returned but was swiftly dealt with, then feeling peckish, he sat up, not quite fully as he would have banged his head, but twisted over onto his right side, leaning on his elbow. With his left hand, he reached into his pocket for a chocolate chip muffin he knew would be waiting for him. After a few mouthfuls, and with little saliva left from the spongey texture, he reached in again and withdrew a glass of milk. He drank down a few gulps before finishing the muffin. Deciding he should probably get up, he turned around and semi crawled out of the shelter.

He could hear Dwellers consistent loud breathing. It was still quite early, maybe he should take care of some emergencies before waking him, he thought. Yes, I'll do it, he decided.

He bent over with his outstretched palm to a tiny little shoot poking through the ground, and immediately his scenery changed as he found himself by a stream, out in the open. Ducking down, but without the tingle in his feet, he slowly looked around for the emergency. It took him a few moments, and he heard it rather than saw it.

A fox. Its head and front paws in a hole along the riverbank, and shaking its midsection from side to side. Ryan quickly leapt towards it and tapped on its behind. As quick as a flash, the fox span round with apparent ease, surprising Ryan who thought it was stuck in the hole. The fox calmed immediately upon seeing him, and then decided to skulk away, looking quite sheepish under his gaze. Ryan watched it go, before peering down the hole it had been in. About a metre deep below the surface, he could see a shaking, terrified, water vole.

Ryan let out a slight gasp, he knew they were extremely rare in the forest, as it began to move, ever so carefully towards him. Not only the one though. It had been shielding others behind it in the shallow escape hole they had found. Getting to the entrance, the large one took its time looking about for other predators. Not seeing any, he hopped out and the rest followed, three other largish ones and five smaller. With a little wiggle of their noses at him in union, they all took off down the water, looking for safer new ground in which to make their homes.

Ryan was very glad he had started earlier, as he was sure there would not be a vole family left if he had waited until Dweller had awoken. Deciding to do another one, as this had only taken five minutes or so, he rested his hand on the grassy bank, and shot off to help bandage up a badger's wounds after what looked like a serious fight. His third emergency was a plant that had been trodden on and needed help straightening up. He had attached a couple of small straight sticks in the ground and tied them to it, acting like a splint, before he returned to Dweller.

The sun had risen properly now, and Dweller was awake, sat eating some breakfast by his shelter.

"Morning" he said, seeing Ryan appear back in his midst. "Glad to see you're keen to get started each day." He said proudly.

"Well, it looked as if you needed a bit more rest" said Ryan, pulling a bacon butty with tomato ketchup from his pocket. "First one was some water voles," he said and Dweller gasped slightly looking concerned.

"Mink?" he asked quickly.

"No, a fox. None of them injured, four older ones and five small. They paddled down the river after it had skulked away." He said and Dweller looked pleased.

"Ah, glad to see them coming back to the area. A couple of decades ago we had a mink epidemic killing off almost all the water voles. It was carnage. Now the minks have died out the voles are able to return."

They finished their food and Dweller asked Ryan if he had done anymore.

"Just an injured badger, which looked like it had been in a fight, and a plant stem that had almost snapped in two that I propped up."

"Ah good job too" said Dweller, looking thankful at his apprentice's progress. "You are starting to take the reins on what will be your forest. I am very pleased to see that. The others were impressed, I could tell."

"Well, I just hope I can live up to the legacy you leave."

Dwellers blue eyes shined momentarily. He had been caught unaware of the compressed emotions inside him until a couple of weeks ago, when the countdown started. Peace and acceptance were needed now he reminded himself.

Ryan downed a cool glass of apple juice and decided to ask Dweller some of the questions that had entered his mind the previous evening.

"Dweller, can I ask you about last night?" he said, curiosity in his voice.

"Yes my boy, please proceed," said Dweller, snapping out of his own thoughts and glad to be back in reality.

"How did the other Dwellers travel to us?" questioned Ryan, suspecting it must something to do with Spruce.

"Ah, well you see as Spruce is the leader of the Council, he is the one who is allowed to open the portals for council meetings. He gets a charmed object to enhance the range of transport as far as he wants, and can connect to the other Council members when the meeting time has come. He gets the charmed object from the magic family in his forest, The Sect of the Glenn, if my memory serves me correctly. It works best on the stumps of fallen or broken trees, as the whole centre of the tree acts as a beacon through the ground, seeking out the council members it needs. All the others need to do is wait by a tree stump and the portal will appear. If you ever needed to contact the council in an emergency, you would need to speak to the 'Sisters of the Wreath', they will provide you with a charmed object to travel to wherever Spruce is."

"Amazing" said Ryan, pleased he would be a Dweller whose forest had a council position. "And what about the Dwellers abroad?" Asked Ryan, keeping the flow of conversation going, keenly soaking up all the information as it was presented.

"Ah well we know that up until about a century ago, Ireland and Northern Ireland would send representatives every five years to travel over and meet with the British Council. This became harder with the development of technology and satellites. But beyond that, we just don't know any more than that." He said tailing off into silence.

They both sat in thought. The shimmers of light in various shades of green, glittering above them, and through tiny gaps, Ryan could see a deep blue sky.

"So today, we will travel to 'The Sisters of the Wreath' and drop back this statue. Then I will get you setup in a main location, making sure animal tracks are clear, tidying up the forest, and picking litter if there is any, as you go. I will spend a bit of time on emergencies before giving you a hand. Then we will eat, before going to another location, whilst also taking care of the emergencies. Later, but before dark, we will walk some of the popular tourist tracks, and clear up any rubbish or dog poo that we find." He said, wanting to show Ryan what was a more normal day for him.

"Sounds like a plan" said Ryan, eager to start. Just then his feet started tingling. Dweller had felt it too. Within a few seconds, voices could be heard coming their way, probably for the shelters they had slept under that night.

"Meet you at the Sisters" whispered Dweller, and they both reached for their nearest trees, vanishing instantly. Within ten seconds, some children had excitedly run over to the shelters, playing games and chasing each other around. Four parents were all stood watching and chatting, whilst a couple of dogs were running around barking.

They both appeared touching the bulbous blackened tree outside the witch's cottage. They walked around to the front door, only to see a sign saying, 'To Dwells, off visiting family, post bag through letterbox please x.' The statue was never going to fit through that small hole thought Ryan, before remembering that there was probably a spell placed on it to accept any size package. He kept his reservation to himself and watched as Dweller stuck the head of the bag in, before shoving the rest through seemingly effortlessly.

"There" he said, taking the sign off the door and posting it through as well. "Right then, let's start at the Minstead one." He said smiling.

"Ah thanks, rub it in why don't you" said Ryan chuckling, as this had been the one he had forgotten about the day before.

"You'll never forget it again now though" said Dweller, his eyes mirroring his mouths happiness.

"Right then, let me take your arm" said Dweller, before twisting as they whizzed through the root system, appearing almost as soon as they had left.

Dweller got Ryan to work, making sure he was happy, before starting off on the emergencies. Ryan plodded along, not enjoying this work as much, but always happy to be out in the forest. He cleared several animal paths that had become blocked with sticks, and collected a whole black bag full of rubbish, which he left by the bins of a farm house, careful not to be seen. He then expanded his works out to cover another area where he began collecting fallen branches, stacking them neatly against a tree. The rubbish was much less in this area. Obviously, people did not venture this way often. He carried on the work, and by the time the sun was high in the sky, he felt like he had done a great deal. After another twenty minutes or so, Dweller popped into view.

"Ah good work, I can see you are quicker than me at clearing up the forest. That is the problem with old age. Though I do feel a younger me may have done it quicker" he said laughing and winking at Ryan.

Struggling to imagine a younger version of Dweller, Ryan sat down at last. What should have been achy tired muscles, were in fact toned and ready for work again. He knew the cloak kept him in action for longer. Without it, he would have been sweating like crazy, needing to stop every few minutes for a drink. Actually, what a good idea he thought, carefully pulling a pint glass of icy summer fruit squash from his pocket and gulping it down.

"Right then, lunch. What are you having?" asked Dweller, who was becoming more interested in what Ryan was requesting from his pocket. Dweller had left the human world over sixty years ago, so had been sort of stuck in the past with his choices. Sometimes he would see a wrapper when litter picking, and often thought he would give it a go, but was usually left with a disappointing taste in his mouth. The last one he had tried a few years ago was a compacted thin sausage shaped snack, filled with chemicals and flavourings in a green foil packet. It had tasted disgusting to him, like a war ration he'd thought, and therefore he had not tried anything new since.

"Oh, just a couple of fajitas" said Ryan, showing him the wraps filled with chicken, peppers, onion, tomatoes, and cheese in a smoky barbeque sauce.

"Mmmm, yes I'll try those" Dweller said, pulling out his own.

Sitting for a while and watching a pair of squirrels running about, they finished their lunch and then rested for a bit, letting their food digest, with Dweller quizzing Ryan on certain facts and aspects of the position he had learnt so far. He did very well, not wasting a second after each question before he was providing the correct answer.

"Very good," said Dweller after fifteen minutes of this. Ryan had just correctly described how to Heimlich a hedgehog, mostly thanks to the animal emergency procedure card he had pulled from his right pocket describing with drawings this very incident.

"Well, I am very pleased," said Dweller. "You have picked up a great deal from me already, but I think you will pick up a great deal more when I am gone. The freedom from a mentor can be just what helps develop you into the kind of Dweller you are destined to become. But for now, duty calls again." He said, standing up and taking Ryans arm. "Let's see, oh yes, the area around Fritham then, if you will."

Ryan turned and grabbed a tree, rotating slightly, and before he knew it was at edge of the field just outside Fritham. They walked up the field a bit further, but this bit didn't seem to need their services at the moment. So Dweller, changing the days plan slightly, grabbed Ryans hand, transporting them a few hundred metres along, to the middle of a shaded area of woodland.

"Ah now see here Ryan, You're in for a treat" said Dweller, looking expectantly around with a grin.

It was all just as normal as any other part of the forest from what Ryan could see, then about a ten thousand little twinkly lights shone, flooding the woodland with colour. It was like Christmas lights thought Ryan, looking around amazed. Each of them was a different colour from the others, and they all began flickering from bright to dull and back again. A small group flew towards them, their light dimming a bit to show their full outlines as tiny people with wings.

"The Fritham Fairies," said Dweller clamping his hands together in delight, and walking forward to the welcome party with Ryan following, still looking up and around at the lights.

"Welcome to our fatherland Dwellers" said the Fairy quietly, but Ryan noticed it looked like he was shouting. He was an older looking man, only about an inch high, with a long white beard, and holding a tiny staff. They were much different to the Pixies they had met near Brockenhurst. The Fairies' features were quite delicate, but they were all good looking, and seemed to expel light from their pores like a character in a comic book who has encountered radiation.

"We welcome you to join us for a feast this evening, so we can be introduced properly to your apprentice." Yelled the old Fairies barely audible voice. The effort to speak so loudly for the Dwellers took his breath away so that he leant on his staff, even though he was fluttering in mid-air.

"We'd be delighted to, your worship" said Dweller, bowing deeply. Ryan copied the action so as not to seem insulting.

Cheering started. It sounded muffled and far away as they were so small.

"Excellent." Shouted the old Fairy, "Celebrations begin at sunset."

"We'll see you then" said Dweller, bowing again. Ryan followed his movement again, noticing a very pretty blonde Fairy smiling at him from beside the old Fairy. She emitted a cool pinkish glow that made her complexion look immaculate. Dweller turned away with Ryan following, just as she winked at him very flirtatiously with her big blue eyes. They left as the welcome party flew back to the main group, and made their way towards where they could see the edge of the woods in the distance. As they got to the last few trees, Dweller was about to say something, but before he could speak, their feet tingled.

"Down" whispered Dweller sharply, grabbing Ryans arm as he descended into a crouch by a thick oak tree. "And keep still" he said warningly.

Ryan did as he was told, barely able to breathe. The last time he had felt like this, He had frozen from seeing Dweller. Carefully he turned his head gently and saw all the lights from the Fairies in the distance had completely gone. Then voices came, louder and closer, as they both remained still, Ryan not realising their cloaks were camouflaging them perfectly against the tree.

"You see my dear Freddy the problems I have had getting rid of them. The local market is too crowded, we need to start selling them in a different location." Said a pasty white bald man, quite thin and gangly, carrying an axe.

"Geoff, if we go further afield, it will cost more, making us lose money." Said Freddy, who was an older respectable looking gentleman in a Jacket and trousers. Pausing to contemplate, he continued,

"Ok, well if their barking is annoying you so much, just board up the barn, but don't drop the price." He said in warning. "People will come to us from miles away for these, and I've got my eye on a pregnant Boxer as well, I'll let you know as soon as I have the location."

"They fetch a bomb" said Geoff excitedly, as they stopped a little way away from the hiding pair.

"They fetch sticks actually" said Freddy, laughing at his own joke, before a cruel smile flitted across his face. "But yes, at three grand a pup, we would hope for a big litter."

"Ok fine, I'll hold out with the king Charles spaniels, but if they haven't all gone in the next couple of weeks, I'll be flogging them cheap."

"Fine, but only ten percent off. People get suspicious if you try too low."

Ryan looked at Dwellers face. It was full with rage, his blue eyes almost flashing from the angle of the light.

"Right then, let's get back, and don't forget to get me that address." Said Geoff as they both walked away out of the trees, their voices becoming fainter.

"Yes, yes I know" was the last words that they could hear from Freddys response before Geoff, with his axe resting on his shoulder, walked towards the village, and Freddy headed to a dark blue snazzy car, that looked as if it had been quickly parked for what was their hurried conversation.

"Thieves and scoundrels" barked Dweller with force, as Freddys car drove off at speed, "The cheek of it, to use the forest as cover for their conversation about stealing animals. Pfft" he said in anger.

"Nasty pieces of work, is there nothing we could do to help the puppies?" said Ryan, hoping Dweller would say yes and come up with a devilish plan to make them rue the day of even considering such foulness. And he was not wrong.

"Well," said Dweller thoughtfully looking back to where the Fairies had been. "We might be able to chat with them," he said gesturing back into the wood, "to help sort our predicament. I know The Sisters of The Wreath would love to get a hold of villains like these. We will let the Fairies know tonight, and they can alert us if they spot anything else going on around here."

"Good plan" said Ryan, wondering what the Sisters would do with those two, each thought sending a shiver down his spine. It is amazing what people would talk about when they thought no one else could hear them.

"Right then, back to our actual work. Let's take ten or so emergencies each and then meet at main location fourteen" said Dweller, testing Ryan.

"The forest near Beaulieu," said Ryan almost at once.

"Correct, of course" said Dweller, leaning against a tree and disappearing.

"Of course" said Ryan smiling, before following his master, disappearing to an area of the forest where an unfortunate worm had recently been chopped in half.

***

The afternoon seemed to fly by, with Ryan dealing with all sorts of issues, from a horse with its tail caught in a bramble bush, to a scarred oak tree that had been used by some teenagers as a place for carving their initials. White sap had leaked from its wounds as Ryan tried to heal them with some special wood paste from his pocket which included soothing and numbing additives.

When he finally landed in the forest at location fourteen, he sat down and took a drink of fizzy orange. Usually, the one to start emergencies first, was the last to return.

As he sat, he wondered how everyone in his life before, was getting on now. It filled him with too much sadness to think of them on an emotional level, instead thinking about their needs and where their lives were headed. Paul would hopefully have taken over the business successfully. His family would have to come to terms with him missing, and hopefully be able to move on. And lastly, he really hoped that Becky and Archie were doing well without him. It was all very idealistic in his own mind, for things certainly hadn't turned out like this in the real world.

Becky had been getting better, thanks to the spells magic enabling her to quickly deal with her emotions and start a routine again, like taking Archie to nursery and making sure the house was clean and tidy. She hadn't been able to go back to work yet, that was too great a step. She had made progress though, which had surprised all that had been close to Ryan, but did make it seem slightly sinister that she could appear to have moved on so quickly.

Paul had not been at work since he had heard of Ryans disappearance. Becky had dropped off some very neat paperwork with the work laptop the day before, but he didn't have time for paperwork. He felt he had lost his best friend and business partner, and didn't feel he was able to continue working without him. How could Ryan be gone? They'd taken the remains of his van for DNA sampling and other testing, but to all intents and purposes it looked as if Ryan had just walked away willingly. Paul did not know what to do.

Ryans family were distraught. It had been leaked that Ryan had been the only one to have life insurance, and combining that with Becky acting almost normal, threw up massive reg flags. Nobody said anything outright, but the suspicion was there, and they discussed it in depth behind her back. They had all helped appeal for his return to them, with baby Archie being at the forefront of the reasons. Although most of them had started giving up hope that he would ever return.

Archie had been his usual self, happy, laughing and wanting to play. It was amazing how untroubled he was, and only seemed to get happier the more that Ryans desperate family descended on them to offer Becky support with him. No, he was the most content, only occasionally remembering 'Dada', which was usually triggered by a photo or Ryans family. Thankfully, he was too young to suffer.

Ryan continued to sit and wait, his mind wandering, birds flying through the trees overhead, and the pure tranquillity that accompanied being immersed within nature. Nothing could be compared with that.

His peacefulness was only broken when Dweller appeared, slightly out of breath and having to bend over to recuperate. Ryan walked over and placed his palm on his shoulder.

"I can feel myself getting older" said Dweller, a fear in his voice, not from the prospect that his time was coming to an end, but that he was weakening, less able to do what he'd been doing the last sixty or so years, to help his forest.

"Come and sit down" said Ryan, worried having noted the fear in Dwellers voice.

Dweller sat, noticing how his knees creaked as he bent down against the tree. The cloak was a wonderful thing that fixed and healed where it could. But it could not hold back ageing, and that was what was happening to him now. As he sat, catching his breath, seeing the birds flying, and the beams of light falling between the leaves, he felt a wave of relief. A feeling so great, partly from the beauty of the forest around him, but mostly from the person crouching in front of him, a face full of concern for him. This would be the right person to help the forest, he knew it.

"Thank you" said Dweller, pulling out a glass of water with a slightly shaking hand.

Ryan sat down on the forest floor cross legged and watched Dweller drink. This man who had shown him so much of the hidden life of the forest, the man who was teaching him how to nurture and take care of it was himself, at his mortal end. And even though he knew he would enjoy looking after the forest, having a mentor with him helped shoulder the responsibility and the tasks, and more than anything, he was good company.

Staring at the old man, Ryan knew he would miss him. Although apparently, he was not gone forever. Seeing how he had settled, Ryan began asking Dweller a few questions which also aided strangely, in taking his mind off his ageing body.

"Dweller, was it true you become a ghost?" Asked Ryan, slightly sceptically.

Dweller chuckled.

"Why? Don't you believe me?" he said, his smile wide, age forgotten.

"I'd never have believed half of what I know now just a few weeks ago," Ryan started by saying. "But ghosts just seem too much of a step up from Fairies, Pixies and witches"

"Well, you'll just have to take my word then" said Dweller with a laugh. "But on January first, I expect to see you, and maybe Pine and the others for my first appearance since I'd been gone."

"But how?" said Ryan, not knowing what to think about this. "How can ghosts possibly exist, and how do you know you will be one?"

Dweller paused as he so often did when presented with a more complex question, arranging the answer in his head for a swifter ease of understanding.

"All Dwellers are tied to their forest for life, and afterlife. They offer knowledge and advice to the current Dweller, and give the ghost councils opinion of what can be changed to better the role and benefit the forest. As to how, I believe that our souls become so entwined with nature, that the forest cannot bare to let us go. Only when a Dweller has decided to, can they pass over in spirit. At the start of this year, there was thirteen Dwellers that still resided as their ghostly doubles, the oldest is from the twelfth century I believe."

Ryan sat in awe listening, before suddenly come to his senses.

"So, they are watching over us all the time" he said, slightly embarrassed that his first moment with the urge, might have been witnessed after all.

Dweller chuckled and had a twinkle in his eye,

"No, not all the time. So don't worry, mistakes can be made and embarrassing things can be done. They're only interested in the forest's needs." He said, and Ryan relaxed slightly knowing that not everything he did would be monitored.

"Have there ever been any female Dwellers" asked Ryan, the thought only just coming to him.

"Well, yes there has actually, but they are not nearly as common. Most women want to start families, and all their time and effort is spent on bringing up children, well that is what it was like in my day. I know now that fathers are much more interactive with the kids." He said, not noticing Ryans guilt that ate at him from the inside. Dweller continued with a dark tone.

"There is even said to be Dweller ghosts of forests long gone, that appear each year in the hope that it has returned." He said with a shiver. "What could be worse than seeing the thing you love disappear for good."

Ryans guilt was extreme now. Dweller had still not noticed, but Ryan seemed pained by it, had he made the wrong decision. Surely the forest needed him more? He would have been happy either way, but this way he gets to help nature grow and feel like he is making a real difference in the lives of not just the animals and plants, but with the people who visit and can experience the beauty and wonder of it all. Slightly calmer, and noticing that Dweller had stopped talking, he looked up into the kind blue eyes.

"I'm sorry, I realise how that might have sounded" he said softly. "I speak for the forest when I say we really do appreciate what you are doing, and it was not an easy thing to commit to, I know. But you are the person who can help sustain millions of lives, and that in itself is a fantastic thing to do. And when you get to an old age like me, you can look back at all you have achieved. All the trees that would not have made it had it not been for your nurturing. And the families of deer that run free around the forest, because you helped heal their grandparents. The thanks and happiness come from job satisfaction, everything else is a bonus."

"I know" said Ryan, failing to hide his real emotion of longing for his fiancé and son. Well, not sure he could call her a fiancé anymore. That thought ate at him a bit more.

"Right then" said Dweller, standing up having fully recovered and wanting to take Ryans mind off his old life.

"Let's do a spot of main location housework, the suns on its way down and we'll be dining with Fairies tonight." He said with a glint in his eye.

"Alright" said Ryan a little happier, distracted. After all, how often did a person have a chance to dine with the Fairies.

They spent the late afternoon clearing branches and animal trails, making gaps in fences, and picking up litter they found along the way. Then they met back at the start having covered a square mile or so each.

"All alright?" Said Dweller, his face orange from the sun dancing on the horizon.

"There was a lot of dog poo over on that trail" said Ryan, looking disgusted and pointing south towards an area of ferns, "picked up as much as I could see."

"Filthy, have they no shame at all!" exclaimed Dweller. "But there's little we can do to prevent it."

"Can we not leave the bags on the New Forest District Councils front door with a note saying more signs for collecting it need to be placed on walking spots?" asked Ryan, wanting to do something.

"I suppose, but they are not likely to listen. Could be worth a try though, but we cannot, get, seen." He said, punctuating the last few words with pauses for effect.

"Next time I will" replied Ryan, with determination.

Dweller turned, calculating how much day they had left. Very little as the sun was touching the land, with the moon up and night approaching.

"Well, I think we should do a couple of emergencies each, and then meet at the edge of the wood at Fritham" said Dweller, rushed by the lack of day left.

"Ok, I'll take the first one though" said Ryan placing his palm on the tree. "I'll see you soon," and with a grin at the prospect of a Fairy feast, vanished.

Dweller followed with a grin of his own, those Fairies know how to party.

Chapter Ten – The Fairy Feast

The emergencies were not bad. It hadn't been too long since Dweller had done them, and no major problems had happened in that time, well none that lived to require saving. Unfortunately, unknown to Ryan and Dweller, a baby donkey had been hit by a car. The driver, a woman in a four by four who had checked her phone messages whilst driving, had ploughed into the animal head on, leaving it lying still on the ground. In a panic, and with no one else having seen the 'accident', she had driven off, her car bonnet crumpled and bumper hanging off. She would later tell her fuming husband that somebody must have hit her in a car park in the forest while she was walking their dog. He bought the story, accompanied by her tears, and thus the poor donkey died without the culprit ever being caught.

Ryan and Dweller appeared at the treeline edge almost in sync. They looked at each other in the twilight, and began walking through the woods, looking for a sign of welcome. Ryan was excited about the feast, but wondered what they would be having, and how? That had not occurred to him before now. Just how? His quietness whilst walking must have seemed suspicious to Dweller, who whispered.

"I'm sure you'll see soon" he said, his face holding a smirk that Ryan could not see in the darkness.

They crept along, following no path, until they came across a single-coloured light, a light that could easily be missed as the moonlight had started to shine through the leaves. The light seemed to float down, like a bonfire ember, the same colour in fact.

"Welcome" came a squeaky tiny voice from the light. It dulled slightly to allow them to see a tiny shining man, with his hands clasped behind his back. He was wearing what seemed to be a leafy toga, similar to what the old Fairy had worn when he had greeted them. Memories of the meeting earlier in the day were starting to become clearer, as though the shock of seeing Fairies had caused him to forget certain things he would usually notice. Like the pretty Fairy that had caught his eye. He remembered she was wearing a two-piece leaf outfit that showed off her slender body and tiny belly button.

"You have been welcomed to our feast in honour of our new Forest Dweller" he squeaked, obviously shouting his loudest. "Now if you'll kindly follow me to our Fairy door, we can begin" he said, floating away from them.

They followed the spec of light through the almost complete darkness. Thankfully their cloaks meant they were not tripping on roots or sticks. After a couple of minutes, the Fairy flew up to a tiny circular purple door, high in a tree, and turned as if waiting for them.

"Right" said Dweller, as if suddenly remembering something. He then rummaged in his pocket and withdrew a twelve-foot ladder. Ryan tried to watch carefully through the darkness, as Dweller climbed up to the door, which the Fairy opened lighting up Dwellers face fully, and it shone with happiness. The Fairy then flew towards Dweller, touching him on the nose. Nothing happened, for a moment at least, as Ryan stood there looking up. Then all of a sudden, Dweller shrank to an inch tall, his body compressing to the part where the Fairy had touched, so for an instant, Dweller and the Fairy were the same size face to face, but Dweller, without wings, began to fall. Before he had dropped below the Fairy's waistline however, he'd been grabbed and flown up to the door. Standing in the doorway and looking down, he shouted in a squeaky voice.

"Your turn, Acorn."

Amazed and with a slightly outer body feeling, he clumsily climbed the ladder. When he was up by the door he looked in and his jaw dropped. The very centre core of the tree was hollowed out into a flight chamber for the Fairies to get about. The outside edge of the tree was filled with corridors and rooms circling around, and with tables and chairs set out all facing into the middle. Light seemed to radiate from all areas making the Fairies all look normal, with just a slight coloured glow.

Ryan was too busy staring to realise the Fairy had flown towards him, until he felt a spark on his nose, and then an incredible feeling of being squeezed softly all over. From his perspective, it was like the tree and Fairy were growing towards him at an alarming rate. Stopping just in time to appear a regular size to his Fairy friend. There was just a moment where his stomach lurched and his body began to drop, but he was immediately helped through the doorway which was pulled shut behind them, leaving the forest as dark and quiet as it had been before their arrival.

Ryan struggled to take it all in, the place was carved beautifully. Sleek smooth wooden architecture was everywhere, with occasional carvings of people who he assumed were previous rulers of the Fairy people. It seemed as if the whole community was there to grab him by the arms, dragging him through to be at the centre of them all. The men were happily shaking his hands and calling congratulations in much more normal sounding voices. The women, who were all very attractive indeed, were placing kisses on his cheeks with coloured lipstick, so after a few dozen he was completely covered. Luckily, he cloak removed them quickly, but still left his face red from embarrassment. Dweller was smiling as he removed his cloak, donning a leaf robe that was provided for him. The female Fairies started removing Ryans cloak too, all excited, stroking his chest and body with their hands while the men cheered him on. The blonde Fairy who he had seen at the first meeting was there, forcing her way to the front smiling seductively. She stood directly in front of him and helped four or five others lift a leafy toga over his head, flying up slightly to reach so his face was mere millimetres away from her scantily clothed busty chest. Succeeding in dressing him, they whisked his cloak away to hang next to Dwellers by the door.

The blonde Fairy then grabbed his hand, pulling him through the crowd, and around the widest corridor that spiralled up to the main table that was on a platform, stuck out slightly for all to see.

"You'll sit here, next to me" she said, smiling and giggling. He reached out and pulled her chair back for her to sit down first, her smile widened at this. He then settled into his own next to her. She could not seem to be able to take her eyes off him, but he loved the attention from this beautiful person. The other

Fairies seemed to be taking their seats around the tree's corridors, all looking up or down to their table. Dweller settled next to the old Fairy who took the centre seat. There were others there on the main table too. What looked to be the wife of the elder Fairy sat to the old Fairy's right-hand side, and some handsome young men were towards the far end. Everyone was happy, smiling as they looked to each other and around to the cheering crowd.

The old Fairy stood up, tapping a glass goblet from in front of him. The noise died immediately. You could cut the excitement in the place with a knife. He spoke with a much deeper crisp voice than Ryan had first heard.

"Thank you all, for preparing this fantastic occasion for our special guests. For the cross over has not happened in over sixty years, and we are all very honoured to be able to witness it." The crowd cheered at these words, celebrating as if they had won the world cup final Ryan thought, with a laugh at the crazy comparison. The blonde Fairy next to him laughed at his laugh, not knowing what had created his pleasure, but pleased he was happy and enjoying himself. He turned to look into her beautiful deep blue eyes that seemed to sparkle with light. She was utterly bewitching, and Ryan felt lust bubble within him, accompanied with the pang of guilt for the one he loved, and the son they had created. His smile faltered, and she seemed to notice, reaching up and stroking his cheek with an understanding kind face. He turned back to the older Fairy just as the cheering died again.

"We are here to thank The New Forest Dweller, for his service to our forest, for we have thrived under his watch, and in turn, helped do our part in maintaining this place we live." More cheering followed this, with the women blowing kisses to Dweller, and the men waving and saluting with happiness, smiles, and laughter throughout. As it all died down for the third time, the older Fairy spoke quickly, so as to finish his speech and let the partying commence before the excitement boiled over again.

"We welcome The New, New Forest Dweller, Acorn, more commonly known at the minute as Ryan. He will be taking over in the forest, and helping to see us into an even brighter future.

We thank him for this, and let the FEAST COMMENCE" he said, hollering the last two words to start. The cheering was wild.

Ryan looked across and saw Dweller drinking heartily from his own goblet, before loading his plate with a fine array of interesting dishes, whilst in conversation with those around him. He looked at his happiest here, with the crowd, the good cheer, and the feast. Ryan could not help feel a twang of guilt that this would be the last time for Dweller, that his time had almost run its course, and a weird feeling that he himself would be in this position one day, who knows when.

He stared down at his own empty plate. It was shiny and gold which reflected his face, but with his features slightly distorted from imperfections. There was another face there too, off to the side but looking at him. He turned his head to the blonde Fairy who was smiling friendly at him, and held up a dish for him to try.

"Chestnut stew" she said, with a cute nervous laugh.

"Thanks" said Ryan holding out his plate as she dolloped a couple of spoonful's on. It had a weird taste at first, sort of like a wet nut roast. But the more he ate, the more he started to enjoy it. Along with the chestnut stew, he had other interesting dishes, like oak leaf greens, pollen balls, bark souffle, fern florets, and a multicoloured dish that tasted exquisite.

"The witches make this for us," said the blonde Fairy taking a bite out of a slice of woodland loaf.

"It tastes incredible," said Ryan. It was one of those flavours you could not put into words, like trying to describe what cola tastes like. "By the way." He added slightly sheepishly that they were eating together and he didn't know her name. "What's your name?"

She smiled wider, as if his interest in her warmed her soul.

"My names Cinthia. Well, my parents named me Hyacinth, but I go by Cinthia" she said, her beautiful blue eyes looking deeply into his, with almost a longing expression on her perfect face. She blinked slowly and turned to her food, aware how entrancing she could be.

Ryan was sort of caught in a daze, she was utterly beautiful and seemed to be interested in him. The usual pang of guilt hit him again though. If it wasn't about Dwellers last days, it was about his family. Well, his previous family, the one it seems he had left behind. His mind snapped back to his plate and he finished off what was left on it before drinking the mead in his goblet.

"I can see it is tough for you, to have left people behind to come here to take care of the forest. It is an incredibly selfless thing to do." She said quietly to him, over the raucous noise of a celebration. But there was a quiver in her voice.

He looked up and saw tears brimming in her eyes, reflecting the blue so perfectly that it looked like they had almost doubled in size.

He took her hands, feeling her warm smooth skin and said,

"I have chosen to do this, not because I wanted to leave my family, but because I believe I can do good for the forest, to carry on Dwellers legacy and those before him. To help look after the animals, trees, and plants to the best of my ability. So that the forest can thrive and grow, and allow me to feel like I have accomplished something truly unique."

She smiled at this, tears blinked away and her cute cheeks and rosy lips had come closer to him as he spoke, like she was drinking in the words.

"You know, I like you very much" she said, with a friendly, slightly seductive smile that stirred up feelings within him.

"I think I like you too" he said, knowing that he did but with his guilt holding him back. "But I have left my family because I wanted to help the forest, not to meet someone else." He said, slightly annoyed at himself.

Her smile changed subtly as she heard this.

"That's a good thing, it really is, but there's no reason we can't enjoy ourselves" she said, as the plates, food and goblets were cleared away, and a Fairy band took to a stage below. "Come on" she added, as they all stood up and Fairies flocked to the dancefloor.

Ryan was pulled by Cinthia down the corridors, but many other Fairies were flying down the central column. They made their way through the crowds of mainly younger looking Fairies, the older ones remained up top, drinking and chatting and watching the frivolities.

The music started. A mixture of rock with a forest twist. It was very easy to get lost in the dancing, the music, the colours that different Fairies were giving off. Also with Cinthia, blonde, curvy, and beautiful, standing across from him dancing, their eyes locked together in happiness, joy, and a little something else.

They danced through the evening, separated occasionally by groups of fellow Fairies that wanted to share the new Dweller, to get to dance, laugh and have fun with him. The music kept going, getting faster and better with each song. The normal tree lights were dimmed but the Fairies lights became brighter, flashing constantly so that they looked like stop motion revellers. It was warm all packed in on the dancefloor, some of the Fairies had flown up and were dancing whilst flying about with one another. Ryan folded his toga over so that more of his body could breathe. A pink light made him stop. Cinthia was there smiling and holding out a drink that he gulped down. A light mead which was slightly seedy but tasted great. Then they danced together again, more fiercely that before, the chemistry was intense. The crowd was swelling and the songs got louder. They were pushed together closer, lights around them flashing, lighting up her beautiful face. They were so close together, arms linked, skin on skin, the crowd almost tearing them apart from the dancing and movement. They pulled each other closer, and Ryan felt his lips brush hers. It was only a split second but it felt wonderful. She looked up at him as they kept dancing, the Fairies around singing and flashing their lights, the music blaring. They kissed again, accidentally, but with no desire to pull apart. He felt her tongue slide over his, she tasted so pure and amazing. Then they pulled away again as the revellers wanted to join in with the new Dweller, to scream words of the songs, to laugh and dance and be a part of the fun, which continued for the rest of the night.

***

Ryan awoke. Very aware that the toga barely covered him, but feeling good considering how long the night had lasted. He looked around the room he was in. Cinthia was next to him. She had been cuddled up in his warmth under a patchwork leaf quilt. Her clothes hanging off her slightly as she slept. Her beautiful features looked relaxed as she lay there breathing gently. Ryan was suddenly worried as he usually had the urge first thing in the morning. He was sure that with the chestnut stew coupled with the amount of mead and grass wine he had drank, it would start to have an effect soon. But then he relaxed as he remembered he hadn't changed out of his undergarment.

Cinthia stirred as he sat up a bit. She reached out for his waist to pull him in close to her, and he let her. It was so nice to feel wanted like this. But not something he felt he should become used to if he wanted to really help as he intended. He looked down to her face and saw her eyes and smile looking back.

"Hey" she said quietly, feeling the warmth from his body and it made her happy. "How did you sleep?"

"Yeah, good" he replied. "I can't remember too much about last night. Did anything happen between us?"

"Well, we danced and kissed, and drank and kissed, and then danced some more" she said, holding him tightly. "Then we all went to bed, and we fell asleep cuddling."

"So, nothing else happened between us?" said Ryan, slightly apprehensively.

She smiled. "No, humans and Fairies can't interact in the way you are thinking. We are about the feeling, the warmth, the happiness, and the fun. Fairies can only mate with Fairies." She said pointedly with an understanding smile. "But that doesn't mean we can't have fun together."

Ryan felt a lot better about the night now, knowing that the only intension was for fun and not for lust or mating. "I had a lot of fun with you last night, and I feel that I could easily do this every night. But I can't. I do not want to get distracted from the work I have come here to do" he said.

"And we'll all love you for that" she said, tilting her head up to give him a quick peck on the lips. "I will not hold you here, you are free to come and go as you please. But I will always look forward to your return." She said with an understanding smile.

With one last squeeze, she released him. He suddenly felt cold, as if left out of her life, as she lay there smiling at him from under the quilt as he sat on the side of the bed.

He heard footsteps, and Dweller appeared at the doorway, smiling and back in his cloak.

"Had a good night have we?" He asked gently so as to not awaken the other Fairies.

"Yes" said Ryan, turning and smiling at Cinthia who smiled back at him, her hand caressing his shoulder before he stood up.

"Here, you'll want this" said Dweller tossing him his cloak. "We've got work to do." Before turning to head down the corridor.

Ryan watched him go for a second before turning back to Cinthia, who sat up immediately and gave him a great big kiss on the mouth, tongue dancing across his for a moment.

"I look forward to your return," she said lying back in the bed.

"As do I," he said grinning, giving in to her enthusiasm. He stood up to remove the toga and don his cloak.

He could feel it working its magic on his liver from the night before.

"Bye" he said with a little wave from the door as she lay there blowing him a kiss.

He exited the tree with Dweller, the awaiting greeter who looked very worse for wear, turned them back into their full-sized selves before wishing them well and closing the door behind him.

They climbed back down a ladder Dweller produced. He had taken the previous one with him when they arrived as he did not want anyone coming across what he knew would be an entertaining evening.

"Ok, emergencies. I will go first" And with that he tapped the nearest tree with his palm and vanished.

What a truly exceptional experience the night had been, Ryan thought, smiling, before he followed his masters' actions, and disappeared as well.

Chapter Eleven – High Winds and A Highwayman

Dweller and Ryan spent the remaining days getting to know each other better. It was a shame it was a timed friendship, but they had both known it would be from the outset. Over the time, Dweller crammed as much information into Ryan as he could, spewing over six decades of forest secrets he had discovered, along with the millennia of knowledge that was passed on through the Dwellers of past. Ryan knew he would not remember everything he was being told, and Dweller knew this too, as he himself was sure that he had forgotten things that his master had shared with him. It was only important to remember the main tasks at hand, Dweller reminded him. Ryan hoped that in the future, certain areas of the forest would trigger the memories of what Dweller had said about it, and thoughts like these would bring him comfort knowing that his master, and those before, had looked after this land like he was doing.

Dweller also mentioned to Ryan, that during the Fairy feast, he'd had a good chat with the leader of the Fairies, the elder bearded one who was called Branch, regarding the two dog poachers they had overheard. Branch had vowed to keep a couple of Fairies posted to the spot, and report immediately if he found out any information, 'which he will pass onto you Ryan', the old man had said purposefully. Ryan vowed that if he heard from the Fairies about this, he would act upon it with as much might as he could muster. Thieves were bad, but stealing innocent little animals was unforgivable.

On the occasional afternoon, when Ryan was doing some tedious tasks, Dweller would sneak off to say his personal goodbyes to each of the groups of the locals. They were all very sad that they would be losing him, but pleased he had found such a good replacement. Ryan noticed him gone, and assumed that is what he must be doing. He had spent such a long time with them that friendships were inevitable, especially when tackling such a monumental task as looking after the forest.

The days started to lengthen, allowing them to work later into the evenings fulfilling the tasks. When the moon started to become fuller, Dweller announced that he would not be helping with the tasks anymore, but would follow Ryan around, making sure that he was carrying out everything he'd been taught, properly. This was called the handover, and Dweller said it was to be his last duty, to make sure his replacement was capable of thinking and acting for himself.

Ryan really enjoyed this increased time with Dweller. Quite often they had gone off to separate emergencies and main locations to help take care of as much of the forest as they could while there was two of them to hand. They talked for hours, Ryan working hard while Dweller chatted about the Fairies and the Pixies, and wondered aloud what the Forest Folk were up to after the party they had attended at their camp the night before. Ryan cleared the animal trails, collected wood from fallen branches and stacking it neatly out of the way, before tackling multiple mounds of dog poo.

Ryan was fuming at the amount. Obviously, people used this spot regularly and never cleared it up. So, he bagged each and every one, forty-six in total, and placed them all in a bigger black bag with a note stuck on it saying where and when this had been collected. That night he tied the bag to the front door of the New Forest District Council Office in Lyndhurst, before disappearing quickly.

The full moon would be the following night, with Dweller saying he would probably be passing over a day or so after. When Ryan appeared back from the poo run, to where Dweller was settling for the night, sat with the lantern that he used regularly, he saw the old man looked tired, and if possible, older.

Ryan sat at his side, beginning to eat a beef stew and dumplings, with the old man just staring into the blackness, in silence.

"These last couple of nights, I can see them coming for me" he said quietly. Ryan, who had raised his spoon to his lips, lowered it, looking around the darkness for any sign of anyone. Upon not seeing anything, he asked,

"Who?"

"My master, and the others, I presume" he said, eyes squinting around as if trying to locate them again. "Momentarily they appear to me, and beckon me with kind smiles. But I am not ready to go yet. I must say goodbye to the Highwayman at least, and then I might feel my duty to the forest is complete."

Ryan sat in silence, stew quickly losing its heat as it remained untouched. Dweller continued.

"I have no doubt you will become a better and more able Dweller than I have been. I can see over these last few years how slow I have become, and the forest needs your youthful work ethic to maintain and progress. I am so proud that you will be my legacy" he said, a tear running down his cheek. Then without another word, he lay down, and almost instantly started snoring gently.

Ryan reached over and dimmed the lantern slightly. He was saddened that in a few days he would have to say goodbye to someone he had grown incredibly close to. It made him think about those he had already lost when he decided on his future. He knew it had been less than three weeks since his disappearance from the recorded world. But he hoped the spell The Sisters of the Wreath had cast, had some effect on Becky's emotions. And indeed, it had.

Becky had been back to work again, with Archie still at nursery. She seemed to act like this was the new normal, and that Ryan had been missing for years, which was strange to hers and Ryans families. They had expected to be having to help and support her through this time, and that she might not heal from this for years, but miraculously she seemed ok, too ok. Her family thought it might be an emotional defence, triggered to make everything feel normal and to escape the reality. But after a full psyche evaluation from the police and NHS medics, she was deemed to be just dealing with the situation fast but well.

The only sticking point was that Ryans life insurance was refusing to payout. It had only been three weeks they had argued, and that as Ryans body was not discovered, it could just be an insurance scam. The police though were keeping Becky up to date on the case, assuring her that once it was concluded, they would have no choice but to pay out the full sum. That at least would set her and Archie up until he was an adult. It would pay off the house, take care of the bills and utilities, and it would still leave a very hefty amount in the bank. The police had come up with several theories about what might have happened, but with some of them proved wrong and the rest unable to be evidenced, unless Ryan or his kidnapper came forward, it would never be resolved.

"Rest assured miss Lewis" the chief constable said to her in his most sincere voice. "If we have no new leads within the next couple of weeks, we'll have to close the investigation."

"I understand" she said, only slightly tearful that her fiancés disappearance would be final, the matter closed. "Thank you for all you and the force has done, I hope he does return, if not for me then for his son."

The constable nodded, placing his hat back on his bald head and standing at the doorway, looking out into the night. With a swift 'Mam', he bowed his head and left.

Becky did feel better about the whole situation. She could not explain it herself, and merely hoped that the process continued to be this easy for her. She had decided when she got the insurance money, she would buy the house next door from the older couple who were planning to move into care homes the following year. That way, she could rent it out and the money from this, along with the house itself, would be for Archie's future, so he could live next door to her, and she would always be able to keep him close. She felt a warm glow inside at this prospect, driven by the spell, it helped her see a nice future where she would not lose anyone else close to her.

Archie was slowly learning new words from nursery. He liked climbing things, and often laughed when he slid down the small indoor slide. He had not mentioned 'dada' for a few days. Becky hoped he would almost forget about the father that was no more, so that it wouldn't cause her the pain of remembering what had happened each time. She knew in the future she would have to explain, but at the minute, she was content letting his beautiful little mind develop without that hindrance.

She lay on the sofa, watching the last episode of the police crime drama that her and Ryan usually ate dinner watching. The baby monitor showing Archie sprawled out in bed, only his legs under his duvet, one arm poking out between the bars. Oh, how she loved him. She just stared at him through the screen, eyes getting heavier, head drooping, and before long her gentle snores had started, with the final reveal of the suspect on tv, missed entirely.

***

The next day was a windy one. Windy but dry. Dweller said that even though the wind kept people out of the forest from fear of trees falling on them, the weather usually led to extra emergencies and much more clearing up around the forest.

"The number of times I've recovered the forest from one storm, before the next hits the following day has been unreal" he said, watching Ryan rescue a pheasant that had been blown into a hedge. "You could be on emergencies all day in weather like this, there's no point working on the main locations when they're only going to look the same again by nightfall."

Ryan worked tirelessly as the day blew by. Dweller watching from a few paces away making sure Ryan was ok with everything, and only a couple of times offering advice on things he knew would be difficult. Towards the end of the day, when the cloudless sky was becoming darker, and after Ryan had helped around fifty saplings be supported upright again by driving a piece of bamboo into the earth and tying them to it, the wind finally dropped.

"Good thing too" said Dweller, when Ryan pointed this out. "Our full moon has approached and we will be able to fully appreciate it in the open. For the Highwayman will be calling tonight" he added with a smile.

Ryan was excitedly apprehensive. The prospect of meeting a spirit that had lingered by its death spot for centuries, was just another thing not many people could admit to witnessing.

"You said he's quite dour, didn't you?" asked Ryan, remembering when Dweller had first mentioned him.

Dweller chuckled

"I did, didn't I. Well, he is quite droll. And he has never forgiven the family that caught and hanged him, even though it was many ancestors ago. But we have become close over the years. He has met many of the past Dwellers, and is full of stories about them and the forest."

"Ah good" said Ryan, now fully looking forward to the meeting.

Ryan took them to one last emergency, an exhausted pigeon that had been flying against the wind all day trying to get to water. Ryan carried it down to a river nearby, and placed it by the edge. It cooed softly to him before drinking.

"Right then" said Dweller, "Let's have a spot to eat before heading to Wilverly. I say this because the Highwayman hates me eating in front of him as it reminds him that he can't taste anything, and he was very partial to brandy in his day."

"Oh alright" said Ryan with a laugh, and he pulled out some chicken and pepper skewers with a side of coleslaw, garlic bread and chips. Dweller chuckled at Ryans varied choices of meal. For sixty years he had rotated between the twenty or so dishes he had been brought up on, occasionally trying new things but ultimately reverting back to what he knew and what tasted homely.

"You know, I will try that one as well" he said, pulling the exact same plateful of food from his pocket along with a large goblet of the Fairy mead they'd had at the feast.

Dweller had liked almost all of what Ryan had eaten, apart from the liquorice he had sampled one evening, but this dish was no exception. Smacking his lips together when his plate was clean and washed down with his drink, he let out a satisfied 'ahhh.'

"Right then, it looks dark enough now. Let's go"

Grabbing Dweller as he touched a tree, Ryan held the fist that was clenched, and twisted slightly as they shot into the abyss.

The full moon greeted them on Wilverly plain, casting its light on the grassland that stretched out in front of them. Dweller began pacing out to the open with Ryan following, eyes peeled for any sign of the spirit they were seeking. They walked for a few hundred metres, away from the dark carpark that was deserted, and out through the grassy plain, to a lone tree that sat at the start of a section of thorny bushes. As they got closer, Ryan saw a dim outline of what could only be described as a dark figure of a man. It could easily have just been someone stood there, bathing in the moonlight. But Ryans feet would be tingling, which they were not. Also, the figure did not seem to reflect the moonlight, but rather let it pass through, so that there was no shadow where it stood.

The reason it was so dark, was from the long black cape and hat it wore, covering a reddish waistcoat with dark trousers tucked into knee high black boots. The head looked slightly twisted and bent to one side, as if the neck had been snapped when alive. The face itself had dark eyes, with a long nose and moustache, but with a smile poking out from beneath it. The figure stepped forward as Dweller and Ryan approached, and called out in a quite a posh droning voice.

"Ah the Forest Dweller returns to me, with a partner no less. Does this mean it shall be our last?" said the figure, reaching out a hand and pretending to shake Dwellers who mimicked the action.

"It does I'm afraid my good sir," said Dweller with a slight nod. "But I'm pleased I am able to say goodbye, for now at least."

"Yes, well we haven't had a full moon on the New year for quite a while actually, so I might get to see you sooner than you think." Said the Highwayman before turning to Ryan. "Blimey, he looks young compared to you."

Dweller chuckled, a glint from the moon in his eye.

"You said that about me too when we first met."

"I am sure I did. I get used to your age as it progresses. I barely notice the changes until a Dweller brings a new recruit along. I myself, do not change. I wish I did. I would love to straighten this old neck of mine back to how it should be, it does nothing for my looks like this." He said before pulling back his cloak to reveal an empty holster and adding, "I'd also have liked my pistol back, long lost to a collector no doubt."

"Well Ryan here will be my replacement, and I must say he has the promise to be the best" said Dweller with a smile. He knew he was telling the truth. When he himself had been an apprentice all those many years ago, he wasn't half as capable as Ryan had shown. When he had started out, he didn't have as much in-depth time with his master, instead he was left on his own for far too long to pick up the duties he supposed would be needed to be done. Why his master even forgot to mention about the English Forest Dweller Council, which was a surprise when the then leader, who was Forest Dweller Pines master, had appeared to him and rather annoyingly had to fill him in. Oh, how he remembered the other ghosts ribbing his master at his first meeting of the ghost council. Those were the days he thought, sighing deeply.

"He does this more now doesn't he?" Said the Highwayman to Ryan, as Dweller snapped out of his thoughts and back to the conversation. Ryan grinned. He knew Dweller was almost there, and if he needed a minute or so to get lost in his thoughts and memories, then he would say he had earned it.

"He does slightly sometimes" said Ryan, and Dweller let out a little titter.

"Well can you blame me. I've got a lot stored in this old head of mine. Which is why I'm glad for someone so young to take over. Speed and endurance are what is needed to succeed, and a good head helps too." Dweller said.

"Yes well, we'll see about that" said the Highwayman with a smirk. "You've got some awfully big boots to fill lad."

"Now Ryan, as you know, Lester here…" started Dweller before the Highwayman snorted loudly.

"I was hoping it would be quite a few more meetings before I am forced to reveal my real name." said the Highwayman, disgruntled.

"Don't worry Lester, your secrets safe with me" said Ryan with a cheeky wink. This perked Lester up a bit, and he let out a sigh and a laugh.

"Oh, I think we're going to have some fun nights together, laddie" he replied, attempting to pat Ryan on the shoulder but going straight through. Ryan expected a cold feeling at the touch, wincing in preparation, but there was nothing at all, just the dullish glowing figure with no other worldly abilities.

"Yes well Lester here is only available after sunset on the full moon night around thirteen times a year. I always try and pop in, or else let him know if I have something planned well in advance. As you know, the meeting of the English Forest Dweller Council are yearly, Spruce will let you know shortly before the next one, and when you should be ready for. The Ghost Council appears only on the first of January throughout the day in various locations. When the time comes, if you want to find us, Root transportation will know where we are, so just ask and you shall appear. The 'Sisters of the Wreath' like long summer holidays, so sometimes they could be unavailable for weeks at a time. Feel free to pop into see them every couple of weeks as I'm sure they would, well, ahem, be happy to see you." He said with a smile. "As for that, the Fairies are usually very busy around pollinating time, the Pixies have many feasts over the Christmas period which I am sure they will invite you to, and the Forest Folk are always welcoming for a more relaxed gathering and chat. I do not think I have left anybody out."

"No, sounds like you've covered it all" said Lester in a droning voice with thinly veiled amusement.

Ryan committed all of this to memory, hoping he would not forget, but sure he would be reminded along the way.

"Yes, and I don't like to be kept waiting" said Lester, sarcastically rolling his eyes.

"Right then, yes, any news I should know about?" said Dweller, in mock anticipation.

"You know, I'm not going to miss this side of you" said Lester with a smirk. "But no not really. We seem to be experiencing a dog poo epidemic, tree growth is at a good level though. And apparently, there is a new Forest Dweller about." His dark eyes resting on Ryan, the smirk still very much visible.

"Ah yes, well the dog poo we are one step ahead on" said Dweller, before launching into the story about what Ryan had done with it. Lester seemed impressed, and let out a rare hearty chuckle when Dweller concluded.

They then chatted for a while about the trees and the wildlife. Lester seemed to be able to view the forest but without being able to interact with it like a living person would. Once they finished this discussion. They settled down on the grass between some of the thorny bushes, lit only in the moonlight. Dweller brought out the lantern and turned it on low, setting it on the edge of them all.

"Right then" Dweller said clapping his hands together, "I take it you know poker do you Ryan?" he asked.

"Yes" said Ryan smiling slowly, as Dweller removed a pack of cards and some poker chips from his pocket.

"Excellent" exclaimed Lester, lying on his side on the grass "This'll be your first of two times playing poker with me and another person."

Dweller snorted as he setup a little stand in front of Lester to show him his cards.

"He needs you to move the chips and shuffle, but other than that he plays his own game." Said Dweller splitting the chips into three individual stacks and beginning to mix up the cards. "You know, as tonight's my last night, do you mind me having a glass of wine Lester?"

Lester winced slightly but allowed it. "Don't tell me how it tastes though" he added, looking away as Dweller procured a large crystal glass, half full with a deep ruby wine.

Ryan, out of respect did the same, and they cheered to Dwellers success, Lester too but without a drink before saying.

"Right then, let's get started."

They played well into the night, laughing, chatting and with the occasional hidden sip of their drinks. Lester loved to bluff Ryan off a pot, but Dweller was too wise to his antics and caught him more than a few times. Ryan started getting tired. They were into the new day and he knew there would be emergencies to attend to when the dawn broke, but he didn't want to be the one to call time on what would be the last evening together for these two.

"Ah you got me." Said Lester, as Dweller turned over his cards. "Eight high I'm afraid, which is not much cop. Well, it has been a good night anyway. I am going to miss you my old friend" he added, emotion threatening to enter his voice.

"And I you," replied Dweller with his aged old smile. "We have had a good few memorable nights haven't we? And you will get to see me again, just not nearly as much."

"That's true that's true," said Lester. There was a slight pause after this as neither knew how to proceed. Dweller broke it with,

"Right then, best be off, duties are calling" he said with a smile. They were all on their feet now, and Lester moved forward, ignoring Dwellers outstretched arm, and gave him what should have been, a very tight hug. Dweller copied the motion and they both stood there for a good ten seconds, not physically touching each other, but feeling the emotion of a long friendship coming to an end. Ryan busied himself by packing the cards, chips, and lamp away into his pocket, and when he looked back, they had stepped away from each other.

"Take care in the ghost world, don't believe them when they tell you what I used to be like" Lester said, smiling with his dark eyes shining.

"Of course I won't" replied Dweller beginning to walk away "I know you too well to have my mind changed." He added which made Lester chuckle.

"I'll see you next moon" said Ryan, turning to follow Dweller in the darkness.

"Watch how you go Ryan. And please do your best for the forest" he added, his voice finally cracking slightly.

"Of course," Ryan called back, catching up to Dweller who was marching silently back towards the car park and trees.

They made it back to the edge of the woodland, and still silent, Dweller motioned for Ryan to take his arm, before they transported over to a section of forest just outside of Lyndhurst. Dweller immediately sank to the floor and Ryan placed his hand on his shoulder trying to see if he needed anything.

"Sleep my boy, I think there is one final sleep before I have to leave the forest, well the living forest." He said in a much older and quieter voice. He had been in good spirits for Lester, but it had taken it out of him, and he needed to rest.

He lay back, his hooded head resting against a stuck-out root, but feeling like he was supported by a dozen of the finest feather filled pillows.

"Night Acorn. I will see you in the morning for our last day together." He said before drifting off into his usual sleep.

Ryan was shocked at how quickly he had changed. He now looked and acted like he was on his deathbed, when just an hour ago they were laughing and drinking.

Ryan lay awake slightly longer, even though tiredness had nagged at him for a while. But worry seemed to lead to insomnia, which caused Ryan to have a very uncomfortable night, knowing that today he was losing Dweller.

Chapter Twelve – A Dwellers Final Duty

Awaking early from his troubled sleep and trying to be motivated for the day, Ryan stretched, rolled over, and stood up. It was pretty early, with the sun barely making it past the horizon, but with the promise of being a beautiful day as his gaze switched to look over to Dweller, who still lay by the tree. He must have rolled onto his side in the night, but was still as cushioned as ever thanks to his cloak. Thankfully he was still breathing gently, apart from the odd snort.

Ryan had a quick glass of apple juice before shooting off to tackle the first emergency. He arrived wearily by the roadside, to a convulsing badger who just wanted its pain to end. Ryan took its head in his hands, and very slowly guided it to release so its suffering was no more. Ominous that the day would start like this, and probably end like it too he thought, laying the badger down away from the road and disappearing to the second one just as a tingle in his feet had started.

The next was some more rutting deer, who were locked in a fight with their antlers entwined so they could not pull apart. Ryan managed to calm them enough to be able to manipulate their heads, moving them around so that they were finally free from the other. Thankfully this time, there were no injuries. They both allowed a quick stroke of their noses, before bounding through the bushes seemingly best of friends again.

The third, fourth and fifth were not needing as immediate a response as the first two, but he dealt with them the same. A rabbit with a broken leg which he bound, a slightly scorched tree from someone's camp fire that needed a good drink of water, and a falcon with a lot of brambles caught in its wings which were painful and stopped it from taking off.

Ryan decided to do a sixth one quickly before returning to Dweller, and he was pleased he did. He found when he got there, a horse that must have only just been hit by a car, had cuts and scrapes along its hindquarters and was whinnying in distress. Luckily, it wasn't too badly hurt, and Ryan managed to patch it up, knowing that with a bit of rest, grass, and water, it would be ok.

Toying with the idea of a seventh, before dismissing it, he returned to the woods to find Dweller enjoying the last bite of his bacon and egg sandwich.

"Well, my dear boy, my time has come." He said in a tired but relaxed voice.

"How do you feel?" Asked Ryan tentatively.

"Tired, accomplished, pleased, and that I know my next transport through the root network, will scatter my being evenly throughout the forest I have served" said Dweller to Ryans shock. "It is an odd feeling I grant you. But a journey that every Dweller has to make, as you yourself will see one day."

"I see" said Ryan, very unsure of what to say. There was silence for a minute as Dweller stood shakily and observed his troubled apprentice.

"Today will be used for answering any last questions you might have. Any niggles that you are unsure of, and any forgotten things that I can remember, which will finally, send us both our separate ways. Yours to a life of selfless servitude, and me, to a peaceful retirement where I will watch over your progress with the council I will be joining." He said, slowly.

Ryan paused, trying to think of any questions he had left. He was sure time would throw up moments where he required Dwellers wisdom, but at this moment in time he couldn't think of anything.

"I take it the pause is to appreciate how well I have taught you over the last few weeks?" Asked Dweller with a wry smile and cackle, which quickly turned into a cough.

"I don't think I have any questions. Well, none off the top of my head" said Ryan, hoping this didn't mean the end straight away.

"Ah well, some might come. Come on, let's go for a walk, it is a nice day after all" he said, leaning back slightly to admire the light green leaves which shone in the sunlight.

Ryan stepped to Dwellers side, as Dweller reached into his pocket and withdrew a knobbly wooden walking stick. He seemed to have aged another ten years since their meeting with

Lester, and it shocked Ryan to see how quickly his life was apparently ebbing away. The cloak was powerless at stopping age from catching up to him.

They spent the rest of the morning walking slowly and carefully through the undergrowth. Their cloaks sliding through the brambles and branches, keeping the leaves and earth away from their feet. They talked most of the time, only briefly pausing to admire the scenery or wildlife. Ryan found that the more they walked, the more questions he would think of.

Finally, after discussing the other dwellers that worked tirelessly all over the country, they reached some open plains.

"Well this seems like a nice place to stop for lunch" said Dweller, sitting down carefully on a thick branch of a fallen tree and pulling out a plate of cheese and pickle sandwiches, several tomatoes, an apple, and a small bar of chocolate. "You though might have a few emergencies to take care of first" added Dweller, staring at the sandwich in his hands carefully, so as to not lose its filling. "After all, a Dwellers work is never done."

"Right you are" said Ryan, happy to get back to helping the forest, and to give him time to think of anything else he might need to know that he had not thought of yet.

He walked over to the nearest tree and just before he twisted into the abyss, saw a large chunk of cheese and pickle falling out the end of Dwellers sandwich and down onto his cloak.

***

After a few emergencies, nothing of which was too serious, Ryan returned to Dwellers side and immediately pulled out and began eating a grilled chicken salad wrap. Dweller, who had finished his food, was sat watching Ryan eat. Slowly he pulled himself up, and walked carefully over to a small pond a little distance away. Ryan watched with interest as he bent forward, clutching his walking stick in his left hand, while the right scooped up some of the water. He then straightened up and turned back towards Ryan, walking carefully so as to not spill any of it.

Ryan swallowed down the last of his wrap, chewing quickly as Dweller approached and sat down next to him. The water in his hand looked slightly murky, likely to be full with all sorts of bugs and germs Ryan thought, with a slightly put off look. He got the impression Dweller was going to ask him to drink it. But the old man himself raised the hand to his lips, swallowing the contents in just a few gulps.

"Does that not taste funny?" said Ryan, quite surprised but relieved it was not him drinking it.

"Ah, it tastes wonderful" said Dweller, his eyes closed and head raised up slightly to the partially clouded blue sky. "It tastes like the forest, warming and comforting."

"What about the dirt and germs though" asked Ryan, still a little disgusted.

"Well, you are forgetting that our marvellous cloaks clean and cure us. Therefore, it is just like I have drunk the purest mountain water, but with the forest's secret benefits." He said, holding his calm position whilst talking, allowing a small smile to spread across his mouth.

"What secret benefits?" Asked Ryan.

"That my boy, you will find out when I am passed. When I have made my final journey, you are to take a drink from the forest water. A stream, a lake, pond, or puddle, it does not matter. But drink you will, and secrets you will see." Said Dweller mystically, lowering his head and staring into Ryans eyes. "Every few days, since I have been a Dweller, I have drunk from the forest's waters. When drought hits, and water is scarce, still I find a stream to drink from. Do this, and you will see." He said, his voice getting slowly quieter.

They stayed in silence for a little while. Dweller admiring the birds singing in the trees, and Ryan sat thinking about what more secrets the forest could reveal. It was a good while before Ryans feet started tingling slowly, and he realized that they had to get moving.

"Let's get back undercover" he said, spotting a couple of walkers in the distance.

They slowly crept back amongst the trees and continued their walk. The tingling feeling began to die down the further they went, until Ryan felt back to normal again.

They spent the afternoon whiling away the time, with Dweller telling stories, and Ryan asking about anything he could think of. Finally, when the sun was on its way down, and the clouds had further covered the sky. They reached a small opening in the trees, with pine needles and fur cones littering the ground, and a grassy hill area out in front of them. The sky was light blue, with a slight purple tinge, when Dweller stopped.

"I feel now is the time" he said, calmly and comfortingly.

"My journey is upon me. Once I travel, my body and cloak will be gone, zapped into all, becoming one with the forest. It has been a great pleasure to serve, and I am pleased I have been able to find you to take over" he said, a tear leaking from the corner of his eye.

Ryan stepped forward and gave the old man a hug.

"Thank you for all you have done for me and the forest. I will try my best to keep up your good work."

"You better" said the old man with a chuckle as they broke apart. "This is my life's work, and a life well spent indeed."

Ryan felt a tear roll down his own cheek, dropping onto the piney ground below. This would be the last time he saw his master in the flesh, and he faced a good six or seven months before he would see him briefly in spirit form again. A time where he would have to prove himself, that he was the one to look after The New Forest.

"The forest thanks you for your service" said Ryan, feeling it was a little cheesy for this moment.

But the old man looked at him calmly and said, "I know it does. It has thanked me every time I have taken a drink over the years. There is the stream just the other side of the hill there, drink from that once I have left, and you will see what I mean."

With a final pat on Ryans arm, the old man stood back and placed the palm of his hand onto his chest to show the Dweller Duties and respect. After a couple of seconds, he turned to a large Oak tree beside him. He raised the same hand to the tree looking back at Ryan.

"Goodbye my friend, and good luck" he said quietly, but with a twinkle in his eye. "You're going to be a great one." Then, with a slight twist, he was gone.

Ryan stood still, staring at the place where his master's kind calm face had been mere seconds ago, before dropping to his knees. The pine needles, twigs, and fur cones would have ordinarily brought pain to a normal person's knees, but protected by his cloak, it was like kneeling on a plump stuffed cushion. There was no big goodbye, no celebration, or fireworks Just a simple farewell, alone with his apprentice in the forest. It seemed like such a underwhelming departing considering what the old man deserved, especially after what he had achieved in his life. But he probably would not have had it any other way.

That was it then, he was on his own.

Well, not totally on his own he thought, as a warmth spread through him. The Pixies and the Fairies, the 'Sisters of the Wreath', the Forest Folk, Lester once, sometimes twice a month, the animals and forest itself, the England forest Dweller council, and the yearly visit from the ghost council. Well actually, he was far from alone.

His sadness at losing his master was slowly easing as he realised he was supported by so many other groups, he got to his feet.

Then, speaking to the forest, he said "Right then, first things first. Let's have a drink."

Chapter Thirteen – The Forest Voices

Ryan walked over the piney ground towards the peak of the hill which was open to the sky but surrounded by the woodland. He could hear the water close by, splish splashing as it cut through the landscape. He reached the top, immediately heading down the other side, towards the line of trees that encircled the small opening. At the bottom of the small hill, just beyond the first few lines of trees, was the stream. Ryan stood at the banks edge, a couple of feet above the water, and watched as it streamed around the bends in the woods, before flowing out of site. The water hitting the edges of the bank made most of the noise, as it jumped up and lapped against the earth. Ryan slowly bent down onto his hands and knees on the river bank edge, and reached out so that the stream flowed straight into his hand. It was only shallow, so his knuckles bumped the stoney basin, but it filled his palm with mostly clear liquid. It was fresher water than the old man had drank, as this was water on the move. Standing up, he lifted his hand towards his mouth, gently removing a rogue leaf that had slipped in from the current. He raised his arm, pausing with the water millimetres from his lips. He let out a lengthy exhale before connecting the water to his mouth, tilting his head back, the cool liquid running down his throat.

The effect was instantaneous. A warm feeling began to spread throughout his whole body, seemingly from his stomach outwards. He started to hear people speaking too, kind voices, saying nice things.

"Welcome new Dweller, we are so pleased you are here."

"Thank you for helping us and taking over the responsibility."

"We all love you, and will protect you like you protect us."

This seemed to keep going, with the voices talking over one another, but all with complimentary words for him.

After a couple of minutes though, warnings and news started to flood through.

"You are going to be magnificent. You will help keep us clean and healthy."

"So many creatures are being killed on the roads, its saddening."

"Sorry we have lost your predecessor, but we're so glad to have you."

"Woodland being chopped down near Ashurst, how tragic."

The voices continued for a little while more, but slowly petered down to nothing. Ryan was stood frozen in a mixture of shock and awe. Had he just heard the forest? It was communicating with itself, and now with him. How extraordinary he thought excitedly. The forest had a voice, and he could hear it.

The warmth that had spread through him had remained, like a candle filling a room with light.

He finished off what was left in his hand, and the voices appeared again.

"You're going to do an amazing job."

"Please keep our animals and plants safe."

"The forest is quite dry, watch out for fires."

A few minutes passed and the voices died down again.

Wow thought Ryan, what a feeling. Why had the old man made him wait before he could drink the forest water? Surely, he could have explained it.

But then Ryan remembered back to when he had asked him.

"Some secrets of the forest, you are meant to discover for yourself, once I have gone," is what he had said.

Well, there must have been a reason. Maybe in time it will come.

Joyed by the new realisation that he was more connected to the forest than before, he walked over to a tree, and disappeared over to Ashurst, to see what was going on with the chopping of woodland.

Appearing at his main location on the outskirts of Ashurst, he quickly had to figure out where the trees were in danger, and it didn't take very long.

There were council workers clearing some woodland along the main road towards Lyndhurst, a road Ryan had driven many times. His feet were tingling like crazy being so close to other humans. So making sure his hood was up, he crept forward for a better look.

The buzzing of a chainsaw was going, and large chunks of tree were crashing to the ground. It looked like they were making space for a new layby.

Not much I can do, thought Ryan sadly, turning to his nearest tree. I think I will do some emergencies before nightfall he thought, seeing that the sun now was very low in the sky.

So off he shot through the root transportation, arriving in an instant at the side of a very dark creature that was in pain, curled up on the forest floor. A bat, thought Ryan, kneeling down beside it, and reaching into his pocket for a guide on bat illnesses. It didn't appear physically injured, at least not from what he could see. He reached down and touched the creature, about to unfurl its wings slightly to get a better look, when he felt it, in his hands, but also in his head. He looked down at its face, which had been shielded by its wings moments before, and its great black eyes stretched open, looking into his. He heard a voice, quiet, but in his mind.

"My insides, they hurt" it said, "oh how they hurt."

"What can I do?" Thought Ryan, hoping it could hear him.

"Help" came the reply.

Ryan gently let go of the wing, and quickly reached for the bat manual. He was too busy trying to help the creature to be in awe of his newfound power.

The list of injuries and remedies flowed past his eyes as he searched for something that could help. The word Rabies jumped out at him, but he ignored it and carried on looking.

The bat was curled over again in obvious pain as Ryan poured over the small book. Finally, he came across a bit about rare issues. 'As bats use their smell and sonar to seek out food, flies, and other small insects, they can accidentally ingest foreign objects that happen to be falling in front of them, most commonly pieces of bark or twigs from trees'.

Ryan looked around. The forest floor was littered with such as you would expect.

He gently touched the bat again.

The New Forest Dweller

"Can you help, please?" came the voice in strained desperation.

"What were you doing when you started hurting?" Ryan thought, initially closing his eyes to think the question but soon adapting to look at the bat.

"I had just swallowed a large may bug, or what I thought was one, when a pain started and carried on through my body." Came the reply.

Ryan reached into his pocket and pulled a tiny glass bottle of ointment with a minute cork stopper.

"Here" he thought, opening the bottle, and holding it up to the bat's lips.

The bat allowed a few drops to be poured into its mouth before laying calmly down, exhausted from the pain.

Ryan looked at the bottle. In tiny writing were the words. Foreign object dissolving and pain relief concoction. Blimey, talk about specialised he thought, placing the bottle down next to the manual. Ryan then sat down next to the bat, waiting. After a couple of minutes, the Bat seemed to be getting better. It wasn't curled over of shaking anymore, just sitting there looking out of breath. It held out its wing and Ryan took it.

"Thank you kind Dweller, thank you. I thought that was it for me."

"No problem" thought Ryan, pleased that progress had been made "I'm just glad to help."

"Oh, help you have" came the voice as the bat looked at him, "Thank you, and I better be on my way now. The diet starts today. Nothing bigger than a mosquito for me."

And with that, it pulled its wing back and took off, quickly flashing through the trees and becoming lost against the foliage.

Ryan sat there pleased for a few moments. Wow, hearing what the animals were thinking would certainly help. It must be from drinking the water. Again, Ryan wondered why the old man had delayed him from trying it until after he had passed.

"He must have had his reasons" said Ryan quietly to himself, pocketing the bat manual and ointment.

Right then, lets go again.

He went to three more emergencies before the light was too dark to see properly. Luckily the last one was only between some fighting bunnies who had been trying to impress a mate before she had hopped off with someone else. Their bruising would heal soon thanks to the cream Ryan had applied. The voices that came to him from each animal was different, with little personalities shining through. This cheered Ryan greatly. He knew that even though he was dealing with their pain most of the time, he could stay connected, not feeling as lonely as he'd first thought.

He decided to settle for the night in an area of woodland which backed onto Brockenhurst golf club. It had been a funny old day, he thought, going through it in his head. He could not believe that only the night before they had been sitting playing cards with Lester. This day had seemed so long.

He stretched back against a tree, pulling a lamp from his pocket, the same style and look that the old man would have procured, and set it down on a dim light. He then reached in and felt his box of personal items. Removing it, he opened the lid, located a picture, and settling down to have a look at it. His little boy smiled at him, so cute and cheeky, oh how he missed him. Becky was there too, her smile more meaningful and content, being cuddled by Ryan and their son together.

"Oh, how I wish they could be here" he whispered to himself, knowing he shouldn't dwell on the past, especially now he was tasked with something so great. Kissing them both in the picture, he placed it back in the box, and then put the box back in his pocket. He sighed deeply just as his belly gave a mighty rumble.

"Quiet you" he said looking down at it. "Dinner for one" he said looking around to the dark quiet forest.

He reached into his left pocket, pulling out simple ploughman's dinner and tucked in. After a few mouthfuls, he then produced for himself a flagon on the mead from the Fairy feast which he gulped heartily. For a while he just sat there eating and drinking, finishing with an apple, before placing the plate, crumbs, core, and flagon back into his pocket.

Right then sleep, he thought, twisting the level on the lamp to off and placing that in the other pocket.

Tomorrows a new day, the first full day for him as Dweller Oak of the New Forest. And with that comforting thought, he drifted into a gentle sleep.

Chapter Fourteen – The socks and the Hounds

Over the next week, Ryan quickly adapted to his solitary role in the forest. He was keen to complete his tasks quickly at the main locations, clearing rubbish and debris, and making sure animal routes were accessible. He also spent many evenings wandering along the man-made paths, hiding the moment he felt a twinge in his feet, before reappearing and continuing the routes. In general, people seemed to care about the forest a lot, but there was always the few that left packets and litter wherever they went.

This evening, he was walking around the Broomy Walk trail just outside of Linwood. It was in a pretty good state, which he was pleased to see. No litter caught in the bushes, no discarded cans or bottles, and not much in the way of dog poo. As he got about halfway round, and the sun was just hovering above the horizon, there came a tiny flash of light which startled Ryan into looking around.

"Up here," called a strained voice as if someone small was yelling.

Looking to the sky, he saw a tiny Fairy, fluttering about head height towards him.

"Oh hello" said Ryan, pleased to have someone to converse with. "How can I help?"

"News from Elder Fairy Branch." Came the voice from the Fairy, the same one who seemed to do all the announcing.

Ryan held out his hand and the Fairy landed softly with barely any weight to him at all. He moved his hand to his ear so that the Fairy wouldn't have to strain his voice as much.

"Thank you, that's very kind of you" he heard, in a much more relaxed tone.

"I'm sorry I haven't been to visit you all again yet" started Ryan. "But I've been ever so busy the last couple of weeks."

"We completely understand" came the voice. "My name is Bark by the way. I am the Fairy with the loudest voice, which is why I am selected as their speaker."

151

"Pleasure to meet you Bark" said Ryan, quietening his voice slightly in case his was deafening to the Fairy.

"Excellent, acquaintances complete, now for the message." He said in a more pompous tone. "Fairy Elder Branch wishes to inform you that the pair of dog kidnappers have been spotted again this afternoon. They were discussing a house in the village of Bank just outside of Lyndhurst that they would be targeting on Saturday night, after one of them has had a good look at the pups tomorrow."

"Aha" said Ryan, pleased that they had been spotted again. "Did they say which house?"

"No, not as such, but they were describing where it was in Bank. Our Fairy lookout could not quite hear the full address from his spot. He said it was past the Oak Inn on your right, and follow the road round. Then on your right would be the house, slightly tucked back from the road. I'm sorry we can't be more help" he added.

"No worries, thank you for this. I'll have to come up with something. We can't have this sort of thing going on in the forest." Ryan said assertively.

"Too right you are," replied the voice in his ear.

Ryan thought for a moment, many wild and ridiculous plans to disrupt and capture the crooks played out in his mind, before a question arose.

"What day is it today?" he asked, hoping the Fairy would know.

"Well, we do not count the days as the humans do, we do it by number. So, for us it is day one hundred and forty-five of the year. Next year is the extra day but this year is only three hundred and sixty-five."

"Ah I see," said Ryan, trying to work it out in his head.

So, the leap year was next year. Thirty days of September, April, June, and November. He had come to Dweller on Thursday April twentieth.

"So, I arrived in the Forest on day one hundred and ten, that means that I have been her thirty-five days. So today must be a Thursday. Blimey, we have two days then." Exclaimed Ryan slightly too loudly.

The New Forest Dweller

Bark winced at the noise. Ryan slowly pulled his hand back in front of his face, and gently said "Let Branch know thank you for this information. If he could keep someone posted there for a couple of days more in case they come back, and I will take care of the pups."

Bark nodded quickly,

"I will relay the message and inform you of any updates. Best of luck stopping those scoundrels!!" he called before taking off, flying around a metre or so away, then with a small flash of light, he was gone.

Right then, the rest of this trail will have to wait. I've got a house to find.

***

Ryan headed to a quiet patch of ground over towards Lyndhurst, and settled down to eat some dinner. He would wait for the it to become much darker and less likely for him to be seen before he would try and locate the puppy house. He was not sure what he would be able to do about stopping the thieves, but finding the house first might lead him to some ideas.

Therefore, it was well past midnight when he appeared on the outskirts of Bank. He kept hidden in his cloak by a tree, surveying the road ahead. The street lights had been turned off already, but thankfully the half-moon hung in the cloudless sky, lighting the way slightly. He crept out from his spot, aware that his feet were tingling from the people that slept in the houses around him. He carefully made his way out onto the tarmac and along the road. The pub was dark and closed for the night, with no sign of any life in the rooms above.

Good, thought Ryan, as he moved silently along the narrow road. He kept his eyes open and ears pricked, with his hood up, and hands covered, as he made his way down the lane which bent gently round to the right. He stopped by a couple of houses and peered into the windows, but these seemed too close to the road to be the one he was after. So, he carried on down, and after a few minutes he saw some more houses on his right just as the road bent to the left. Could these be them?

Carefully he trotted towards the first one, quietly through the long gate, and silently, thanks to his cloak, over the stones and towards a wide black window. He peered in.

"WOOF" came a loud bark, just the other side of the glass.

It scared the life out of him. Ryan jumped backwards onto the stoney driveway, accidentally hitting a car he had avoided on his way in. The alarm started and lights began flashing. The dog started barking louder now, able to see a proper outline. Ryan scarpered for the exit just as a light flickered on upstairs. Panicked, he vaulted the gate, hiding just the other side of the large hedge. He could see a couple of lights come on in the other houses around. He knew he should use the hedge and disappear. He grabbed it, and was just about to clench his free hand, when he heard it. Some little yowls from puppies, the next house along. He chanced a look around the hedge to next door. The light was on upstairs and the owner was looking through the curtains, over at their neighbour who was stood at the lounge window fumbling with their keys. After a couple of seconds, the alarm stopped. The owner of the car opened the front door and a large heavy dog pounded out, sniffing furiously. Ryan thought better of it to hang around any longer, and grabbed the bush once again, disappearing over towards Bolder.

He sat down, breathing heavily in relief at having found the house whilst avoiding detection. Blimey that big dog had made him jump. It must have been watching through the window as he approached. Ryan laughed nervously to himself, pleased to be out of there and safely concealed back amongst the trees. He reached into his pocket pulling out a beer, hoping this would calm him down from the adrenalin rush he was experiencing. With any luck, the owners would just think it was deer or something, but it would be good anyway for them to be more aware at night, considering what Ryan knew was about to happen there.

Sipping his drink from a green glass bottle, and relaxing so that his breathing got back to normal, he laid back against the base of a tree. Right, what to plan for these thieves? Alerting the police? No, they would never show up on a whim if a crime had not even been committed yet. Alert the owners? He would have to leave a note or something as he could not afford to be seen so early in his Dweller days. Well, I will sleep on it, he thought, and maybe scope out the area tomorrow. Hopefully I will be able to catch a glimpse of the one who is coming to view the pups, probably the short one of the two, Freddy.

Ryan remembered the dark blue car he drove, and clenched his fist at the thought of what people like that did. He finished his beer and lay down further, flicking the bottle into his left pocket and sighing deeply to himself. In the morning, he hopefully would have thought of something. And with only a few more dastardly plans for what he would like to do to Freddy and Geoff, he fell into a troubled sleep, dreaming that he was chased by an enormous hound, with ugly hooked nosed men that tried to catch him. His cloak kept him too comfortable to awaken from this, and he spent the rest of the night, running through his mind.

***

A song from a little bird began, rousing the others around it. Their joyous twittering announced that daybreak was upon the forest, and most of the animals were relieved for the light again. The bats, badgers, and other nocturnal creatures, retreated to their homes, as the rest of the forest began its preparations for a day ahead.

The noise of the birds started to awaken a couple of forest campers, middle aged guys who had headed into the forest with a couple of bottles of vodka, some potatoes and sausages, where they had made a fire, and slept rough for the fun of it. They had conversed and drank well into the night, passing out with the fire still flickering away, keeping half their bodies warm, while their backs faced out into the cold dark night. Groggy headed and grumpy, they awoke fully to the growing noise of the forest anthem, knowing it would not get quieter from then on. They cleared up their rubbish, with one of then stamping out the dying embers of the fire, kicking dust and dirt over it to make sure it wouldn't rise again. They then took their belongings, in silence, back through the woods to their homes, where after a quick goodbye, each went into their houses and collapsed on their beds, snoring almost before they had landed.

In a different area of the forest, with a similar melody being sang by the birds, Ryan awoke too. For a moment, he allowed a brief time to stretch and reflect on his exhausting sleep. Reaching up to rub away the hooked nosed men from his memory, he sat up quickly as something wet touched his hand. Looking out slightly blurrily now to what it could be, he saw a baby deer, face almost touching his own, and looking directly into his eyes. He reached out a hand and stroked it.

"Good morning, what a beautiful day it is, thank you for becoming our Dweller," came a childlike voice in his head, the moment he made contact with the fawn.

"It's a pleasure," thought Ryan back, and the fawn blinked in understanding.

"I don't suppose you could help my mum, could you?" It asked in a slightly quivering voice.

"Of course," thought Ryan, getting up and hoping this wasn't going to be a Bambi moment.

"She's sprained her ankle you see" said the fawn, leading Ryan over to its mother a short way away. She was crouched down laying low to the grass, looking slightly weary.

Ryan let go of the fawn and reached out for the mothers' leg to take a look. But just before he touched it, a large deer with massive antlers jumped out in front of her, shielding her from Ryan. Its eyes looked weary but resilient, and Ryan took a step back, not having witnessed an animal that didn't want help since he had come to the forest. They stood still for a moment, Ryan looking at the Stag in the eyes, with it looking right back. The fawn slowly moved to its mothers' side, and the Stag turned to it, snorting as if in warning, adding a string of grunts to the message. Ryan saw his moment when the stag had turned its head, gently placing a finger on the Stag.

"Your mother will be fine, we don't need a new Dweller to help us with this, look what happened to your uncle buck, lost his eye completely now because of it." Came an angry rant in Ryans mind followed by a "Hey!" As the Stag noticed Ryans finger gently on its neck, and it drew back slightly breaking the contact.

Ryan was shocked, they didn't trust him, a Dweller. Well, the Stag didn't. The fawn seemed to, and the mother, though weary, was willing to let him help. Ryan stayed still, watching as the Stag nudged the mother with his nose until she stood up, gingerly on her front right foot, before they slowly walked away into the forest. The fawn gave a longing look back, but followed its parents before Ryan lost sight of them in the trees.

"Well, that wasn't what I expected" said Ryan quietly to himself. "Ah well, let's get on with some creatures that do want it" he said to himself, reaching for the nearest tree.

He did around a dozen emergencies that morning until they started becoming less serious. He wanted to get over to Bank to check out the house sooner, but this had kept him busy until mid-morning time. He had not even had time for a drink or bite to eat as he had rushed to try and get as many done as possible. Finally seeing to a frog with a slight fever, he had applied drops to it which would hopefully return its blood to a natural cool feeling, he headed over to a location just outside of Bank.

Appearing on a hilly area of trees, he started walking along a ridge and down towards the houses, his feet starting to tingle as he went. The cloudy sky blocked out the direct sun, but it did not seem to offer much in the way of rain though. It had been quite dry since he had entered the forest, and this showed by how many plants and saplings he was having to get water for during his emergencies. It was five this morning and there were bound to be more the longer the rain held off.

As he made his way through the trees and occasional grassy patch, he spotted some horses trotting over to him. They came right up, showing their beautiful grey and brown coats, whilst whinnying softly in welcome. Ryan held out his hands and immediately received hellos and congratulations for being the new dweller in his head.

"Thank you" he replied, making sure he touched each of the five horses, to allow all of them to show their appreciations. "Always feel free to seek me out for help or comfort" he added, trying to start moving on.

"We will" came the replies, as the horses turned and started to trot away. The bond was broken, so Ryan carried on along on his way, down a slope until he was only a couple of hundred metres from the house, with a good view of the road too.

"And now I wait" he said quietly, crouching down by a tree and making sure his cloak was tucked around him in case of any people walking by.

He waited in position, until the cloud hidden sun had crossed the midway point of the sky. He was keeping his mind busy, looking at the views of the surrounding forest, and sorting a couple of animal issues when they found their way up to him. A bird with broken wing had appeared shortly after he had settled, followed by a squirrel with a tail full of thorns, and then a barn owl with a pulled neck muscle. He treated them all, whilst continuously keeping an eye on the house and road. But it was not until early afternoon did he see what he was after.

A fancy dark blue car came down the road, past the pub and houses, and around the bend. It parked in a layby a little way past the house and the man that got out, was walking back towards the bend. Ryan could see a new black coat, which was stretched around Freddys short rotund build, as he trotted eagerly along the edge of the road to the house, his greying hair bouncing atop his head.

Right then, I need to get closer thought Ryan, not wanting to miss anything. He was just about to stand up and stretch, when his feet started going crazy. He froze, just as a couple in their late thirties walked past his tree, both dressed in posh walking gear, with knee high designer boots.

"And so, I said to the office, surely you can do without me for one little meeting. But nooooo, I have to attend on Friday, and lead the pitch to save the boss's arse. Well at least I'll be in his good books and probably get another raise. Then we will book that holiday to Bali the week after." Said the man, a mocking tone used for his work talk, before laying on a simpering voice when talking about their holiday.

"They never could manage without you," said the blonde-haired lady, her hair tied back in a ponytail which swished as she walked. "I'll start looking for flights when we get back then" she added, their voices tailing off as they got further away.

Ryan unfroze. That had been close!

Careful not to follow the couple closely, and keeping his eyes peeled for anyone else, he began his descent towards a bush partway between the house and the car. Once there, he turned his back to the bush so he faced up the way he had just come from, keeping his ears pricked for any noise of Freddy coming by.

The wind whistled gently over the hill and through the trees, ruffling the leaves on the bush he was hiding behind. His cloak did not seem to react to the wind much, rather it just hung and moved with him, only occasionally pressing against him if a big gust blew.

Barely a few minutes had passed when there was an opening of a door to his right. He could he some muffled voices saying goodbye, and the sound of a dog and a few puppies yowling before the door snapped shut. Then muffled footsteps getting closer.

"Geoff" came the voice quietly. "Yes they have got them, I have just been in and put a deposit down on one. They are wanting three grand a pup and there is nine of them plus the runt." He said excitedly, his voice getting louder as he approached before starting to die down when he went past.

Ryan could barely hear the garbled talk coming from what must have been Freddys phone, before Freddy answered the voice with.

"Yes, all on for tomorrow night, I have said I will be collecting Sunday. But I'll only be collecting my deposit back if you do your job right" came Freddys voice, which was almost too quiet now for Ryan to hear. Within a couple of seconds, the voice stopped completely, as the car door slammed shut and the engine roared into action. That was it.

Ok, I know when, where and who, thought Ryan, now I just need to think of what to do. After a few minutes of thought, he decided he should get close to the house, to see if there was some way he could leave a note or something. He heard the car pull away, the noise of the engine disappearing after a few moments. Ok, let's go, said his internal monologue. Ryan touched the bush with his palm, focussing on a tree the other side of the house, vanishing and reappearing there moments later. From here he had a much better view, and was able to see into the back garden.

The patio doors leading into the house only reflected the white light coming from the clouds. To the side though, he could see a washing line, full with a mixture of adult and child clothes. Surely, he could slip a note into a sock or something without them noticing? Yes, I'll do that he thought pulling a sheet of paper and pen from his pocket. He scribbled the words down and then reread it to make sure it was legible and had all the details. It read,

Warning,

I have overheard a guy called Freddy and Geoff talking about stealing your beautiful puppies, and wanted to make sure I could put a stop to it. The police will not react to a theft unless it has taken place / in progress. Saturday night is when Geoff is planning to do it, so please be on the lookout and phone the police the moment you see anything. The short guy that popped round this afternoon and left a deposit is Freddy. He said he will be back Sunday to get his deposit back as there will be no puppies to buy. He'll need stopping too so that no one else has to go through this.
I hope you can,
Kind Regards.

Ryan finished reading and folded the paper carefully. He then placed the pen in his pocket, and carefully made his way down to the rear fence of the garden. He didn't want to hop over it here, just in case they were looking out of the patio doors and saw him. Instead, he crept along the back of it, before turning right at the corner and heading down the thick hedge that went along the side of the garden which led to the washing line. This end of the house only had a single misty bathroom window looking out, but he still had to be aware of any neighbours that might be watching. He feet tingled constantly being in such close proximity, and he had to rely on his senses in case someone came close. When he got level with the washing line, he climbed over the six-foot wooden fence which butted up to the end of the hedge he had just walked past. He landed lightly, keeping his eyes and ears alert for detection. Not disturbing the stony section the washing line was situated in, he walked forward, reaching out with the letter, and tucking it into one of the child's pair of socks so it stuck out noticeably for them to see.

Sighing with relief, he was about to turn back when he heard the patio door open, and a female boxer dog sprinted out on the lawn to go to the toilet. It had to be the puppies mum Ryan thought, frozen to the spot and hoping she couldn't see him. All of a sudden though she paused, about to crouch to empty her bladder, but she had looked around and seen him, stood in the shadow of the house. She gave an excited bark and sprinted over to him, and layered slobber over his cloak which was quickly absorbed in.

"Shhhh" said Ryan, quietly panicking as she barked again. "Here, fetch" he said, grabbing a pair of men's socks, rolling them in a ball and launching them down the garden. She turned and sprinted after them just as a woman's voice called,

"Ruby No, leave those clothes alone! Alex, she's got a pair of your socks off the line! I will have to bring it all in again."

Ryan sensed his feet tingling out of control as he heard the woman step out onto the lawn to come and collect the clothes. He reached out quickly grabbing the hedge and instantly reappeared next to the tree behind the garden. That was close, he thought, seeing that the woman had just turned the corner to the house and started removing the clothes. She was too busy placing them in the basket to notice the letter, before then spending a few moments getting hold of Ruby to retrieve the now soaked through pair of her husband's socks. A man appeared at the door, quite tall with brown hair and eating an apple.

"Ah Ruby you silly thing," he said in a loving voice as she bounded up to him looking for a fuss. "At least they weren't Timmys socks" he said laughing, as he turned to go back inside as the woman and Ruby both stepped across the threshold. He closed the door.

Well, they have a warning Ryan thought, still relieved to be out of there. He wondered whether the old man had this many close calls or whether he purposefully went out of his way to avoid human trouble. He probably did have a few thought Ryan, remembering how angry he had gotten when they'd first overheard Freddy and Geoff. Right then, a spot of lunch before some more emergencies and forest work. Then tomorrow night, I will be back to make sure that whatever Geoff is planning, doesn't go as he intends.

***

The rest of the day and the next seemed to fly by. Ryan continued his duties, sorting emergencies and visiting several main locations to do a bit of general clearing work. When sunset began, and the clouds started darkening, Ryan decided it was best to head over to the spot he was at the day before, on the hill, and able to survey the road and house. Once he reached it, he sat down and ate some dinner, watching the view slowly restricting in the darkness, and the lampposts starting to light up. The house with the puppies was quiet and dark, but there were still cars in the drive to suggest the family was at home. Ryan tucked into his chilli con carne, knowing he was in for a long night. Once he finished, he placed the plate and cutlery in his pocket, and withdrew a small glass of orange squash. No beer tonight, he would need a clear head. He watched carefully for the remainder of the evening, as the occasional car drove past, and at one point, a lone dog walker went up the way of the pub. The pub goers were enjoying a busy Saturday night, but once it closed and the people had dispersed, Ryan knew it had to be past midnight.

He waited, warmly concealed in his cloak, eyes searching the darkness as the wind started to pick up around him. The trees swayed, and a couple of leaves and twigs dropped, but silence continued. Ryan felt himself becoming tired, and carefully helped himself to a chocolate bar and cup of tea as he waited, hoping the energy and caffeine would help keep him alert.

A slight flash appeared, the other side of the house, up where he had been the day before writing his warning. It looked momentarily like the light of a phone, before it was hastily covered. It could have been a Fairy he thought, wondering if Bark or any of them would be joining him. He stood up, dropping his cup silently into his cloak pocket, trying to make out any outline in the blackness. THERE. Another slight flash before the light was gone for good. Definitely looked like an electronic light.

He needed to get closer, he thought, hardly daring to breathe even though he was a couple of hundred metres away. He decided on a quick plan, and then disappeared to the other side of the house, to the tree which was behind the light.

Even though he arrived with the smallest pop, he still crouched down, trying to get his senses back under control. A faint whiff of honey played across his nose as he tried to make out a figure.

Then he saw him. Dressed in black, with a large cotton black sack and balaclava covered head. Geoff was stood at the fence at the back of the house, around twenty metres down from Ryans location. The position of the houses blocked out most of the street lights, and as the sky was clouded over, there was no moonlight. He stood and watched as Geoff carefully climbed over the fence, and began to creep over the lawn to the back patio doors of the house.

Ryan thought he saw a flash of light from the window above, and so must have Geoff, as he moved to the side, back against the brick wall, frozen still. He stayed for a couple of minutes making sure that there was no one awake, before he crouched down, and looked to be fumbling around in his pocket.

Looks like he's got a toolkit for picking locks thought Ryan, deciding to climb down the hill carefully and making his way to the back fence to get a closer look. He could see the crouched figure fiddling with the lock, and after a few more minutes, he reached up and pulled down the handle.

It had worked, he had the door open and was pocketing his tools again before silently creeping into the house. Ryan tried to make out what was going on inside, but it was far too dark to see anything.

Then, the light switched on. It was like the scene from a horror movie. Geoff's horror movie. For there was the next-door neighbours big dog bounding towards him with loud thunderous barks. It leapt, forcing Geoff off his feet, and falling back onto the living rooms cream carpet. The dog pounded his chest and tried scratching at his head just as Alex and the next-door neighbour burst out from behind the sofa and descended on him with a golf club and a hockey stick.

"Out of the way Rufus" called the next-door neighbour loudly, as the big dog leapt off Geoff's chest. Geoff tried to rise but was whacked a few times by the pair of men. Fear must have made him oblivious to the pain, as he scrambled to his feet, launching towards the door, leaving the two men in his wake. Rufus wasn't so slow to react though. Just as Geoff had felt the cold air of the night hit his face, the dog was at his feet, tripping him and biting a hold of his arm. He was pinned to the floor by the dog but kept wriggling, trying to get free as Alex and the neighbour jumped on him trying to restrain him. Blue lights and sirens started outside the front, as the police cars had silently responded to an emergency call that had come through five minutes before. A couple of burly officers ran around the side gate, over to the struggling group. The neighbour had to release Geoff to hold back his dog, stopping him from going for the new pair of strangers which left Alex alone trying to contain Geoff, a much bigger bloke than he was. Alex got an elbow to the jaw just as Geoff made it to his feet before being tackled to the ground and cuffed by the officers.

"Right then you big brute, you're nicked" said the officer pulling Geoff to his feet and removing the balaclava. Geoff was red faced and frightened, this was not his first offence.

"Thank you officers for responding so quickly" said Alex through a stiff and swelling bloody lip, before turning to the neighbour and saying "and you too Jeremy. If it hadn't been for you and Rufus, he'd have gotten away."

More lights came on inside the house and other neighbouring houses due to the noise. A light came on for the garden too which had previously only been illuminated by the living room light that poured out the patio doors.

A small female office ran around the side of the house and Jeremy had to restrain Rufus again, almost pulled over by his immense strength.

"Cars ready boss, let's get him in. Would you mind a quick statement please sir?" She asked turning to Alex and Jeremy, not sure who's house it was.

"I'll leave this to you" said Jeremy holding Rufus by the collar, "I will get him back inside mine, and then pop over for a tot of whiskey if you fancy."

"Yes, I need it" said Alex gratefully, patting him on the back.

Just then Rufus turned his head in the direction of the rear garden fence. Ryan who had been watching this all play out with glee, suddenly saw he could be in the spotlight next, and bent down quickly to hide just as Rufus gave off a bark.

"What is it boy, someone else?" came Jeremy's voice.

Ryan, crouching and thinking fast, decided to try and make it to the side hedge so he could escape. If he headed up the hill, he would surely be spotted. Thankfully after a few silent hurried steps, he made it, disappearing to a safe part of the forest moments before Jeremy peered over the fence.

What an excellent result, thought Ryan, before taking a bit of time to calm down a bit. He helped himself to a celebratory jug of mead. Now for a bit of kip, before returning tomorrow to watch Freddy get what's coming to him.

***

The following day, after sorting his emergencies in the morning, Ryan headed over to his initial spot in Bank, on the hill watching the scene below. There were a few scuff marks in Alexs lawn from the night before, but nothing much else suggested what had gone on. Ryan was about to settle down for a long wait again, when Freddys car came around the bend, parking in the same layby as before. Excellent though Ryan smiling to himself, he does not know about Geoff yet. He root travelled from the tree to behind the bush by the road, and listened as Freddy closed up his car and almost jogged along to the house.

"Geoff, give me a call. I am just about to pick up my deposit and ideally wanted you to confirm it had all gone well. Call me back straight away," came Freddys flustered voice.

Ryan had to stifle a laugh as the man went past before he heard a tap on the door.

"Good morning, Anne, I'm here to pick up, OH NO," cried Freddy. There was a patter of footsteps, sounding like he was trying to make it back to his car.

The New Forest Dweller

"Not so quick there fella," came the voice of the burly policeman who must have been waiting inside the house. "We've got some questions for you."

"NO, I HAVEN'T DONE ANYTHING" screamed Freddy as he attempted to free himself from the policeman's grip.

"Well, people normally don't run and scream when they are innocent. Anyway, your pal Geoff has already confessed it is you helping him out. You'll both be going away for a long time" he said, dragging a screaming Freddy back towards the house.

"Brilliant" said Ryan clutching the bush.

"It is brilliant, you're such an excellent Dweller" came a voice in his head from the bush he was touching.

"Thanks" Ryan thought back, slightly embarrassed but trying not to laugh.

The siren of a police car started up the hill as it came to collect Freddy and the officer.

Well, I am glad that is sorted, let's go and let the Fairies know, he thought, pleased he might get the chance to see them again. They must hear the good news.

Chapter Fifteen – Fairy Friendship

He appeared at the edge of the wood on the outskirts of Fritham, and quickly proceeded to walk off the beaten path and towards the Fairy tree. He had not gotten very far, when he saw a flash of light, and a Fairy sitting on a branch above. Ryan could tell from the light that it was Bark, who must have been stationed to keep watch in case Freddy and Geoff returned.

Ryan strode up to the base of the tree as Bark fluttered down to him.

"Both arrested and all puppies saved" said Ryan triumphantly. Bark did a little flip in the air with pleasure.

"Oh fantastic, come on, let's tell the others" Bark shouted, leading Ryan through the trees to the right one. It took a few minutes, and once they were there, Ryan removed a ladder from his pocket this time, and climbed up to Bark who was hovering at the tiny open door. He ascended, getting head height with the Fairy, who flew towards him and tapped him on the nose. His body shrank upwards again, and just as he felt himself starting to fall, Bark grabbed his hand and forced him through the opening. Before he could focus on the busy interior of the tree, there was an excited squeal, and all of a sudden he was embraced tightly with a face full of blonde hair. Giving a slightly nervous laugh to this welcome, he hugged her back. It felt good to feel wanted like this he thought, as the broke apart looking at each other happily.

"How've you been? What've you been up to? It feels like you haven't visited in ages?" she said, bombarding him with questions before giving him a great big kiss on the cheek.

"Yes, I've been alright" Ryan said smiling at how concerned and genuinely caring she was. "I've come to give elder Branch an update on the Puppy poachers" he said, looking around to see if he could see him.

"First, let me get you into your toga," she said smiling widely showing her beautiful white teeth, before pulling him off to a side room where, after a quick kiss on the lips, she helped him remove his robe. She couldn't resist one quick cuddle with him as he stood in nothing other than his undergarment, before she lifted a new leaf toga over his head.

"There" she said biting her lip, "all ready."

She then turned and pulled him by his hand back out into the bustling core. It looked like a very busy office, but with Fairies flying here there and everywhere, conversing, and holding samples of pollen and seeds. They climbed up around the spiral so that they neared the area they had sat for the feast. Ryan saw the table was pushed back away from the edge, and an older group of Fairies were sat around discussing important issues. There were papers, maps, charts, and samples all spread across the surface of the table, with Branch sat at the far end, deep in thought. Suddenly, he noticed Ryan and Cinthia approaching, and his face lit up momentarily with a smile, before asking anxiously.

"How did it go with the dog thieves?"

"We got them both" said Ryan happily, and the table cheered and began clapping. Cinthia placed her head against his shoulder with a smile on her face, thankful that the puppies would be ok.

"Brilliant work from our new Dweller" said Branch, once the cheering had died down. "Your predecessor said you would be one to watch, and he was not wrong. Ah Bark there you are, all good news, no need to keep someone stationed at the position anymore" he said, clapping Bark on the shoulder as he appeared at Ryans side having followed them up.

"Yes, brilliant" said Bark, happy not to have to wait in the tree any longer for people who may or may not return.

"Right then, I'll leave you with Cinthia if that's ok Forest Dweller Oak?" Branch said smiling. "We've got some work to finish off, and I know she's taken a liking to you."

Cinthia blushed awfully pink, almost the same colour as her light.

"Oh grandpa, stop it," she said in a mock telling off, before leading Ryan away, back down the stairs.

"Always feel free to visit, I'll send word when the summer festival is going to happen," called Branch behind him.

The cheering, which had started and ceased from above, continued down through the core of the tree as word spread about the success of 'operation puppy' as they had called it. Ryan received many claps on the backs and kisses on the cheek, as they walked down to a canteen area to get some food. Cinthia was dying to know all the details, so Ryan relayed all he could remember. She squealed and giggled, gasped, and applauded throughout the story, her beauty enhanced with each expression, and left Ryan with flutters in his chest as she hung onto his every word.

"You are so brave and clever to make sure those pups stayed safe" she said, once he had finished his story and started tucking into a leafy nut salad that had been made for them.

"Well, I'm not sure I did much apart from send them a warning" said Ryan, trying to remain modest and looking down at his plate.

"But you made sure they didn't get away" she said, making him look up, her eyes locked into his, her chest heaving excitedly. She reached out her hand on the table and took his in it. She was intoxicating in her love for him, and he almost felt powerless to resist.

Just at that moment, another strong male Fairy, with long auburn hair walked in.

"Congratulations Dweller" he said meaningfully, clapping his hand on Ryans shoulder. "Top work indeed. The forest needed someone young to invigorate it, and you seem just the guy. I am Augustus by the way, but most of the guys call me Aug." he said, grabbing a plate of chestnut stew and sitting down at the table with them, oblivious to the hand holding and the slightly annoyed look Cinthia shot him. Aug continued, "Yes the whole tree is talking about it, but then again, not much exciting stuff happens around here."

"I'm just glad to help," said Ryan pleasantly to the good-natured Fairy who smiled back at him. Ryan and Cinthia released hands and ate the rest of their salads quickly, as Aug filled the silence with chitchat and general news that was going around. When they had finished, Cinthia stood up and took her and Ryans bowls over to a table filled with other used cups, dishes, and cutlery. She placed theirs on top and turned back, grabbing Ryans hand to take him somewhere else.

"It was nice to meet you" said Ryan, looking back at Aug who smiled and waved happily. They were all so friendly, and no one seemed to have a bad thing to say.

"Right then, I know you'll want to be on your way, but I wanted a quick chat somewhere private" she said, leading him down the spiral, before getting to a small room that seemed to be her own. Closing the door behind him, she darted forwards, pulling him into a close embrace, kissing him deeply, her arms caressing his waist. He felt their tongues battling in his mouth, and her beautiful aroma filled his senses. She truly was something else. They stayed locked together for a few minutes, until Ryan pulled back for air. Cinthia's slightly ruffled hair stood out on one side, as she seductively licked her thick luscious lips, tasting him on her still, making her smile. She then pulled him in for a cuddle and they sat down on her bed, still holding one another.

"My parents are wanting me to settle down" she said, head on his shoulder looking at the wall behind him, her voice slightly shaky. "I'm happy where I am at the moment though" she continued, her voice slightly stronger. "I love thinking about seeing you next, and know that even if we couldn't carry on my family line, we could still have fun and be together." She finished, sounding hopeful.

Ryan paused for a moment. For him it was nice and welcoming having someone who was all over him with love and caring, but she was prepared to give up any future children to be with him. He leant back slightly so they could look at each other. A single tear was already rolling down her pink cheek, dripping down to her bosom.

"Listen Cinth, you know I have feelings for you, strong ones. But I have had to leave someone I love to come here to take care of the forest. If I could have it my way, I would want her and my son to be here with me. But for me the job has to take priority. I also don't want to stop your chances of a family for a relationship with me, where we can only see each other once in a while. It would not be fair to either of us. I am sorry, but I only want the best for you" he said, finishing kindly and hoping she wouldn't be too emotional.

She smiled at him, a wavering empathetic smile.

"I understand" she said slowly. "I just sort of hoped something between us could have worked out. But I know what you are saying. I am still quite young, and I know my parents do want to be grandparents one day. Oh Ryan, what we could have been eh."

"I know. You are so incredibly beautiful, you'll have guys lining up for you though" he said, and she chuckled at this, another tear leaking out her brilliant blue eyes, her face trying to be happy.

They spent the next few minutes chatting, all the while holding hands.

"Right then" said Ryan, moving to stand up. "The forest calls, as always" he said smiling.

"Thank you, Ryan. If this is to be the end of my chance of an us, I wish you the best. And please do always feel free to visit and come to our festivals. They are fun and I could introduce you to a couple of friends of mine if I am taken by then," she added with a cheeky smile, half hoping he'd regret his decision and scoop her up in his arms. Instead though, he replied with,

"I look forward to seeing you all again, and I am happy to celebrate, but I don't wish to have even a casual relationship. I was engaged before I came here, and I think if I cannot be with Becky, I don't want to be with anyone unfortunately" he said, hearing the words himself, and feeling sorrow at the thought that this wouldn't be happening.

"And I completely respect you for that." Cinthia said, standing up and arranging her clothes to make sure they covered her as they should. "Well, I'm sad its goodbye for now, but I'll always look forward to your visits" she said, walking over to the door and opening it. They exchanged a brief hug, purposefully avoiding kissing again, and Ryan strode out into the bustling corridor, with Cinthia leaning on the door, watching him go. Her heart was feeling like it would pound out her chest, but she was relieved to have talked, knowing she would have to move on.

When Ryan had got a little way away, he looked back, just as her door closed shut. Sighing, he turned to the exit, removing his leaf toga, and climbing into his robe, immediately feeling the effects of comfort and cleanliness spreading over him. At the door, he was greeted by a different Fairy, who helped him out onto the ladder, and made him return to his natural size. Thanking him, as the Fairy flew back in and closed the door, Ryan climbed down the ladder, thankful that it hadn't been noticed during his time in there. Getting to the base, he pocketed it, gave a final sigh, and disappeared off to an emergency.

Chapter Sixteen – Heatwave

The next week and a half was hard. Even though he worked on throughout the day, often skipping meals, Ryan couldn't shake the feeling like he had lost someone close to him again. It was more the fact that he was coming to terms with not seeing Becky or Archie again, rather than losing Cinthia. But having a chat with the latter had reinforced the point that this wasn't just a short-term commitment, and that he had in fact signed up to a lifetime of servitude to this amazing place.

The work itself tried to keep his mind busy. There had been such little rain since he had joined the forest that when any downpours did occur, though only for short bursts, he knew it meant that emergencies would at least be less plant related.

In fact, Ryan felt he was cheating a bit on this front. He had picked up a bucket from the road that must have fallen off a vehicle, and was using it to carry water to thirsty plants, as the cloak would not produce anything that had the capabilities to deal with the magic of the forest water. Plastic buckets which were man made and had no soul, were perfect for the task however. Thankfully it was a black bucket, and blended in alright with the environment. Ryan left it in a secure location, and every time he needed to transport water for plants and shrubs, he would quickly shoot off to collect it. It did mean only one trip per plant rather than several trips with cupped hands, and thanks to the lack of rain, the need was becoming more frequent. In fact, when any rain did seem to fall, it wasn't enough to turn the grass from the yellow straw colour it was now, back to the green it had been in the spring.

Ryan noticed the ponds and lakes had shrunk dramatically, and the rivers were flowing slower and shallower. All this dry weather led to only one thing, the risk of fire.

The New Forest District Council had been putting notices up at every car park, warning against open flames and barbeques. Ryan had seen them, all new and shiny, stuck to car park entrances and fence posts. Thankfully, he had been on hand the day before, when a few teenagers were smoking in the wood by Beaulieu station railway, dropping their cigarette butts in the grass before leaving for the train. He had been on emergency duty at the time, and was able to put out the small patch that was smoking, before it spread to anything else. It did worry him how something as small and simple as that though could start a huge fire.

He vowed to increase his emergency patrols, so that he would do about ten smaller sessions a day, instead of his usual three or four longer ones. This would allow him to catch any flame quicker to stop the spread. He had decided he would do this until the next good heavy rainfall, but the cloudless days and increasing temperature did nothing to say it was going to change.

The only thing that pleased Ryan today, was that he would be dropping by at Wilverly tonight to meet Lester again. He did wonder if it would be a little awkward being there on his own, and wondered if Lester would feel it too, considering his predecessor had been to the previous eight hundred meetings or so. However, it was someone to chat to, get news from, and have a laugh with he thought, as he bent down to snip a hole through a new mesh fence that went straight across an animal route.

That was not to say he was lonely. The forest and animals communicated with him regularly, and it was nice to hear their thoughts and praises. But it was good to mix it up a bit. He had found that he needed to have a drink of water every few days or so, remembering how the fourth day after his second drink he'd just stared at a horse, thinking words, and wondering why he wasn't getting a response. The horse must have assumed he was a bit weird as he had stood there, hand on the its head, staring into its eyes without actually doing anything for the sore hoof. Ryan was able to laugh about it afterwards though.

Something he had noticed when full of the waters magic though, was how much easier it was to help a dying animal. It had a happened a few times now, and he was getting much better at relieving their pain so that they could rest in peace. It was not a pleasant thing to be good at, but it did help reduce the suffering of a creature that just wanted the end to come quicker.

He also liked to hear of any news that the forest would pass on. It was usually surrounded by thanks and praise, but often extra information was weaved in between. He had been made aware of a large gathering over in the woods towards Sway one night, and was able to clear up once the forty or so partygoers had left, so that the rubbish which was strewn about didn't blow all through the forest. He did not like the fact that people would do this, but did appreciate the forest wanting help and handily provided the information to do this. He would have found it on his next main location visit, although by that time, it would have blown through the forest.

He continued working through the day, flitting between emergencies, and tidying work. He knew he had not popped in to see the 'Sisters of the Wreath' or the Pixies for a while, and vowed to catch up with them over the next week. They would know that he was busy though, starting out on the forest tasks after your mentor has just passed was usually the busiest time, and the one a Dweller needed to do alone to find his own routine.

When sunset came, which he watched from a ferny hill between Burley and Bransgore, he decided to sit down and eat. He hungrily tucked into a chicken burger and chips, following it up with an ice-cream, all the while watching the yellow, turn to orange, and then red, as the last few light particles passed through the atmosphere. He laid back once he had finished, looking up at the darkening sky, and able to make out the twinkling dots of stars that spread across the deep blue canvass.

Right then, Lester would probably have appeared by now, he thought smiling and sitting up. Time to say hello again.

Lester was indeed there when Ryan wandered across Wilverly plain again. His slight luminescence highlighted his outline and features, and Ryan saw he was looking pleased when he approached.

"Ah, good to see you are a Dweller who will keep visiting" he said, moving forward to give Ryan a mock hug. Ryan copied the action. "I've had a couple of Dwellers in my time that only visited a few times a year, and one I only saw three times ever." He said in a grateful tone. "It can get lonely appearing on these plains you know."

"I imagine it would with no company" said Ryan, standing back slightly to end the fake hug.

They settled down on the grass between some thorny bushes again, sprawling out in the darkness, neither of them feeling the cold of night. Lester gave Ryan an update for the forest, much the same as he had done for his predecessor, and Ryan listened carefully, amazed at what Lester knew and reported on. After several minutes of updates, Ryan broke out the cards and chips, and they had a good long night of poker together, chatting about life, Lesters history, and what he could tell Ryan about the previous Dwellers.

All in all, it was a nice evening. Ryan did have a slight suspicion that Lester was being nicer than usual to encourage him to keep returning, but it might be that they just didn't know each other that well yet. After quite a few hours, Ryan finally said that he should get some sleep. Lester, not wanting to give off a wrong impression to alienate the new Dweller, whom he liked a lot, agreed it was late.

"So, I'll see you next month?" he asked jokingly, but with a hopeful undertone.

"Of course," replied Ryan casually, smiling as he stood up and leant in for a hug goodbye.

"Well, from what I've seen, you're doing a mighty fine job with the forest. Dweller John would be proud of you" Lester said smiling, as he had not used the old man's name in decades.

Ryan returned the smile as they broke apart once more.

"So, I take it he is no longer Forest Dweller Oak?" Asked Ryan, looking into Lesters dark eyes.

"No, he will now be Forest Dweller John, reverting back to his old name. For you are the new Forest Dweller of the New Forest." Said Lester, chuckling slightly before adding, "The New Forest Dweller Oak is your official title though. The name passed down through the centuries. Forest Dweller John is called this now, as could you imagine the confusion on the ghost council if they had a dozen or so all called Oak, it would be mayhem" he said, chuckling again.

Ryan laughed too.

"Ah I see, yes that does make sense" Ryan said.

The New Forest Dweller

"Right then, you best be getting off. I will see you at the next full moon. Take care now" said Lester, watching Ryan as he turned away and walked back across the plain to the trees at the car park.

John had told him to appear here and walk the distance, just so that Lester could see you coming. He had let slip that the first time he had gone to see Lester alone, he'd appeared via root transport at the lone tree, which was little more than a sapling at the time, only to scare the ghostly highwayman, who had been casually checking his frilly white underwear. Ryan had laughed when he told him the story, and had to promise not to repeat it to Lester even once he had passed. 'He was embarrassed with me even a year or so after,' he had added.

Ryan got back to the line of trees by the stoney car park. He could only just see the white signs of warning against flames and barbeques in the darkness. He was glad the council tried to keep on top of it, he did love the forest, his home.

***

The warm weather carried on through the month with only the odd shower which was soaked up quickly by the plants, leaving nothing for the rivers, lakes, and ponds. Ryan had dealt with several animals that had been very dehydrated, bringing his bucket of water, sometimes having to cup his hands for the smaller animals. The plants dehydration was taking more of a back seat in the emergencies list, as there were simply too many to try and help. Many of them would have to wait on the rainfall to replenish their liquid levels.

As the sun set on the longest day of the year, Ryan finally sat down for the first time, having been on emergencies again for the whole day. He had only sorted a couple of injuries, spending the majority of time providing water to plants and animals all over the forest. Surely the weather had to change soon. It hadn't even gotten to the peak summer time, July and August, knowing this as he was counting the days as the Fairies did now.

Having seen the warm weather, and what it was doing to the forest, Ryan had visited the Pixies the previous day to see if they could help with the water situation.

"We have had all of our scouts out for a couple of weeks," said tiny king Gadbre. "Theres about a thousand give or take who are spreading water all over the place, but as you know, the forest is drying up. Lakes are now ponds, and rivers are streams."

"Is there anyone who could help with this?" asked Ryan, knowing the forest must have seen hot summers before and made it through.

"The witches. Whoops sorry, the 'Sisters or the Wreath' might be able to assist in some way, but if I spare anymore of our clan, we will start dropping out of the sky," he said looking sombre.

"I'll go and have a chat with them" replied Ryan, hopeful as Gadbre nodded vigorously so his crown slipped down slightly. "I'll see what they can do" he added, bowing before turning away.

"Keep us updated," called out Gadbre from behind him.

Back in the present, Ryan knew he would have to pop in and see the 'Sisters' in the morning. He had not expected to be tied up all day with emergencies. They would be able to help he thought comfortingly, as he settled down in a stick shelter for the night. Hopefully they can help.

***

He arrived at the 'Sisters' cottage just after he had finished his fifth emergency the next morning. When he had seen the sixth had been a plant which was browning from days of sun and no liquid, he knew he'd sorted the main injuries and should seek out the 'Sisters' to find out what they could do.

Marching around to their front door and knocking loudly, he waited.

"Pleased to see you back," came a voice as the door creaked open, revealing Flo with her bright orange hair.

Ryan walked in as she held the door open, through the curtains, and into the very warm living room.

"Blimey" said Ryan, glad his cloak was dealing with his sweat, "What's going on in here then?" he said looking at the large cauldron that was bubbling away in the fireplace. Flo followed him in, and stood smiling at him like a proud mum. Another voice began.

"Well you see we're due to be going away on our holiday soon" said Gwen, appearing with her purple hair from around the corner. "And we didn't want you to worry that the forest was getting too dry, like your predecessor did so often. So, we are mixing up a few potions of what we like to call, Cloud Magnet."

"Yes" said Flo taking over, "what it does is, when you drop a vial of it around the forest, it will slowly draw in all the clouds in a twenty-mile radius so that they condense together overhead and provide rainfall."

"You should note though," said the white-haired Dotty, appearing from the stairs "that you should only use one at a time, otherwise you are stealing clouds from another part of the forest."

"And," began Gwen again, "we'll probably only be able to make three solutions of the potion, which is to be used wisely and only when you can at least see some clouds around."

"Yes" said Flo, "It does not work without them. The potion will draw them in for around an hour, before allowing a steady rainfall, if there is one, until they have all wrung themselves dry."

"Understand?" asked Dotty, as Gwen began to stir the mixture which was quickly shrinking below the lip of the cauldron, smoking as it changed colour and size, finally just leaving a tiny pool of silvery blue liquid that Gwen carefully filled into three individual diamond shaped vials before stoppering them with tiny corks.

"Perfect" said Ryan, smiling as he took the vials and carefully placed them in his right pocket.

"We are going away next week for around a month. Oh, we cannot wait. We will be on a beach in Brazil, drinking cocktails and meeting the locals" said Flo, blushing slightly but looking excited.

"Yes, no magic when we're there, but my word it'll be fun like always" said dotty, whipping an inflatable rubber ring out of thin air before making it disappear in her hands.

"We'll see you when we're back" said Gwen, wiping out the last blemishes of the potion from the bottom of the cauldron before adding, "get the cleaner elixir Flo or this will rot the pot."

"Well thank you ladies" said Ryan, as Flo pulled down a small red glass bottle from a crowded shelf and poured a couple of drops out for Gwen. "The forest will miss you, but have a nice time and see you when you are back. If you see any rain on your travels, let it know the forest could do with it" he said, smiling and winking at them as the cackled.

He left, Dotty holding the door for him before it sprang shut again.

Looking up to the sky, he just saw a vastness of light blue, with a bright patch where the sun was burning. Sighing, he knew it would be another day of emergencies until he would be able to release one of the vials. At least he had a backup now which he was thankful for, patting the pocket the potions had disappeared into.

Chapter Seventeen – The Forest Folk Return

Ryan was clearing a small burnt patch of gorse bushes that had caught fire the day before. There was only around twenty of them that it had spread to, but it had badly burnt a group of fleeing rabbits who'd had to wait a while before he could help them out.

The weather had not changed much over the two weeks since he'd picked up the vials from the 'Sisters of the Wreath', but himself, the Pixies and now the Fairies too had been battling on with the hot weather.

In those two weeks, it had only rained once without aid. A downpour on the evening after he had picked up the vials. It had lasted a good few hours, but the forest was so thirsty it barely managed to introduce a hint of green back before the sun bleached the plants and grass to yellow. Just a few days ago though, Ryan had used the first vial of Cloud Magnet. It had worked as well as he had hoped, collecting, and amalgamating and faint whisps of cloud overhead so that they slowly turned a deep grey, before emptying themselves over a good portion of the forest. Like the natural rain though, it still was not enough. It had only lasted an hour before the clouds were spent, and the last whisps had dissolved into the atmosphere. He was only willing to use them sparingly, only if the forest became too parched again.

Ryan thought about all the immediate effects of the rain, pretty much all the dehydration emergencies ceased, with injuries, illness, and disease becoming the main concerns again. It had also allowed Ryan to get back to some main location work, and he was shocked at how quickly he had fallen behind thanks to all his time being taken up just keeping the forest alive.

The Pixies and Fairies too were granted a couple of days rest as they had been tirelessly distributing what small amount of water there had been, to places that were in greatest need. He had visited both of their magical establishments as soon as he had distributed the vial, to let them know what he had done and so that they could hopefully get out of the rain.

He had also seen Lester again a couple of nights ago, and even he could not remember a time with this lack of rain, as they discussed the forest water shortage during their card game.

The only group Ryan had not seen for a little while, other than the 'Sisters of the Wreath' who were now on holiday, was the Forest Folk, who were usually found wandering the plains. They were masters of becoming undetected, thanks in the most part to the piece of magical property that the 'Sisters of the Wreath' had provided to keep any normal humans away from their camp. He couldn't remember seeing them since John had passed, and did always keep an eye out for them if he was on open land.

In fact, it was they that ended up finding him. He had been enjoying a comforting sleep, kept cool by his cloak in the morning sun, his hood up, and back against a tree, when some of the children from the group had run over and leapt on him, waking him quickly as he stared around trying to see what was wrong.

"Oh, you cheeky little things" he said, laughing as they skittered away through the trees, and out of his reach as they knew they'd be tickled.

"Morning Dweller," said some of the older men who were leading their horse drawn carts over the uneven ground.

"Ah good morning" replied Ryan, pleased to see the Folk once more. "It's nice to see you lot about again, it's been a while."

"Ah yes" said Herbie, a straw haired toothy guy who was slight of figure, but with a great strength due to hard living and lots of manual work. "Been away we have. Visiting a tribe from down Devon way, the Dartmoor Folk." He said smiling goofily.

"Yes, needed a partner for young Jack you see" said Ted, an older balding man who was bent over double but still fit and strong. "So now we have a new member of the group, she's called Rose" he said, pointing over to a few carts which were being pulled along behind them.

Ryan saw a young couple walking hand in hand beside a horse, both looking happy, newly in love.

"Ah glad to see they both like each other," said Ryan smiling at the group as they halted the carts.

"Right then, you don't mind us setting up rest here do you?" Herbie asked, walking over and shaking Ryans hand. Ryan got a strong herbal smell as he approached, and it seemed to linger with the whole group as the started unpacking their stuff, setting up camp.

"Not at all" said Ryan smiling, "At least I know where you are, and I'll pop back later if that's alright with you?" he asked.

"A Dweller is always welcome to our table" Ted said, and the growing group all nodded enthusiastically.

"Excellent" said Ryan stretching, "Well I better get on with some work. I will pop by this evening and perhaps stay with you all tonight."

"We look forward to it. I will get Mable to start a stew" said Ted, walking to his cart and popping his head in the door.

Ryan saw a few folk wave him off as he disappeared for some morning emergencies, and was immediately thrown into a sad situation.

Laying in the long yellow grass, he found himself peering over to where people had abandoned their cars, and were gathered around the shape of a pony lying in the road where it had been hit. Too many were lost like this.

He would never be able to get to the animal, as he saw one of the people on their phone asking for the verderer to come and either help the animal, or end it. The New Forest Verderers were people who officially look after the forest for the council, but also deal with animal fatalities, road closures due to trees coming down, and trying to preserve the natural landscape. They were the ones who were the most likely to ever spot a Dweller, and often they would tell stories of cloaked figures and the old man of the forest, usually when something unexplained or unusual happened. The person hung up the phone and turned back to the increasing number of people, as more of them got out of their cars that were held up by the traffic.

I'm going to have to go to the next one thought Ryan, knowing there was no way he would be able to get to the animal when there were dozens of pairs of eyes around it. His feet were tingling enough as it was. With a small sigh, and quick prayer that the verderers would attend quickly, he grabbed a handful of dry grass and zoomed off to the next one.

A half dozen or so more he completed, until the dehydration victims started appearing again. The Pixies and Fairies would be out in force to help, he was sure. He was desperate to check on the foal, so made a purposeful transport back to the long grass which was still trampled down from where he had lain before. He looked out to the road, but all he could see was the usual few cars making their way across the landscape. Ah he thought, hands pressed into the crushed hay like grass, they must have taken the body away.

"So thirsty" came a faint voice in his head, before he realised that it was the forest speaking, the grass announcing its feelings.

"When will the rain come?"

"Foal killed not far from here."

"Plants and insects dying in the forest"

Oh, so the foal did die thought Ryan glumly, raising his hands to make the voices in his head stop. Poor thing. Well, I better get back to it.

He shot away to near Frogham, and started to check on the animal paths and general state of the area. He walked around the location, removing litter and the occasional dog poo, checking the paths and wildlife to make sure it wasn't being damaged. Often people would hang tire swings from a tree branches, which even though it was a type of littering, he allowed, as it brought happiness to the children and often made them want to return.

He spent the rest of the morning checking over the area, before settling down for a spot of lunch after midday. Positioning himself so that he was near some houses without being seen, but so that he could see the everyday workings of normal people. An old man who had walked with his cane up to the village shop for a paper and loaf of bread, an old lady who had taken her small dog out on a very short walk up to the red phone box and back, which seemed about all she could manage, and the postman, who drove along and dropped some envelopes through a couple of letterboxes.

Taking another bite of his cream cheese and tomato sandwich, he saw he was being watched after all. A blackbird was perched on the ground, a few metres away, patiently waiting. It was staring at him as he ate, before flying up when it was seen, and resting gently on his knee. Ryan placed his sandwich on the porcelain plate it had appeared on, and lowered it down onto the ground. Then reaching out with his hand, and stroked the birds head feathers.

"I'm struggling for food," said the voice immediately in Ryans head. "The insects that usually hang around the stagnant water have disappeared, and the worms aren't popping up much due to the lack of rain."

"Ok" thought Ryan unhelpfully. Then thinking quick he added, "let me try and see what I can do about that."

He reached down into his right pocket and withdrew a pamphlet on the feeding habits of the forest animals.

"Ah black birds, yes here we are. The blackbirds' normal diet is insects and beetles, worms, spiders, and snails. And in the winter, fruit, berries, and seeds. I see," thought Ryan looking at the bird and realising both his hands had been on the pamphlet. He reached out and relayed this message again to the bird.

"I know, but there seems to be a lack of anything at the minute. People are not even watering their gardens" came the voice back.

There must be a hosepipe ban in place then. That wasn't good considering it was only July and August was usually hot too.

"Right then, what about bird trays and berry bushes?" thought Ryan.

"Not many people are going outside and filling up the bird feeders anymore. I've managed to have a drink from a bird bath a couple of times, but it tasted disgusting" it said with repulsion in its voice. "I'm only asking as I have three hungry chicks back at the nest."

"Right then, wait here while I find you something" thought Ryan, standing up as the bird hopped off his knee.

Ryan remembered that when his grandparents used to live in Burley, they had a beautiful cottage, an apple tree in the garden, and a horse paddock round the back which was lined with blackberry bushes. I will try there, he thought to himself this time, reaching out and connecting with a tree.

When his grandparents had to move into care homes, they had sold their house to the wealthy next-door neighbour who had kept a hold of it, renting it out to those who wanted to live in the forest with their horses close by. The outside had not changed much thought Ryan, as he appeared in the corner of one of the paddocks by the blackberry bushes. He bet the inside had been updated considerably, remembering back to his childhood. Looking back to the bush, he could see that the berries had not all ripened yet, but there were several that were almost there, so he picked those ones carefully. Once he had a dozen or so, he looked over to the garden where he knew the apple tree was. He would have to be quick to make sure he was not seen.

Right then, three, two, one. Grabbing the prickly blackberry bush and being transported thirty metres to the trunk of the apple tree, he looked up. There was movement in the windows of the house. He grabbed a single apple that hung on a low branch which was weighted down with so much fruit, before he disappeared back to the blackbird.

"Here you are my little friend" said Ryan out loud, carefully placing the apple and berries on the ground. The black bird grabbed a berry and flew off immediately in the direction of its nest. Ryan, glad he could have helped, sat back down, and tucked into his sandwich again. By the time he had finished, the bird had completed a couple more trips to and from its chicks. It hopped over to him, seeing he was about to leave, and tilted its head to one side. Ryan reached out a finger and stroked it gently.

"Thank you kind Dweller, this should see my family through a few days at least. Always feel free to return and say hello." Said the voice in his head, before the bond broke and the bird flew off, with another blackberry clasped in its beak.

Ryan stood satisfied for a few moments. This is what it was all about. Helping nature to survive and progress.

He was thankful to be able to do this every day. There were things he missed, notably Becky and Archie, but the forest seemed to be able to display its love, beauty, and thanks to him in many ways, which helped validate his decision to be there.

The rest of the day passed quite quickly, with not many serious emergencies to sort out. After dealing with a bloated cow, where he had needed to consult the manual regarding releasing a build-up of gas, he returned to main location work for the majority of the afternoon. As the sun started lowering, he carried out one last lot of emergencies before heading over to the Forest Folks camp.

The moment he arrived, he could smell a delicious stew, which was bubbling away in a large pot sat just above a carefully arranged and guarded fire. The Folk that saw him arrive called out welcome, as he strolled into the opening they had left in the middle of the carts which formed a ring around them. Some of the children were playing games with sticks, and the older women were in ancient looking wooden rocking chairs, some with babies asleep on their chests as they knitted and weaved wool and other materials into clothes and garments. It was nice to be part of a group like this, one that all cared for one another, with only the need to better the lives of those around you. Some of the men were sat on the ground, smoking long pipes, and drinking brownish liquid from a selection of very dented metal cups.

"Here, have one" said Ted, holding out a drink for Ryan to take. He thanked him and sat down taking a swig. It was like a rudimentary alcoholic brewed tea, which was sharp on the tastebuds at first, but the more he sipped, the better it became. He could feel his cloak working its magic, filtering and cleaning his insides of the alcohol so that he remained level headed even when the others started getting louder and laughing harder.

As the evening progressed, he was made to feel so welcome by them all. He was supplied with a big bowl of stew and a massive piece of freshly cooked bread. The guys all constantly topped up his drink and offered his puffs of their pipes. He was also treated to stories of the past Dwellers by Ted, as the children sat around him oohing and aahing. After a few stories, and once the children had all been put to bed, some of the guys and girls started playing songs on wooden instruments which were beautifully carved and sounded exquisite, while other folk got up and danced around the fire, singing and laughing all the time. They liked being in the company of their Dweller, and he was made to join in with the fun, late into the night.

Chapter Eighteen – Drought

Over the next two weeks the heat persisted. There were several showers of rain during this time, but nothing like what was needed to quench the thirst of the ground. In many places, large cracks had appeared in the earth, simply caused by the forest trying to drain what was left of the water. Surely it cannot keep going on like this thought Ryan desperately, having spent yet another day watering plants and providing animals with a drink from a highly depleted lake.

He had used another vial of Cloud Magnet, but there simply was not enough moisture in the air. Over the hour, it had drawn in enough clouds to make a single pearly white one, that barely covered any of the forest, before the magic forced every drop out of it, so it faded into nothingness, depositing the smallest amount of water onto the forest floor.

Ryan had been on high alert for fire again. Twice he had caught the noise of fire engine sirens screaming through the forest to deal with small isolated bonfires and barbeques. The owners had been slapped with hefty fines for risking it in such a dry environment.

It was getting towards the end of July now, day two hundred and two to be precise, and the day was another hot one with very little cloud cover.

Ryan looked up, as he had done frequently over the last few weeks. Not enough to warrant using his last vial, he thought, desperate to not waste it like he felt he had the previous one. He had just finished what felt like the thousandth water supply emergency of the day, and wondered whether he should keep going with it. Yes, every plant and animal saved is a good thing for the forest, he told himself, trying to keep his motivation up. It was hard, as ninety nine percent of the time he was alone with only the forest and animals for company. Even the communication had stopped between them temporarily, as Ryan did not have the heart to take even a small amount of water away from the forest at the minute.

As he rubbed the chest of a squirrel that seemed to be struggling to keep going, he had caught a glimpse of movement and looked down to see several more animals, lining up patiently for his help. The squirrel seemed to be having a serious heart attack, and nothing Ryan did from the manual he was looking at seemed to help. The squirrel passed in his hands, lying motionless finally, having been unable to communicate with him, and Ryan sadly not able to provide a quicker easing.

A tear dropped from his eye, hitting the ground. The first water that had fallen in the forest in three days. Gently placing the squirrel's body at the base of a tree, he turned back to see who was next. Four or five of the animals were quite badly dehydrated, so he shot off across the forest with his bucket, and filled it from the remaining few inches on what had been a large forest lake. Upon returning, the four or five had turned into almost a dozen. He placed the bucket down for a few foxes to drink from first, and he cupped his hands and offered it to a hedgehog that drank gratefully. After a couple of minutes, several of the animals had dispersed back into the wilderness and he was left with a duck with a broken wing, and a millipede who had been severely injured by a bird or something. Ryan was about to start on the millipede, who seemed most in need, but the duck leant forward and swallowed it hole.

"Now really" said Ryan out loud, exasperated. "You cannot eat creatures who are awaiting my help. I am not providing a buffet line for you" he said sternly to the duck, pointing his finger.

Making the duck wait, he turned back to the bucket which only had the last dregs at the bottom. Though it would have been mixed with all sorts of saliva, he tilted his head back and drank what was left. Even the duck looked disgusted. The cloak worked overtime to remove the parasites and animal residue from Ryans body, as the liquid slipped down his throat.

"So thirsty."

"We need water"

"When is the rain coming again, I didn't get any last time."

The voices coming from the trees and plants were painful to Ryans ears. They sounded croaky and dying, like if a human had spent a few days wandering the Sahara. What could he do apart from reassure them?

"Rain will come soon, it can't stay like this forever" he said aloud, not wanting to promise specifically.

After a few minutes, the initial thought voices that came from drinking became silent. Sighing with relief that he didn't have to hear that all the time, he turned back to the duck that was tolerantly waiting. Reaching down for it, he heard the duck's voice.

"For your information, the millipede was here for you to put it out of its misery, and as you weren't listening to it, I thought I'd help it out."

"I'll have to take your word for that I suppose" thought Ryan, narrowing his eyes in suspicion. "Right then, this wing." He placed the squirrel manual that had been left on the ground back in his pocket and immediately withdrew one on duck wings. Scrolling through to a broken wing section.

"All I can do is string it up and let it heal itself" said Ryan, pulling out a see-through bandage, "and you'll have to go easy on it for the next week or so." He added, strapping the wing up and around the duck's neck.

"Thanks Dweller" came the ducks voice in his head. "I really was just helping the millipede." It added, looking deeply into his eyes.

"Ok, I believe you" said Ryan, giving it a little kiss on the head, "thank you."

He placed the duck down, and it waddled off, quacking happily, and in search for the rest of its friends.

Ryan returned the bucket to his usual safe spot, even though he knew he would be needing it again before the day was out, and continued helping the animals and plants around the forest.

That evening, when the darkness had spread across the sky, and the twinkling of the stars appeared, he lay on his back out on the dry plain.

He removed the picture of Archie and Becky from his pocket and hungrily stared at it, missing them immensely. It had been a tough time, and his mind had been focussed on the weather so much it had taken his thoughts away from the ones he had left behind. He wondered if they still thought of him, missing him, and wondering what had happened. He stared at his little boy in the picture for what seemed like hours, sad he would not get to hear the excited 'dada' again, or even see how much he'd grown. His past made him feel sad, and he made a vow to stop looking at his old belongings as it was getting more painful, and filling him with a regret he knew he shouldn't have. Tucking the picture away, and forgetting he had not eaten since the morning, he drifted slowly into a troubled sleep.

**

Archie had been picked up by Becky from nursery that day. He was so happy to see her, and cried out 'mama' whilst running from one side of the baby room to the other to give her a big hug.

"Oh my little boy" she said, scooping him up and holding him against her. "Have you been good today?"

"He has," came the voice of a carer who was changing one of the other kids' nappies. "A little cheeky at times, but ate all his food and had a long nap" she added.

"Ah thanks" said Becky, smiling at the woman, "Ok, we'll see you again soon" she said, turning to go with him in her arms.

"Bye Archie" were the calls of a few of them. Archie waved slowly, more interested in the thumb he had just put in his mouth.

Getting back home and bathing him, she realised she was happier at the minute than she had been in a long time. The payout on Ryans insurance had come through a few weeks back, which meant she was able to pay off the house, take some leave from her job, whilst keeping up with the bills and shopping. She knew she would have to go back at some point, and the hospital had promised to keep her position, mainly because they needed everyone they could get.

Archie splashed about, playing with the bubbles, and watching his little toy duck propel itself through the warm water.

"Cheeky" he said, making Becky look round to see Fearne the cat wondering in, making sure she did not get too close to the splash zone, but wanting the company.

"Yes, she is cheeky" said Becky, smiling at the little boy who looked so happy at the appearance of the cat. "She is quite cheeky, but not as much as you" she said, tickling his underarms. He let out an excited laugh and caused a bit more splashing.

The spell that had been cast on her was wearing off. Her natural happiness with her son and lack of stress from the financial side was helping immensely, meaning that the power of the emotional side of the spell was not needed anymore. It would cease to work in a couple of weeks and she would be back to her normal self, without the after effects of the major trauma usually left on a person when losing a loved one.

She had not considered dating again, instead she spent more time with her family, and planned exciting things to do with Archie and some of her close friends.

When she tucked him into bed that night, she just watched him close his eyes and drift off to peaceful sleep, lullabies playing in the background. All was well with them both.

***

Ryan persisted the next few days. More animals kept seeking him out for help, and he had to keep popping off to refill his bucket. The lake had nothing in it now, and he had to dig down a bit just for the hole to fill up with murky water for him to take. Yet another day had come with only thin whisps of cloud blowing through the sky above, nothing to suggest any change was coming.

Getting back to the animals, Ryan noticed three deer holding back from the rest of the animals. He put the half full bucket down, and watched as several birds took sips, followed by a couple of rabbits and then a badger. Finally, the Stag, Doe and baby deer moved forwards, each taking a few quick sips of water. The baby deer nodded its head to Ryan, and he returned the action. The mother looked like she was walking much better now, as they followed the Stag back through the trees. Very strange behaviour, he thought, but not dwelling on it for long as a frog had just hopped into the bucket and could not seem to get out. He rushed over to its aid.

That afternoon he met with Gadbre the Pixie King, and Bark the speaker for the Fairies.

"There just seems to be no water left" shouted Bark, standing on Ryans left knee as he sat with his back to a tree, his legs raised up to support them.

"We've found the same" said Gadbre, looking sympathetic, towering over Bark from Ryans right knee. "Some of our lot are living off root wine at the minute. They can't even fly straight anymore."

"Rain is coming," said Ryan which made them both look sceptical at this sudden prediction.

"How do you know though?" Bark virtually screamed, his voice only just travelling to them both.

"From this" said Ryan, and making sure he didn't accidentally shake his legs, he carefully pulled a newspaper he had found in the early afternoon by the side of the road, from his pocket.

The headline read, 'Drought Over?'

"Excellent" squeaked Gadbre and they both looked immensely relieved. "We've never known it as bad as this."

The article from the local paper read that heavy storms were due a few days from now.

"Well, this papers two days old, so hopefully it should be tomorrow" said Ryan, thankful to provide the information but knowing that thunderstorms could bring on other disasters for the forest. He was mostly pleased though that the drought would be ending, helping them all to relax from the onslaught of a thirsty forest.

"Ok then, we will get all of our scouts in tonight. They have had to dig for water to try and spread it around to those most in need. We have lost a couple of experienced Pixies doing this, but we've had to keep going. They will all be pleased with this news though" said Gadbre, readying himself for flight.

"I'll return and update King Branch" shouted Bark, "We'll see you soon Dweller."

And with that he took off, flying a couple of metres, before a tiny flash and he was gone. Gadbre also flew off, at greater speed than the Fairies due to the size, but without the ability to pop and vanish as the Fairies did.

Hopefully, the forest should get a good soaking tomorrow.

Chapter Nineteen – Fire

Unfortunately for all the kids and teenagers, the good weather was coming to an end only a week or so into the summer holidays. It meant that this would be their last night until who knew when, for them the camp out once more. The original group of six teenagers who had gone before were all keen again, making plans on text and socials, organising who brought the drink and where they were going to meet, inviting more people who'd had to listen jealously of their previous outing.

They all gathered at the edge of the forest, by a pub in the village of Bashley before walking out, trying to find a secluded place to have a good time. There was about twenty of them, and they laughed and joked as they made their way through the dry grass before reaching trees. One of the long-haired guys had a boombox on his shoulder, playing some loud repetitive music while holding a bottle of beer in his other hand. The sun was still up for a little while, giving them enough time to find the right spot where they could chill out, smoke, and drink the night away.

Once they had found an open space between the trees, they set their stuff down, and some of the guys started to collect fire wood, while the girls sat on a fallen tree, chatting and giggling while watching the boys. The one with the boom box, made sure to sit it carefully on the edge of the fallen tree, and wrapped its long carry strap around a sturdy branch to stop it falling.

Soon, a mound of firewood was made in the middle of the clearing, with an extra pile a short distance away. One of the original party goers got it going with his lighter and a bit of scrunched up bit of paper, and they all watched it spark into life.

For the next couple of hours, the music played louder, they ate half cooked sausages on sticks, and had cups of alcohol mixed drinks.

When evening had well and truly settled in, the partying began to get more rebellious. Groups of them were smoking and kissing, the girls sat on the boys' laps, while the long-haired guy who controlled the music was smoking a joint a little further away. A few of them were dancing, two guys with a girl they both fancied, moving enthusiastically to the music to compete with one another, as the loser would likely to sleep alone that night.

The evening started getting wilder, and the two drunk guys started fighting, neither of them having yet won the affections of the girl. They brawled by the flames of the recently restacked fire, sending bottles to the ground in the effort of defeating the other. All of a sudden, a blue flame lit and shot across the floor. A bottle of vodka and rum had been knocked down, and the liquid has run towards the fire, catching alight, and shooting back to its origin. The group leapt up, the girls trying to get out of the way while the guys threw drinks at it. Drunkenness did not improve accuracy, as the fire found its way to the bottles by the tree, flames flying higher at the pool of the initial spill, and starting to light the underside of the dead dry tree.

Smoke started coming from the grass as well, spreading out in a circle from the centre, as everything was so parched, it immediately became fuel for the fire. The girls screamed, grabbing their stuff, and the boys ran to help them get out the way. The boombox could not be retrieved by the long-haired guy, who had his hand burnt as a flame shot up through the core of the tree. Swearing, he leapt backwards, seeing the light of the fire lick the plastic, making it sweat. The fire seemed to be spreading outwards in all directions, feeding on the mass of dry debris in its path. The group ran for it, circling round the fire to all be together, and then running back the way they had come, leaving crackling and roaring flames in their wake.

***

It was gone midnight and Ryan awoke. He'd had a strange dream, and had woken up thirsty. He lowered his hands to the ground to push himself up for a drink when he heard it.

"FIRE, Fire in the forest."

"Please help us we're dying."

"Alert the services, FIRE, FIRE, FIRE."

"SHIT" shouted Ryan aloud, and he sprang up looking around. He immediately knew how bad it was as he saw light on a horizon where only darkness should reside.

He quickly pulled out the last vial of Cloud Magnet and dropped the liquid out on the ground, then transported over towards the light.

Arriving, he saw in shock how large it had already become. As far as he could see left and right, the flames were spreading over the ground, and with no water to stop them, they would just keep going. What to do he thought hurriedly, not knowing how he could stop it. John had said alert the services. Call the Fire brigade. He pulled out his old phone from his pocket, stepping backwards as the flames started getting closer. Rabbits, foxes, badgers, and all sorts of other animals were sprinting away from the flames, with birds overhead relocating to trees in safer parts of the forest. He pushed the button to turn the phone on. Thankfully it had a small amount of battery left, but no sim. He let out a distraught yell. His sim must have been cancelled. AH, but I think I can still make emergency calls from a phone with no sim. He hit nine nine nine and listened, ignoring the mass crackling, and crashing as trees succumbed to the fire and fell, the leaves and branches adding to the flames. Ryans cloak was working hard to keep him cool, and he could feel the heat on the tip of his nose and fingers.

"Hello, which emergency service do you require?" Came a female voice down the phone.

"Hello, Fire Fire Fire in the New Forest, it's out of control, you'll need to send everyone you have." Shouted Ryan feeling sorry for the call handler.

"I see, and where abouts are you?" said the voice, keeping calm yet he could hear her typing away furiously.

"Between Bashley and Wilverly in the New Forest. They won't miss it." He answered a little quieter than the last time.

"Ok, I'll alert the authorities and someone will be out shortly." She said professionally. "Please get yourself to safety." She added before he hung up.

Turning the phone back off and tucking it into his pocket again, he thought manically about what to do next.

"The Sisters" he cried out, grabbing a tree and transporting over to their cottage.

Running around the dark side of their house, he got to the front door.

A sign attached to it on a hook said,

'Gone on Holiday, any matters of urgency will have to wait for our return, no leaflets or junk mail please.'

"Shit" he said again, forgetting that they'd gone to Brazil and would not be back for a couple of weeks.

"Pixies then" he said, knowing they would be the closest ones to the fire and need warning anyway.

He ran back round to the blackened bulbous tree, and shot over the forest to where the Pixies resided.

Running through the trees shouting 'Fire, Fire," until a Pixie watcher flew down to him looking shocked. Ryan didn't wait for him to ask, but instead shouted,

"Fire over towards Bashley, get everyone, need water!!" he cried and the Pixie nodded feverishly, zipping off to the top of a tree. Ryan heard clanging, and saw them all emerge from the tree tops, some looking groggy, but others alert. Gadbre flew down to him, looking shocked.

"What is it Dweller, what news."

"Fire" said Ryan, hardly able to speak the word anymore, "Over towards Bashley, massive, you won't miss it. Need water."

"PIXIES," shouted Gadbre immediately, and they all flew into order. "You heard our Dweller, get water and STOP THIS FIRE!"

"YES SIR" they all said in union, before flying off, roughly in the same direction.

"I've dropped the last vial of Cloud Magnet" said Ryan and Gadbre looked pleased.

"Good work Dweller, we will need all the help we can get. Have you tried the sisters, or the Fairies?" he added.

"The sisters are on Holiday" he said, as Gadbre swore, "but I'll go to the Fairies now" he said, thinking how he also needed to find the Forest Folk and make sure they got out of the way.

"Go then, we'll start the prevention and evacuations." Shouted Gadbre and Ryan sprinted to the nearest tree, vanishing the moment he touched it.

Landing at the tree next to the Fairies one, he pulled out a ladder and climbed two rungs at a time in his haste. There was no one on the little door, so he pulled it open and shouted 'Fire' through the hole.

Unfortunately for Bark, who was just returning from a quick wee break back to his entrance watch, he received the full blast of Ryans shout, which knocked him out completely.

Not being able to help, Ryan watched as the Fairies inside awoke and tried to help the poor unconscious Bark. Their lights were all dull at this time, but one bright pink one flew to the front. Cinthia stood there, looking worried and shocked as a full-sized Ryan stared in at them.

"Fire, towards Bashley," he said softly to her and she nodded.

Turning to the crowd of Fairies, some of who had pulled Bark into a chair, she shouted.

"Hear that Fairies. Our Dweller needs help. Let's go, be careful not to get burnt."

Ryan leant back, as thousands of tiny Fairies flew at his face, funnelling through the hole and swinging around him, their lights flashing bright now, before they started popping into nothingness, as they disappeared to where the Pixies were trying to hold back the flames. Cinthia stood there, in the doorway, looking stunning and fierce, her expression softening as she looked into his eyes.

"I've got to go warn the Forest Folk" he said quietly, and she nodded. King Branch came up behind her.

"You've got the lead on this Hyacinth, show them you're the Fairy to lead them" he said, only just loud enough for Ryans ears to pick up.

"Right then, I've got to go" he said, nodding to them and sliding down the ladder and quickly pocketing it. He looked up just in time to see a flash of pink as Cinthia shot off to help with the fire. He did hope she would be ok. Pulling his thoughts together, he ran back over to the nearest tree. Not sure where they would be, he simply thought, Forest Folk, and he did, to his surprise, disappear.

King Branch watched him go. He was proving to be a very efficient Dweller indeed. Sighing, he was sorry that his Cinthia could not be together with him as she so clearly wanted. But he was pleased that Ryan had made it clear that the forest had to come first. Anyway, she was beautiful, intelligent, and a leader. She would make a fine wife and mother to one of the Fairies he had suggested she try dating.

"Your Highness" came a voice behind him, and he turned to see a very groggy Bark, sitting up in his seat.

"Ah Bark there you are. There is a major fire in the forest that the others are dealing with. Please guard the front door and relay any messages and updates that come through."

"Certainly, your highness" he said immediately, quite embarrassed that the king had seen him slumped asleep in the chair. He had no idea how he had gotten there, but took up his position outside the door straight away, on alert for any returning Fairies.

Ryan appeared in darkness next to the Forest Folk Camp. He could see light on the horizon and knew they would have been in serious trouble had he not been there to awaken them. He began walking forward into the centre of the carts.

"What you doing here Dweller at this time?" came a voice to his left.

He looked round and saw Jack, stood ready, lowering a bow and arrow they must use in case of intruders, even though their magic statue from the 'Sisters of the Wreath' kept all other humans away.

"Fire in the Forest" said Ryan loudly, "Look on the horizon, it's spreading this way, you have to get out of here." Jack nodded, stuttering to agree.

He pulled up a large pot, the one they used to make stew, and started banging it with a piece of wood.

"What in the blazes Jack" said an angry Ted, appearing half dressed from one of the carts. His tone and manor changed when he spotted Ryan there.

"What is it? What's wrong?" he asked quickly.

"Fire, near Bashley, you need to leave" said Ryan as Jack stood there trying to sputter the words out.

"FIRE, FIRE, FIRE, the forests on fire" shouted Ted, rousing the whole group.

"Thank you Dweller, we will all get to safety. Do you need any help" said Ted, staring into Ryans face.

"I've got the Pixies and Fairies onto it, along with a potion from the Sisters." He replied, readying himself to join the others.

"Ah good" said Ted, hauling some items together as more of the folk ran around tidying up and packing things away.

Ryan left them to it, getting to a tree and vanishing over to the edge of the flames. He saw Pixies pouring tidy buckets of water onto the ground, trying to form a line to halt the oncoming fire which had spread to Wilverly, Sway and almost Lymington already. The sound of sirens rang out through the forest, as other reports of fire had flooded in on the local emergency line. Every firefighter on call in a thirty-mile radius was now on their way to tackle what was being described as devastation in the forest. Animals that had been running from the flames were hot and tired, the Pixies helping carry the smaller ones to safety while the Fairies were spread out, trying to use their magic to slow the fire. The clouds were swirling in the sky above, shutting out the lights from the stars and moon as they got heavier and denser.

Ryan was just about to step forward to see how he could help, when a massive Stag leapt towards him, the doe not far behind. It was manic and pawing the ground desperately as Ryan grabbed its head.

"Our son, our son is trapped, oh please help us Dweller," came a frightened shouting voice in his head.

"Where?" replied Ryan immediately.

"We were encircled by the flames somewhere back that way, he wasn't quick enough to get out, please get him," came the hysterical voice.

Ryan withdrew his hand, looking at the doe as he passed her and sprinted towards the flames, ignoring the calls from the Fairies and Pixies to hold back. Reaching the edge of the fire, he proceeded in at speed, flames licking his cloak tastily. He kept going, feeling himself becoming warmer and warmer, the feeling in his feet becoming more real with each step. After a few hundred metres, He broke into a small clearing, surrounded by burning trees, but centring on an earthy patch which is thankfully where the baby deer stood shaking, looking terrified, and turning quickly, as it wasn't able to see a way out. It had a nasty burn on its rump, and was calling out for its parents who couldn't save it.

Ryan darted forward, and the deer sprang towards him looking thankful as he was its only symbol of hope. There was no way of transporting out of here though with everything burning, he'd have to run through the fire again, but surely the deer wouldn't survive that. Looking down at its small body, and cute black eyes that stared up at him, he made his decision. He pulled out a large jug of water from his pocket, before pulling the whole cloak over his head and wrapping the deer in it. He poured the water over himself, so it soaked his hair and ran down his body, before he picked up the cloak carrying the deer, and turned towards the flames. He was very aware his feet were now on the forest floor and the heat was sucking all the oxygen from around him, it was the only way though.

He ran, faster than he could have believed, flames catching him all the way, the water helping at the start, but soon disapparating. His toes and feet were bleeding from sticks and thorns, but still he ploughed through the burning forest, not sure anymore which was the right way, but needing to keep going straight. The deer bleated in his cloak, kept cooler and better than it had been, as the magic of the cloak cleaned its body fully. He continued, with screaming muscles, as burns started worsening across his body, flesh scorched and dry, his mind screaming. He couldn't go on, but he must, he must. The edge of his cloak caught fire. The magic had finally succumbed to the heat of the environment, and in his desperation for the animal inside, he tried to pat the flames out as he ran, but his body was protesting from more movement, and he just had to keep going.

Then it was there. A cool breeze shot over his face. His tired aching body launching through and out onto the yet to be burned part of the forest. He stumbled a dozen or so metres further, before releasing the baby deer from the smoking cloak, collapsing onto the forest floor as the flames slowly approached. But just before he lost consciousness, he felt a drip hit his cheek, as the Cloud Magnet gave way, and the heavens finally opened.

Chapter Twenty – Charcoal and Rain

Ryan awoke with a start. His body was so sore and tender, aching all over. He could barely feel his feet at all from the burns and scratches. He gingerly got up, noticing how his cloak, which lay beside him, and his undergarment, which he was still wearing, were both soaked from the rain that poured down. Their magic must have been destroyed he thought as he slowly placed the cloak over his head, noting the holes where the fire had burnt through. It was drenched, but cool against his scorched skin. With a sudden realisation, he placed his hands in his pockets, but there was nothing to grab, it had all gone.

Thankfully it wasn't pitch black anymore, the sun must be on its way up, and as he looked around to see where he was, he saw Cinthia sheltered in a hole in the tree next to where he had been sleeping.

He assumed the fire had been quelled by the rain, but had to check with her first.

"Cinth, hey Cinth" he called softly.

She stirred and turned over, her big beautiful blue eyes opening and staring at him for a moment before they focused.

"Oh good you're up" she shouted, smiling happily, and flying out to hug his cheek, "I thought you were gone."

"Not quite yet," he said, stroking her gently with one finger "Is the fire out?" He asked, remembering that was why they were in this situation.

"Yes, the rain has been so heavy, its refilling the lakes and rivers too. Our thirsty forest is drinking it up and thankfully it put out all the fires. There is a lot of destruction though." She added, flying backwards so he could see her biting her lip.

"How did I get here?" he asked, looking around at the damp wood.

"About thirty Pixies lifted you onto the back of a Stag, and he brought you here, away from the fire. The baby deer survived and was very thankful." She said, looking adoringly into his face. "You risked your life to save him. That was ever such a brave thing to do." She added.

"It's what us Dwellers do" he said, feeling every injury start to throb worse as she laughed.

"Well, I best be getting back to help with the clean-up." She said, holding out her palm in a halt and saying, "You do not have to do any of it, us and the Pixies have agreed to do it, as you have already done so much. Thank you Dweller," she said lovingly, as she sped forward, and gave him a tiny peck on the cheek, before a flash, and she had vanished.

Ryan stood there for a while, in the rain, sopping wet, before deciding to head over to the 'Sisters of the Wreaths' cottage. He at least thought he could wait there as shelter under their small porch to protect himself from the rain. He started walking, forgetting that he didn't need his cloak to transport. As he made his way much more carefully towards Burley, realising how well his cloak had worked at stopping him stepping on stones and branches, or getting caught up in thorns and sticks, he remembered that he only needed to be a Dweller to use the root transport. Slapping his head, and regretting it due to the pain, he reached out for the nearest tree.

Arriving at the bulbous blackened tree and walking around to the front door, he saw the slightest glimmer of the rising sun on the horizon through the clouds. Dawn was here. And so it turned out, were the Sisters.

The sign had been pulled off the door and a light was on in the window above. Ryan knocked, slightly surprised at his good fortune that they were in.

In an instant, the door was opened, and a sunburnt Gwen peered out to him for a second, before letting out a squeal and pulling him in.

"He's here, he's here." She said, calling to the others. "We have only just got back and been looking for a sunburn solution."

Flo and Dotty appeared in the room and both ran over and hugged him.

"What an exceptional Dweller you are," said Flo standing back.

"We saw the Fire on the news a little while ago and knew we'd have to travel back to help out" said Dotty, pulling the drenched Ryan further into the cottage where the fire was crackling away. He gave it a shifty look, having spent the night trying to stop one.

"From what we hear, you couldn't have done more than you did." Said Gwen, and the three of them stood there, watching him staring into the flames, thinking about all the wildlife and animals he'd had to hear burning in his head as he was caught in the thick of it.

"Do you know," he began slowly, looking round at them, hair plastered to his face, cloak dripping on their chair and floor, "How far it spread in the end?"

They all glanced at one another, which gave him an uneasy feeling in his stomach. It was Flo who took lead.

"Well," she said starting slowly. "It spread back to New Milton, and onwards to Bransgore, Brockenhurst, Lymington and just the edge of Burley before it was doused by the rain."

Ryan felt the air exhale as he sighed. That was a big area, a lot of destruction.

"The firefighters saved the towns and villages, but the forest was where it had spread worse anyway" said Dotty "The Pixies will have to find a new home. Their wood got a blasting just before it rained."

Ryan didn't want to hear anymore. He knew many had perished. He had only been a Dweller a few months and already a massive chunk of the Forest had been destroyed.

He didn't know how long he sat in silence, dripping on one of their chairs, but it was Dotty that came up to his side, making him look up at her, red eyed.

"I take it, your cloak got damaged and is no longer working?" She asked politely. "And your undergarment too?"

Ryan, suddenly felt very uncomfortable, knowing he must have released his bladder in the time since his undergarment had ceased to remove the waste. He nodded, and she bustled away upstairs, clunking around, and knocking things over, before trudging back down and laying out in front of him, a brand-new cloak and undergarment.

The New Forest Dweller

"We have made them for all the past Dwellers, just in case they got theirs destroyed, and each of them stayed in their originals up until their final transportation. You on the other hand are different." She added, smiling at him.

Slowly he stood up, shaking the wet cloak from his body so that flecks of water sprayed everywhere. He then removed his undergarment, Dotty and Gwen averted their eyes fully, but Flo had never been able to resist a peak of a nice pert bottom, had a little peek. He pulled on the new undergarment, feeling his nether regions tingle in anticipation, before lifting the cloak over his head. In an instant his whole body was clean and dry, the burns repaired, his lungs cleansed from the smoke, and feeling like he could conquer the world again, instead of the defeat he felt in his previous wet outfit.

"Well?" Asked Gwen, as the three of them stood there, waiting and watching.

"I feel great" he said, truly believing that it was not over. He had conquered this and would help rebuild, the forest would survive, but not only that, it would flourish.

Turning to the three of them, he gave them each a kiss on the cheek, Flo went bright red, before saying,

"Thank you ladies, and now, I have work to do."

And he left, back out into the daylight, with a small amount of rain still falling, but he was cosy and dry in his new cloak.

With the faintest of hopes, he reached into his right pocket, searching for his old belongings, but they were not there. Well that concluded that he thought, momentarily sad he had lost his pictures of the ones he loved dearest, but there was so much to do now he couldn't dwell on it."

And with that, he spent the rest of the day, clearing the mounds of ash, helping bring down destroyed trees to aid with rebirth, but also so they didn't fall on other plants and animals. He was assisted all day by the Pixies and the Fairies, who were working tirelessly to wash the charcoal away and leave fertile ground for a fresh start.

Around mid-afternoon, he saw Spruce, Pine and Ash, his fellow Dwellers on the England Forest Dweller Council, stomping up the Hill. He thanked them for coming to help, and they offered their condolences to those that had been lost. They then stayed for the rest of the afternoon and well into the evening, making sure all was ok and knowing that it wouldn't rear up again.

"Not with this weather" croaked Ash, lifting his hand up as the gentle rain had continued.

***

Over the next couple of days, Ryan continued the work. The Pixies had set up temporary accommodation in the Fairies wood, and had been made to feel very welcome. Ryan was back to doing emergencies, getting through a backlog on the first morning after the fire, seeing to more than a hundred animals that had suffered burns that needed cream. The young deer was about number eighty on his travels, and it gave him the biggest hug, licking his face all over as he felt a tear fall from his eyes in happiness. The doe as well came over after he applied the cream, and he stroked her head.

"Thank you Dweller, Thank you so much. You risked your own life for our child's. We could never repay you." Came her calm voice in his head.

The Stag, slightly sheepishly, wondered over too, as the baby deer pranced around, a cool feeling on its rump from where the cream was working.

"Thank you," said the Stags voice, much more relaxed this time, when Ryan reached out for his head too. "Thank you so much. We all owe you our lives, and our forest."

"You are all very welcome." He said for the eightieth time that day. "I am your Dweller, The Dweller to the Forest, The New Forest Dweller. If I cannot help you, then I am not doing a good enough job."

"Thank you Dweller" came his voice again, "We look forward to seeing you again." Then they turned and started walking away. The baby deer gave a final prance and lick, as he bent down to say goodbye to him, before he too walked back into a greener forest.

There were very few trees and plants to treat for burns. Those that had only been licked by the flames, had received most of their recovery when the rain had fallen, their roots sucking up the water, filling themselves up, letting the liquid and time heal them.

As he got through yet another burn victim, he thought about how could it have started, should he go looking for the origin. He supposed yes, in case it was something that could start up again.

So, that evening, when it became too dark to see to the animals, he transported to the edge of the black wasteland, and began walking. There were no living trees, grass, or plants here now. The fire had seen to that, which meant he could not transport through to where it had begun. Instead, he pulled a lantern out of his pocket, like the old Dweller once used, and began his search, deeper and deeper into the burnt area, trying to find the epicentre.

He walked for around an hour, noting how the fire had spread outwards from a certain area that must still be a little further along. Finally, he reached a small circle clearing which had only one burnt out tree in. He saw a melted plasticky residue on the floor, some scorched glass bottles, a few of which had crack and shattered, with one that looked like it was quite clearly a strong alcohol. He checked around the whole circle and concluded, the fire had spread out from this location.

Anger seethed up inside of him like he had never known. The destruction of thousands of trees, insects, plants, and animals, had all started from humans. Humans who were not even meant to be having fires in the forest anyway.

He paced around, the hem of his cloak brushing the floor but remaining black free. He then picked up the bottle. What had he expected, it to be a natural fire? They had probably camped out because the rain was coming, he thought, knowing he was right.

He marched back the way he had come, hoping his emotions would remain forever so that he could pour the blame onto someone else instead of feeling like it was still on him.

"ARGHH" he shouted, falling to his knees.

He couldn't accost anyone. It would reveal himself to the world and that was the last thing he needed at the minute. How could they though? They knew the forest was so dry and yet they still had a drunken party.

He knew he had been a teenager once too, but he would not have dreamed of being so reckless.

He needed to do something, send a warning, he couldn't let it happen again.

"Not on my watch." He said out loud without even the trees to hear him. He began walking again, reaching the edge of the destruction before grabbing a green piece of grass and travelling over to Lyndhurst, to the New Forest District Council Offices. There he wrote out a long note and attached it to the bottle, leaving it on the step by the front door. Then, still hooded, he walked away, disappearing at the first instance to a secluded spot where he could spend the night.

Chapter Twenty-One – Local News

'DRUNK TEENS SET FIRE TO FOREST' read the headline on the local paper Ryan had scavenged from a bin in the dead of night in Brockenhurst, a week after the fire. He continued to read the article from the day before to the listening group. They were all there for this forest meeting, The 'Sisters of the Wreath', The Forest Folk, the Pixies, and the Fairies.

'Around twenty teenagers are being questioned regarding the fire that decimated a large area of the New Forest last week. The group, who have admitted to drinking and partying, also confessed to an illegal fire getting out of hand when a fight broke out in the group. Millions of pounds worth of damage has been done to buildings and vehicles, not to mention a vast ancient part of the forest which has been destroyed. For their own protection, the underage teenagers cannot be named. The oldest of the group, though Dougie Stevenson, who turned eighteen the week before, has been questioned further on his involvement in what happened. He said 'I was just there for the vibes, ya know. I love my music, and having a good time. It was some of the younger ones who lost control and split the drinks everywhere which started it all. I lost a good stereo in the fire man.' Dougie has since been charged with supplying alcohol to his underage partygoers. No other formal charges have yet been announced. We also spoke to the Chief Fire Marshall who was at the scene...'

Ryan put down the paper staring around at them all.

"Well, we know now what started it" said Ryan, with no triumph in his voice at getting to the truth. "Teenagers it was."

Silence continued in the group. Finally, Ted spoke.

"Well, most of us survived." He said glumly, knowing that the Pixies had lost around thirty and the Fairies, eight. "All thanks to you Dweller." He said, and all the eyes turned back towards Ryan.

"It wasn't enough though was it." He replied to them all. "I think we need to do more in the future to help stop this sort of thing from happening again."

"What would you have us do?" Asked Flo.

"Yes Dweller, we're yours to command." Said Gadbre, and each person there seemed to puff out their chest, ready for his orders.

"Well," he started, not sure where to lead it. "I suppose, if we do get a severe drought again, we need back up. Backup potions from the 'Sisters of the Wreath'" he said, nodding to the three ladies, "Backup lookouts across the forest when the lakes and rivers have dried up, to spot any potential dangers day and night." He said looking to the Fairies and Pixies who nodded. "And maybe," he said turning to the Forest Folk, "Help with some of my tasks in the meantime. I am going to be busy planting and nurturing the forest back to health, and I would appreciate you guys helping tidy up after the other humans on your travels. Just the litter and dog poo mainly, but it would help me out a lot" he said, and the whole group of them nodded, pleased to be of assistance. Often, they felt the least useful of the Forest group, but by given this task, they would prove that they were up to it.

"Right then" continued Ryan, "Let's all get some rest. The summer is almost over, and we'll need all our energy, as we still have a lot of work to do."

***

Over the course of the next week, things slowly began to change. The blackness of the burnt area had received a good few rainfalls, which reduced all the ash and charred remains down into the soil, and amazingly, green shoots started to appear. The rebirth of the forest had begun.

The Pixies had decided to remain in the Fairies forest, at least until the New year where then they would move into another wooded location, the other side of Brockenhurst. It would be closer to the area of destruction which meant they would work through the nights at the start of the year to help speed growth along in time for spring.

Ryan was a bit nervous about the prospect of meeting Lester again, what with the whole area still pretty much devoid of life. But Lester knew about what had happened, as he was made to watch silently over the forest for most of the moon's cycle. He had seen Ryan run through the fire, being scorched all the way as he rescued the baby deer. The courage he showed, and his love of the forest and all of its inhabitants was unlike any he had ever seen in another Dweller. Lester would never admit that he watched this though. He had winced all the way knowing the pain that Ryan would have been in. It was his privilege to know what sort of Dweller they had. A great one.

He had felt funny that week. He wasn't sure if it was because of what had happened in the forest, or pride at having seen how its inhabitants responded to the call to help. Either way, there was a faint light in his eyes whenever he tried to look to either side. Maybe his vision was being restricted because there was less forest for him now to see? Or that his part of the forest had been burned so bad it had affected him? He was not sure, but he certainly wasn't going to trouble the already overworked Dweller with it.

They played cards again all night, after talking at length about the rebirth of the forest and how it would hopefully play out. He kept his updates on pollen levels, butterfly numbers and other things he had noticed quiet until their next meeting, knowing that they had only this one main thing to discuss this time.

About halfway through the night, Ryan laid down his hand, showing a full house and beating Lesters three sixes, when he remembered something. Pulling the most recent newspaper from his pocket, which had another headline 'TEENAGERS CHARGED WITH ARSON', he flicked through the first few pages, resting on an obituary for an old lady from Lymington.

"Do you know this lady?" Ryan asked, doubting Lester would.

The ghostly Highwayman stared at the image for a few moments, his neck slightly twisted where it had broken upon his death. He tried to shake it no, but didn't quite manage it to one side. So Ryan continued,

"Her name was Edna Heckingbottom. She was the last in line to a very old family indeed. She sadly passed away several days ago, and some of her possessions have been put up for auction when they cleared her house."

"Right," said Lester slowly, with the faintest recall that he had heard the surname before somewhere.

"Do you recognise any of these?" Ryan asked simply, turning the page to about a dozen different interesting pieces that would be going to auction next month.

Lesters eyes scanned the page, not changing at all until he got to the last item, a well-polished silver Pistol. His eyes widened at the sight of it. He tried to reach out and pull the paper towards him, his hands passing straight through the page.

Blimey thought Ryan, it must have been interesting if he's forgotten he is a ghost.

"My goodness" said Lester looking up, "That is my Pistol. But that means, surely." He turned his eyes to the side, and the light got brighter. Then he turned more, and it started to lighten his body which shocked Ryan into jumping back, still clutching the pages. Lester became lighter and brighter the more he twisted, almost completing a full one eighty, before stopping. He then turned back and became his black barely visible spectre.

"What on earth was that?" said Ryan, completely astounded, his eyes struggling to adjust back to the darker form.

Lester told him about the light in the corner of his eyes that week.

"And that must mean" he said ready to conclude. "That as she was last in line from the family that murdered me, my bounds to the earth have been released. I am free to go on, if I so wish."

Ryan stood there looking shocked and amazed. He went a few moments before asking the first question he could think of.

"Well, why don't you?"

Lester looked sheepish, squirming slightly before he gave his response.

"I have grown to love the forest. Forced to live here for hundreds of years. It hasn't always been easy. But if I go on, there is no way back." He said, short sentences matching the sudden thoughts that were coming to him. "At least I have the choice now" he said, looking up pleased.

"Well, whenever you do decide to do it, you have to spend one more night with me so that I can say goodbye properly." said Ryan, making sure Lester understood. He was very fond of his ghostly highwayman friend. His wit and dour nature were a stark contrast from the others in the forest. He would miss these evenings when he was gone.

When the night did come to an end, they both stood up and pretended to hug like usual.

"Please don't disappear before our next one" said Ryan, hoping he wouldn't, but not wanting to come across as selfish.

"No, I won't" said Lester smiling, and he stood back, watching Ryan walk away, back through the darkness, trying to find life to transport from. "I don't want to miss what's to come with you, Dweller." He said quietly to himself, very much looking forward to the next time they saw each other. He was showing he would become a great one.

Chapter Twenty-Two – Walk Through the Woods

Hilary was a woman in her very late forties. Fifty-six to be precise, but only ever saying late forties to people she didn't know very well, or anyone who cared to check her dating profile. She had long blondish hair that was usually tied into a professional bun, secured up on the back of her head, and walked in low heals, but with confidence and purpose. Her eyes were tired from having just completed another twelve-hour night shift at the emergency response centre in Southampton, and she was walking back to her car where she had parked on the second floor of the staff car park.

She got in and plugged in her phone, before turning the car on. It was only seven in the morning, and there might not be anyone in, but she thought at least someone should try.

No one in the office seemed to care about the call that had come through early, alerting them to the humongous fire that had spread across the forest, but she did. She had taken the call from what sounded like a young guy, and thought he deserved recognition for his swiftness. It was only thanks to him that the fire crews were about to save so many people from all the houses and villages. Not one recorded death or injury from a fire on that scale was unprecedented. And it was thanks to this stranger's phone call, which came a full fifteen minutes before the rest started flowing in, which allowed the fire crews to hold back the flames when they spread to the edge of civilisation.

She was slightly suspicious that it could have been one of the teenagers, calling it in due to guilt of starting it. But on having read the reports on them in the papers, she had concluded that not one of them had the decency to ring and own up to their mistake. Instead, they had run, trying to hide from the authorities, who had managed to round them all up thanks to the group text chains they had been in.

No, this guy was separate from that, and had probably, without knowing, saved many lives. She was determined to find him, if nothing else to give her thanks, for her daughter and baby granddaughter lived in Sway, one of the villages right at the heart of the fire. She could not bare thinking about what could have been.

She tapped in an address that she had sneakily found on the police database that was linked to the phone number. Pressing for the quickest route and then accepting. She began on her short journey to the registered house.

Four hours it had taken her to go back through all the calls to find the right one. She must had relistened to it about twenty times, writing the number down and trying to get a clue about who he was, but nothing came through. Even when she had tried to call the number multiple times the day before, it just kept saying 'this number is no longer in use.'

Leaving the city, and seeing all the cars tailed back coming the other way to go work was satisfying to see. Serves them right for having normal hour jobs she thought, smiling, but with a twinge of jealousy in her mind. Her night shift wouldn't last forever, just one more week.

As she followed the directions, through to a nice-looking estate of houses, she pulled up outside the right one, looking to spot any signs of life within. It was half seven now, and there were a couple of lights on in the windows. Well worth a knock then she thought, turning off the engine and opening the door.

She walked over the pavement, and then her shoes crunched on the stones up to the front door before pressing the doorbell. She waited patiently for about ten seconds, as a black and white cat rubbed itself along the inside of the window to a dining room. The door suddenly opened, and there stood a brown-haired woman, with a blonde-haired toddler in her arms.

"Hello," the woman said to her. "Can we help you?"

"Oh hello," replied Hilary, smiling at the boy who was about the same age as her granddaughter. "I hope you don't mind, but I just wanted to see who lived here and thank them for their call in to the emergency services a couple of weeks ago."

The woman looked confused. Putting the boy down so he could run off into the lounge shouting 'cheeky' whilst chasing the cat.

"I'm sorry, I think you must have the wrong house." She said, still looking confused.

"Oh, I do apologise. I was given this address as the call came from this number." She said, sliding a piece of paper with the number in front of the girl who did not look that interested in the seemingly crazy woman at her front door. For a moment her eyes moved across the strip of paper, then the door opened a tiny amount.

"Where did you get this?" she said, a tiny stutter in her voice which Hilary missed.

"Well, the call came through on this number a couple of weeks back letting us know that the forest was on fire. I work at the emergency service response, and just thought I would follow up and give thanks from the whole department to the nice young man I spoke to" she said, noting how the woman's face was turning from confusion to shock.

"But that number was my partners," she said, stuttering quite noticeably now, a tear appearing in her eye.

"Oh, I am sorry dear. Did he leave you?" Asked Hilary shocked at the tear, before realising she had said out loud something she was probably only meant to think.

"No" said the woman, letting out a small cry, both eyes welling up now. "He disappeared several months ago. The police have never been able to find him, and I've assumed him to be dead." She said, both eyes leaking.

"Oh, I'm so sorry dear" said Hilary, embarrassed but trying to comfort her. "Here," she said pulling out a tissue. Then wishing she could just get back in her car she said "It must have been someone else then, they must have reassigned the number, I'm so sorry to have bothered you." She said sympathetically patting the young woman on the arm before turning back to her car. She quickly started the engine, just wanting to get out of this embarrassing situation before it was reported. She didn't exactly have clearance to search on the police database, but had done it out of thanks for the young man that had reported the fire.

Becky stood in the doorway, another tear hitting the ground as the car rolled away and round the corner. She closed the door and went back into the dining room to see Archie sat down in the lounge watching the tv.

"And in local news, it seems that the old man of the forest, is now the young man of the forest. Bob Davey, a local nature enthusiast, managed to capture a few pictures on his camera of a young man with a brown cloak, out and about in the forest, the morning after the fire."

"Drenched he was, from head to foot. I'd only gone out as the rain would have meant some beautiful wildlife pictures. I didn't even know about the fire until that afternoon."

"Davey's photos seem to show a young, brown-haired guy dressed up pretending to be the forest legend. Oh, there always seems to be someone who wants to dress as a hero. That's all from us this morning"

"Dada" said Archie suddenly, looking at the screen and smiling. Then, in a much quieter and confident voice he again said "Dada."

Becky, who had been standing round the corner from the television, walked out just in time to catch a teary glimpse of a dark-haired guy in the rain, before the image changed to the closing credits.

"Dada" said the little boy, excitedly getting up and running around.

"No squidge. It's not dada." She said, sad that this is how it would be.

Archie turned to her, and very crossly said, "Dada." She smiled at his change in tone, as he ran off still saying the occasional 'dada.'

What a strange last few minutes she thought, wiping the last tears from her eyes. She hadn't felt this sad about him since he had disappeared.

Straightening up, and back in control of her emotions she turned to the little boy who was still charging about, and then, not quite sure why she felt like it, she said.

"Right Archie, shall we go for a walk today in the Forest?"

***

Ryan had awoken early again as usual, and almost immediately began wolfing down some food and drink before starting his day. It looked cloudy overhead again which was good. The downpours over the last couple of weeks had gone some way to healing the forest, so that the cracks that had appeared in the dry earth were sealed, and the river ran normally with the lakes almost back to full.

He had noticed too that the forest in general was looking cleaner as well, and it wasn't just the Forest Folk to thank for this. He had seen on his travels, groups of mostly older retired people with high visibility vests, walking around the tracks in the evenings, like he had done before the fire, picking up litter and poo. Each had printed on their backs 'The New Forest Legends.'

It did confuse him at first, seeing the groups out in the evening, but over the days, he had spotted many different people all across the forest, each adorning the same name.

He was pleased and rather touched that they had started this, the idea based on the legend of the old man that looked after the forest (or young man now, but he of course had not seen it on television, and the pictures hadn't made it to the local paper yet). But it showed there were decent people out there who did take pride in the wildlife and environment. Little did he know, that groups like this had been set up and started all over the country, in some mass eco awareness movement. Spruce, Pine, and Ash had all witnessed their own forest legends walking through, helping to carry out their work. Not only that, but it seemed to have spread further, so that there were legends all over now, for different regions, all devoted to keep their area clean, championing anti littering.

It had a great benefit of freeing up time for the Dwellers, as with much less clearing up after the humans, they were free to cultivate areas and plant new trees and plants.

This new movement had inspired councils to increase the fines for littering and not picking up dog poo, so that it was as frowned upon now as any other illegal activity. Ryan had seen the new signs that had gone up alongside the 'No Barbeques and Open Flames' ones, this time reading 'Littering is a Criminal offense, One Thousand Pound Fine, No Excuse'.

He didn't quite know how big the movement had become through his simple sighting, played out by the media as just a guy dressing up as a legend, but in turn inspiring real people to get out there and actually make a difference to the land we live in.

He travelled off to his first emergency of the day, a field mouse that was currently being toyed with by a cat at the top of Beaulieu high street. It's terrified little squeaks making the cat enjoy its capture, then releasing it for a second, before the cat pounced on it again, pleased with its technique.

"Get out of it" said Ryan quickly, surprised at having materialized in the village, but knowing the Forest would not have let him unless the coast was currently clear. His feet still tingled being in this close a proximity, but he only needed a few seconds to shoo the cat away, which let the mouse escape up the hill and into the long grass.

The cat gave him a grumpy look. It was only young, he saw, and would probably learn from this to not play with its food next time. Ryan disappeared off to his next one by holding the small strip of grass he had appeared from, just before a car accelerated up the quiet village cobbled street.

He then arrived at the edge of the fire damaged forest, to see a hawk on the ground about fifty metres away. He ran through the blackish brown remains of the ground, which unfortunately had no green shoot to allow him to transport closer. As he got there, he saw that the hawk itself was not injured, but the rabbit it had just pecked the eye out of had already perished. He let out a sigh. He could not be angry with the hawk, it was in its nature. John had told him there would be times when you were called to an emergency, where one animal was about to eat another, and sometimes you'd be able to help, but remember, that one animal saved, could mean one going hungry. The likelihood was that if that animal had been on the hit list before, it probably would be again. The old man had said after the first couple of years, he had stopped intervening, as it was all part of the ecosystem that kept the forest alive. In this particular case, there was nothing he could do anyway. He reached out and stroked the hawks head gently, and it allowed him to, before hearing in his head,

"I'm sorry Dweller, I've got a family to feed."

"No worries" he thought back, "it's all just part of nature."

Then he turned back to the living part of the forest, ready to continue his work.

About ten or so other emergencies later, when thankfully the last one was just a lost dog in the woods that he helped via root transport back to its owner that was walking along with a screaming child in a pushchair. He kept hidden behind the tree as he approached, with the owners calls for 'Charlie' the dog to return. He had released the dog, and it sprinted back to his owner, who cried out in relief as she immediately put him back on his lead to avoid losing him again. The child stopped crying at least, seeing the dog return again.

He sneaked a peak from behind the tree, feeling sadness that the child was probably around Archie's age, the mum similar to Beckys. Guilt flooded up inside him, and he turned, disappearing to a part of the forest to be alone. Sitting on a tree stump, he pulled out a sausage sandwich with ketchup, eating away while staring into nothingness, thinking about the family he had deserted. In a way, he thought it a good thing that his first cloak had been destroyed, meaning that he couldn't look back and dwell on the past. But in another, there was a yearning that he thought would not be quelled with time. He missed her, and his little boy.

A tear dripped from his eye, hitting the top of his cheek, and rolling down to his clean-shaven chin, hanging there until the second one followed it along the same path, joining together, and dropping to the forest floor. He was glad no one could see him.

***

Becky pulled up to an empty car park on the outskirts of Burley, reversing carefully up towards the wooden guide post. She turned the engine off and got out, removing the pushchair from the boot, and then going round to the side door. Archie squealed with excitement as she opened it. His toothy smile radiating happiness as she placed his shoes back on his feet, he always pulled them off in the car. Then, placing him in the pushchair, began their walk along the path and into the deeper forest.

Pine cones and sticks had to be dodged by the wheels of the pushchair, so that Archie didn't have too bumpy a ride. Becky began breathing heavier as she started going slightly uphill, and thankfully she thought, no one was around to see her take off her jumper as she got hotter. Archie was enjoying the view of the trees and the scenery, his thumb dipping in and out of his mouth frequently, in between the 'oohs' and 'ahhs' as they went.

Finally, after about twenty minutes, she got to a spot where she could unstrap him and let him have a run around. She did this, carefully making sure the brake was on the chair, and that he wasn't going too fast to fall over in the little clearing.

He let out so many funny noises as he felt the freedom to look and explore whatever he wanted, bending down to inspect the grass or pick up leaves, occasionally making Becky jump forward as she thought he was going to put something in his mouth, before cheekily smiling and running off further.

***

Ryan finished his food with dry eyes. He had made his decision, the right one for the forest. He had to look at the bigger picture when it came to the world. He had wanted to stay in the life he had, it was comfortable and fun so he had thought. But it would have been a selfish thing to do, especially when he had been given the opportunity to do so much good as he was doing. No, he must put his family from his mind. He knew the 'Sisters of the Wreath' had the potion which would allow this, and thought he would ask for it next time he saw them. The guilt was too much to be living with daily.

Standing up, he wondered whether to start doing some work to help rehabilitate the forest, or do a couple of emergencies first. He would be distraught if he picked the first option, and there was some poor creature, tree, or plant somewhere in desperate need since his short food break. So, when he touched the nearest tree, he thought emergency, twisting and disappearing with the faintest pop and waft of honey.

The moment he landed by a great old oak he began looking around. There was no sign of wildlife in distress nearby he thought which seemed odd, and instead he looked round for a plant or tree that was dying. Nothing. Very odd he thought again, scratching his chin.

He was just about to touch the tree again, when he heard a squeal. He paused as it sounded human, before realising that his feet weren't tingling so it must be a pig or something. He headed up a slight hill, before catching sight of two humans in a little opening in front of him. He immediately jumped behind a tree, confused, and terrified that his legs had stopped working. How would he be able to tell in the future if anyone was getting close? They were working this morning he thought, his mind racing through reasons why they would not be now. Taking a quick look around the tree again to confirm, as they were only twenty or so metres away. He saw a woman chasing after a little toddler, who was laughing at his mummy trying to get him.

What was different about this he thought, hands on the tree as he moved back round to be hidden.

"Go and see them" came a voice in his head from the tree, surprising him, as he thought his question had been only for him to figure out.

"I will then" he replied in his mind, releasing the tree and stepping out.

He stood there, his hood up, but not pulled right forward, so the light played off his face, staring as a little figure turned to face his mother and him. The air shot out of his lungs as he recognised the little boys face.

"Archie" he said in a whisper, as the boy reached and hugged his mum, not having noticed Ryan a little way away. Ryan couldn't move. He just stood there, drinking in the sight of his son, his happy beautiful little face. Archie let go of his mum, looking round again at the forest with wonder, and spotted the figure. There was a pause.

"Dada?" came the little voice, questioning.

"No, no dada anymore" said Becky, heartbroken at how he had remembered his dad in such a joyful moment. Ryan pulled his hood right down now.

"DADA" came the excited squeal from the boy and he ran past his mum, who turned to see where he was going. She froze, seeing Archie running towards an unknown figure.

The New Forest Dweller

"Archie, NO." She shouted, taking off after him. She managed to catch him quickly, holding him back about ten metres from the figure as she looked up at it. Her eyes temporarily not believing what she was seeing, but then it clicked, and the last remnants of the spell gave out, breaking it completely.

"Ryan?" she said nervously.

"Yes babe" he said, hardly believing what was happening.

"Dada" came Archie's voice again, and he broke free from his mothers' clutches, stumbling towards his dad, arms out for the biggest hug he could give.

And then he was in Ryans arms, being lifted into the air and squeezed tightly. Ryan felt his eyes release the tears he had been holding back, as Becky, with her memory back of what had happened before he had left, rushed over, angry, and happy, and tearful, and you name it, she was it. She held him tightly, sobbing, and unsure if this was real, but feeling safe.

"Dada" came Archie's voice again as Ryan gave him kisses on his cheek before turning to Becky and giving her a big kiss.

"Oh, how I've missed you both." He said, tears of joy running down his face, landing on his cloak but due to the magic of emotions, allowed to run right down to the ground.

"We've, missed, you, too" said Becky through sobs, hardly believing it, and having to release him to get a better look. "Have you been here in the forest the whole time? Why didn't you contact me? We all thought you were dead?" She said wanting answers but trying not to be mad. "I can't believe it. But I am just so glad to have you back."

He paused for a moment, words stuck in his throat. He couldn't go back. The forest still needed him. But the forest must have brought him here for a reason.

"You are coming back, aren't you?" she said, her bottom lip quivering at the silence.

He looked into her teary eyes, and at Archie's happy little face at holding his 'Dada' again. He tried to choose his words carefully.

"I am bound to the forest," he started saying, and Becky let out a little cry. "But I want you both in my life, to be here with me." He said, willing her to say yes. She regained control again for a moment.

"What, just live in the forest? With a one-year-old?" she said, looking uncertain and a little shocked.

"Well not actually in the forest like I have been doing. But maybe buying a place, a secluded house in the forest, where I can return to you each night?" he said, hoping she agreed. It was her turn to pause, but only for a split second.

"Yes, yes of course, we've both missed you so much. I do not want to risk losing you again" she said, and he let out the biggest smile, pulling her in and kissing her again.

"We will find a nice house in the forest to buy. Your life insurance paid out so we can easily afford somewhere now. But what about Archie? And nursery? My family and his schooling? What would we do about that?" She asked, questions instantaneously popping into her head, making her not sure what to do.

"Well, I would have to remain missing." He said to her slightly surprised face. "I can't risk people knowing I am here carrying out the forests work and bidding. I am The New Forest Dweller, Oak." He said proudly.

"But what about my family, and yours? School and everything else?" She asked, wanting answers now.

"You can continue living your life, taking him to nursery and seeing family and friends. But I need to stay hidden, at least for a while. The less people that know about me the better." He said, cuddling his little boy tighter, as he had put his thumb in and was pulling Ryans ear. "We can still be together and raise our little boy here." He said.

She paused to let this all sink in, making sure it would all fit and work. Slowly she answered.

"I best get the house on the market then, and look for another."

He let out the biggest smile, his heart leaping and full, the happiest he had ever been in his life, getting his family back and becoming part of the new one in the forest. He could not wait for it to begin.

Chapter Twenty-Three – A Forest Reborn

Ryans jubilation showed in his face for everyone to see. Becky had indeed put the house on the market, and was looking for something that suited her needs in the forest. She had been hard pressed not to spill the beans about Ryan to anyone, remaining tight lipped and only telling her family she just wanted a change of house due to the recent unhappy memories. She had found a cute cottage between Minstead and Lyndhurst, and had her first offer accepted by the thankful son of an old couple that had to go into care. Luckily, she had just enough left from the insurance to buy it outright, meaning that she could rent out their old place to provide a bit of income to take care of the bills and Archie's nursery costs. The move wouldn't happen until around the start of October, which gave her plenty of time to pack up their belongings and arrange a company to move everything for her.

She was reluctant to ask Ryans family or hers for help moving, as she didn't want the questions of why she was keeping his stuff, and there was also the possibility that she might let it slip that he was still alive. Archie had been babbling about 'Dada' a lot recently, which was brought up by the nursery staff, but she said to them it was just as she'd had some pictures printed that she had shown him, which made them all sympathetic, and with no follow up questions thankfully.

Ryan himself had to be careful around Becky too to start with. He had not revealed too much about his work in the forest, especially not the magical community he was now a part of. They had met a dozen times again in the forest, she would let him know when they would be there, and he would come and meet them in the right location at roughly the right time. He did have to keep pulling the new watch she had given him out of his right pocket to make sure he didn't run too late. She had given it to him on the third meeting, as otherwise he was waiting around a lot as he really didn't want to miss them.

The forest itself seemed to mirror his emotions. Green buds were now springing from the ashy ground, hiding the blackness in a sea of green. The transformation was astonishing. The Fairies and Pixies were working wonders encouraging things to grow. The Forest Folk kept up their end of the bargain, often having to watch out for the Forest Legends that were also unknowingly helping them out.

Together they had planted, thousands of trees, hoping they all wouldn't be killed off by the winter, with the Fairies promising to keep nurturing them. The 'Sisters of the Wreath' procured several mighty mulch potions, which was like plant feed on steroids. When it was spread around the new section of forest, it helped plants and trees grow much stronger and quicker than normal. Animals began returning as well, starting with flies, bugs, and spiders. Birds ventured out into this area, not staying long due to the lack of housing, but making the most of the insects. Before long, rabbits had made fresh burrows, and other creatures came, joining the new forest ecosystem into the old. It would not be long before it was all one again.

***

"Happy Birthday my little man" said Ryan, picking Archie up as he walked towards Becky who had arranged to meet him for this moment.

"Dada" said Archie, hugging him tightly before pointing into the forest.

"Hey babe" said Ryan, leaning over and giving Becky a kiss and cuddle.

They then walked hand in hand, along the path, Ryan a few times having to nip into the trees when he felt his feet tingle, before rejoining them again slightly further along and making sure he did not use his cloaks magic or the root transport in front of her.

"Why can't you just wear normal clothes so you can just walk with us?" said Becky when he reappeared for the third time. He thought about it for a moment. He didn't want to be far from his cloak in case he was needed, and definitely did not want to be spotted by anyone he knew. He said this to her, adding that his face had been plastered about as a missing person for a couple of months and someone might recognise him. She had agreed, and they continued their walk.

"The burnt bit of the forest looks good now" said Becky looking up to his face. "It was on the news about how well it's recovered and how quickly its growing."

"Ahh, good" said Ryan, hoping they hadn't drawn suspicion in the rapidness of the regrowth, and thinking he should call a meeting to maybe let nature continue from here for a while. "Yes, I've been working hard to help it along." He added casually.

She stopped, holding his hand still, making him turn to her.

"What is it you do exactly?" she asked, remembering all the animals that had come up to him in the forest before he had disappeared.

"I will let you know, when you move into the new place." He said looking into her eyes.

"Promise?" she asked.

"Of course," he replied, not sure what she would think, but knowing she would rather know the truth.

She looked pleased, and they kept going, Ryan still holding Archie in his arms, who let out a small sob as he was still a little emotional from tripping over when he had tried to follow his dad into the wilderness a few minutes before, when Ryan had hidden from unknown people coming along the same track.

When they finished their walk, Ryan kissed them both goodbye, with Becky saying she was going to see her family tomorrow but would be back at midday the following day. He accepted, just so pleased to have them both back in his life.

Once they had gone, he disappeared over to an area where some kids had left stick dens up, and sat down in one. He started eating some food, helping himself to a celebratory bottle of beer for his sons second birthday, as the light began to fade.

Becky filled him in with all that had been happening to the rest of the people he had left behind. Paul had unfortunately had to close their business, not able to cope without Ryan running it, and instead joined a local building company and was doing well by all accounts. She also said that Ryans family called often, always happy to facetime and come and see Archie, offering sympathy and help if she needed, which she always declined.

It was comforting to go to sleep now, knowing that wrongs in his conscience had been rightened, and that the future was definitely looking bright.

He had even been happy for Cinthia, who a few days before when he had seen her, had told him she was in a relationship with one of the other Fairies, a nice guy called Lea, his name short for leaf, and they were even expecting a baby together. She had looked excited and a little nervous when she had told him, but he was so genuinely happy for her, pleased that she had found the right partner, which also aided in his relief of his guilt.

He lay in one of the stick dens, staring at the point where they crossed, before shutting his eyes, and quickly drifting off into a pleasant sleep, the forest peaceful around him.

Chapter Twenty-Four – New Years Day

Becky had gone to her family for Christmas and New Years, returning for just a few days in between to see him, but not staying too long as it might arouse suspicion with her family, who had said they would have her for the whole holiday. He had enjoyed seeing them, taking a few hours out of each day to spend time with them, thanks to the Forest Folk and Forest Legends who were still picking up the tasks of keeping the Forest clean and clear of rubbish.

New Years Eve finally came around. Ryan had been slightly apprehensive about the meeting with the ghost Dwellers due to what had happened in the summer. At least the forest had grown back well, the plants and grass pretty much back to how the had been, and trees replanted in the same locations that they had been before, thanks to the Fairies, Pixies, and Lester, who spent all of his time watching over the forest, and knew it like the back of his hand. In a few years, hopefully it would look like the fire had never happened at all.

He joined the Fairies for their New Years Eve Party in their tree. The Pixies had their own quiet get together across the wood in their temporary homes. They, like the Forest Folk, had offered for him to join them in their party games and celebration, but Ryan had already agreed to attend the Fairies Party, and to meet Cinthia's new baby. Fairy pregnancies were quicker than human ones, and she had given birth only shortly before Christmas. The Forest Folk were having their usual singing and music festival, with plenty of drinking and smoking of pipes, the children allowed to stay up all night to welcome in the New year. The 'Sisters of the Wreath' had gone away to spend the holiday with and old wizard relative who lived in the north of Wales, they wouldn't be back for a few days, but had left a summoning potion with him this time in case of emergency. He hadn't needed it yet thankfully, but the night was young and after all, he would be partying with Fairies.

As he entered their tree after sunset, he was pulled through by many hands, having his cloak removed and donning a new leaf toga which was quite brown and dry. The moment it was drawn over his head, he saw a little family coming towards him. The happy cheerful guy called Lea, embraced him like a brother, clapping him on the back with the pleasure of seeing him. Ryan copied his actions as he liked the guy a lot, before his eyes moved to Lea's wife, Cinthia. Her beauty seemed to have grown since he had attended their wedding in November, her pink glow radiating from her pores as she held, wrapped up in her arms, a tiny little baby boy. He leant forward and kissed her on the cheek, giving her a quick squeeze before stepping back. She was smiling tearfully, still so full of emotions from the hormones of the pregnancy, but pleased he was there. She held out her little baby boy for him, and he carefully took him into his arms, staring down at the tiny face that looked inquisitively up at him, smiling. He'd inherited his dad's brown hair, but his mums' big beautiful eyes and rosy cheeks. Ryan stooped slightly and gave him a tiny kiss on the forehead. He giggled cutely, snug in his blankets being held by this friendly stranger. The crowd, who had almost fallen silent, cheered. Ryan lifted the boy slightly above his head, and the cheering increased, with Lea and Cinthia hugging and laughing as Ryan showed off the baby to the crowd. Bringing him carefully back down to his chest, Ryan moved forward to pass him back to his mother.

"Congratulations, you two. He really is beautiful." Ryan said, as he transferred the baby into her arms.

"We've named him, Acorn" said Lea, looking down at the little boy, "A name you used to have, and hopefully, won't be used by another Dweller for a long time."

Ryan smiled at this, his eyes becoming slightly hazy. Cinthia and Lea laughed at his emotion, pulling him in for a group hug.

"Right then." Said Lea, "let's get this party started."

The celebrated well into the night. Cinthia had taken Acorn to bed before she returned to join in with the revelry, dancing away with Ryan, Lea, and the rest of the crowd. Ryan had a great time. He danced with so many groups of Fairies, accepted and drank drinks of all different flavours, listened and moved to all the new songs to celebrate the years end, and saw every colour he could imagine shining through the core of the tree.

Near dawn, he fell asleep on a large double bed, just as the music and partying finally began to die down.

***

After only a couple of hours sleep, he was awoken. Looking up groggily, he saw it was Bark who has nudged him awake.

"Bark, how good to see you" said Ryan, sitting up, his leaf toga almost bare from how dry and dead the leaves had been.

"Hello Dweller, I am glad you look like you have had a nice time. But I thought you would like to get up to meet with the ghost council, they should have arrived by now." He said, knowing that it would be an important meeting after such a year.

"Ah yes, thank you Bark, I'm glad you got me up for that" said Ryan, patting him on the shoulder in thanks.

"I have your cloak here, and I will see you out the door. But please do feel free to return later" he added, not wanting to seem pushy, like he was telling a Dweller what to do. Ryan did appreciate the waking. He turned slightly, removing what was left of the leaf toga and slipping his cloak back on. He felt its effect instantaneously as it cleared his insides of the alcohol from the night before, and made him feel spritelier and more awake. He looked up, seeing that Lea and Cinthia were cuddled up in the bed next to him, still both fast asleep. He was pleased for the two of them to have one another like he had Becky, it was such a relief to not have the burden of someone else's love on his shoulders when he couldn't give it back. Smiling, he turned away, following Bark back to the entrance before being made back to his normal size and climbing down the ladder.

Straightening up at the base of the tree, he placed the ladder back in his right pocket, raised his hood, and walked towards the nearest tree, heading to complete a few emergencies, and to think over what he would say to the ghost council.

Thankfully, there was nothing major for him to sort that morning. The only serious case in the forest was for the humans to deal with. A drunk driver had crashed on their way home, but the scene was being dealt with by a police car and ambulance, as Ryan watched for a minute from a bush a little distance away, after he had helped a treat a nearby foxes' injuries from a fight.

After the fifth emergency he attended, he decided to take the plunge and visit the ghosts. Lester had said they were a funny lot, some quiet and thoughtful, while others were more outgoing and sociable. He rarely got to see them though anymore, only when there was a full moon on New years day, which happened roughly every twenty-eight years. And even then, there was only a couple of hours crossover and that's if they travelled to Wilverly to see him. They always did though, thankful for his service throughout the years to the current dweller.

Ryan held his hand on the tree, not sure what phrase or word to think to be taken to where they were. 'Ghost' he tried, but nothing. 'Dweller John,' Still no luck.

"Oh come on, I just want to see where the New Forest Ghost Council are." He said out loud.

That did it. He hadn't expected it though, which is why he arrived upside down, and unceremoniously crashed to the ground on his head, thankfully softened by his cloaks hood.

He heard a lot of laughter around him as he started getting to his feet, his hands on the ground so the voices in his head started momentarily. Once up, he looked around to see about a dozen pearly semi translucent people were there, floating slightly off the floor.

Ryans eyes met the one in the middle, who smiled kindly at him, eyes twinkling.

"Forest Dweller Oak, I am very pleased to see you. The rest of the council here, well, they are very pleased to meet you too" said the central figure smiling. His old mentor.

Ryan stepped forward, so happy to see him looking so fine in his white cloak. Offering a mock hug like he did for Lester, which was copied by not only Ghost Dweller John, but by each of the other thirteen that lined up to do it too. Dweller John introduced each one as they stepped forward, clasping their hands around thin air for a few moments before moving on.

"It's so great to see you again Dweller John" Ryan said, seeing the beaming smiles of all those that watched him. He was about to say something else, when he remembered the voices, the ones he had only heard for a split second before he had gotten to his feet. So, with quite a quizzical look he asked his old mentor the first question he could think of.

"Why was I not allowed to drink the forest water before you had passed?" he asked.

He had pondered this when he had first had a drink from the forest, and again a couple of times since.

Dweller John, looked relaxed as he answered.

"Aha, you seem to never cease with your quest for knowledge and answers. A good trait to have, as it displays willingness to help and understand. The short answer is, we would then be in each other's heads, which could be very uncomfortable at times I assure you." He said, with a grimace to the white figure next to him whose cheeks became, if possible, an even pearlier white in embarrassment.

Dweller John continued, looking back to Ryan.

"The forests water, allows connections between all that drinks it. It spreads messages, information, news, and love throughout. Now you can normally choose when you want to connect, simply by placing your palm against the ground or touching any animal or plant. But with other humans it is different. You can hear each other's thoughts constantly until the effects of the water have worn off from one of you. Thankfully myself and my mentor were only connected for a day, which if we are honest, was still a day too much." He said sheepishly.

The ghost next to him actually put his head in his own hands, shaking it as though trying to remove the memory. Ryan decided that no follow up questions were needed, and simply laughed along with all the other ghosts around them.

"Right, we have a lot to discuss" said Dweller John, straightening himself up when things had finally settled down. "We want to firstly thank you for saving our forest, your actions certainly stopped it being completely burnt down. After this we will discuss your upcoming first full year which officially starts today. So shall we, oh I don't know, go for a walk?" he asked, his usual wise smile flitting across his face, for he knew The New Forest Dweller had a big year ahead of him, one full of hard work, but one he knew he was certainly going to enjoy.

The New Forest Dweller

A few months later…

The air was crisp and cold over the frozen land, but deep beneath the surface, a flame resided. The summer fire had ignited a thin vein of coal, and it was determined not to be extinguished. Over the many months, and after splitting off in multiple directions, it slowly made its way towards Boltons Bench in Lyndhurst, catching a thicker, richer seam, burning hotter for longer, and starting the process to awaken, the Bisterne Dragon.

Printed in Great Britain
by Amazon